THE MANCHURIAN'S TRAIL

J.C. FIELDS

Cover Design – Jaycee DeLorenzo
Publishing Coordinator – Sharon Kizziah-Holmes

Paperback-Press
an imprint of A & S Publishing
Paperback Press, LLC
Springfield, Missouri

ISBN -13: 978-1-960499-96-7

OTHER PUBLICATIONS
By J.C. Fields

The Sean Kruger Series
The Fugitive's Trail
The Assassin's Trail
The Imposter's Trail
The Sean Kruger Boxed Set
The Cold Trail
The Money Trail
The Dark Trail
The Virtual Trail
The Ominous Trail

The Michael Wolfe Saga
A Lone Wolf
The Last Insurgent
A Matter of Payback

Dakota Storm
A Storm Does This Way Come

DEDICATION

For Sean, Megan, Ryan and Miranda.

ACKNOWLEDGMENTS

My first novel, *The Fugitive's Trail*, was published nine years ago. The book you hold in your hand is number nine in the Kruger universe and my fourteenth title. A lot has happened during those nine years. First, I became a full-time writer versus having to write at odd hours of the morning, night and weekend because of my day job. Second, I've been able to gathered a strong team of professionals who have assisted my quest to be an independently published author. I owe a huge debt of gratitude to the following individuals.

Sharon Kizziah-Holmes, owner of Paperback Press, became the first person to support my writing and has been instrumental in my growth as an author. Thank you.

Our critique group, Shirley, Sharon, Lori, Michael and Conetta has been a major factor in improving how I put words together.

The editorial team, Kate Richards, Nanette Sipe, Shirley McCann and Tina Vyborny, continue to file the rough edges off my manuscripts and polish them into readable gems.

Jaycee DeLorenzo continues as my cover designer. Thank you for your talent and knowledge of producing an eye-catching cover.

To Judge Tom Pyle, retired Associate Circuit Court Judge and his twenty-eight years' experience as a JAG officer. Thank you for being instrumental in shaping the court scene chapter. Your expert input and great advice is appreciated.

Dr. Clarissa Willis, my foreign rights agent. I am looking forward to your success as you take *The Michael Wolfe Saga* to Europe.

I want to thank, Paul J. McSorley (voice actor) and his wife Nikki (dramatic background music). These two have been instrumental in producing all of my novels into audiobooks. It is a testament to their talent these recordings have been so successful.

And again, last but not least, my wife Connie. She believed in the dream from the beginning and never once uttered a discouraging word. She is the love of my life and a true partner.

PROLOGUE

Berkeley, CA
Summer 1985

The new father appeared in the doorway of the small apartment bedroom used as a nursery. Until larger accommodations could be found, this claustrophobic space would have to serve as the baby's room and study for the two college students. The young woman sat in an old wooden rocking chair purchased at a local flea market. She held the four-week-old infant to her bare breast as she moved the chair back and forth.

The new mother stopped watching the baby and directed her attention to the child's father. His expression alarmed her. "What's wrong?"

"I fear I may have placed all three of us in danger."

The young woman stiffened. The baby broke its attachment to the nipple and whimpered. Before saying anything, she stroked the little girl's head and made soothing sounds. When the child returned to suckling, she frowned. "What the hell have you done?"

"I spoke to my father."

"Why would you do that?"

"I could no longer live with the lie I've been living." The man's English revealed a slight British inflection from attending boarding school in Hong Kong, his native Mandarin barely discernable as he spoke.

She studied him for any sign of deception. Seeing none, she turned her attention to a small window next to the rocking chair. "I thought we discussed this and agreed after the birth of our daughter, you would cut off all contact with him." Her voice barely above a whisper, she turned back to glare at the man. "Why? Why would you call him? What were you thinking? Did you bother to think about the consequences if you told him he had a granddaughter?"

The father shook his head. "I spoke to him because of you and our daughter. He would find out eventually. I had to tell him."

"Really." Her voice dripped with sarcasm.

"Yes. I told him I would not return to China and that you and I have plans to buy a house outside the city. I also mentioned I would be working with my friend, Steve Wozniak, who started a new company and needs engineers."

"What was his reaction?"

The young man stared out the window.

She sighed, stood, and placed the now-sleeping baby in a crib. After covering it with a blanket, she pulled a T-shirt over her head to cover herself and turned to glare at the baby's father. "That bad?"

"I believe we should pack very quickly and leave."

She stared at her husband. "And go where?"

"Your parents' house in Austin."

The young mother sighed and began packing the baby's needs.

He turned to leave the nursery. "While you pack the baby's bag, I will gather a few things for us."

She nodded but did not look at him.

***

An hour later, the mother peered out the apartment's second-story street-side window. Her attention fixed on her husband as he carried two duffle bags across the street to a yellow Toyota Corolla.

Multiple cars lined the crowded street in front of their apartment building. As soon as he finished loading the car, she would bring their daughter and join him. The second he reached the vehicle, a white Ford van screeched to a stop next to him. Four men dressed in blue overalls jumped out of the back and rushed to her husband. She saw him start to turn as the four converged on where he stood. The attackers appeared to be the same nationality as her husband.

She muffled a scream when two men grabbed his arms and another struck him on the head with an object she could not identify. Her husband slumped, supported by two men holding his arms; the fourth man grabbed the victim's legs and raised them. They rushed their quarry back to the side of the van and threw the body into the open cargo door. Three of the attackers scrambled in behind him. The fourth man directed his attention to the window where the mother stood. Tall and lanky, his pockmarked face turned in her direction. He displayed an icy glare, relaying his message with clarity. *Don't interfere.* With his warning given, the fourth man climbed into the van, and it sped off.

Stunned, she did not move from the window. When the reality of the situation dawned on her, she turned and walked straight to the bedroom where her daughter slept. She threw the diaper bag over her shoulder and picked up the young child. Grabbing her billfold and car keys, she stuffed them into the diaper bag. After stepping out of the apartment, she left the door unlocked and rushed to the street below.

Arriving at the Toyota, she unlocked the doors and placed the baby in the car seat in the back. She ignored the duffle bags her husband abandoned on the street and started the car. The tires squealed as she drove south. Her destination, Austin, Texas.

PART ONE

Present Day

CHAPTER 1

Southwest Missouri

JR Diminski parked his light-gray Toyota Camry on the right side of the garage, his normal spot, next to Mia's Honda CR-V. The house, located on a quiet street in a sleepy part of town with a shaded fenced-in backyard, suited the couple and their soon-to-be six-year-old son.

The time approached seven in the evening when he walked into the kitchen. Mia's back remained toward him as he entered. She appeared unaware of his arrival as he watched her slam a cabinet door shut and curse.

"What's wrong, Mia?"

She shook her head causing her long black ponytail to flip back and forth. Reaching for an open drawer on the left side of the sink, she hesitated and then banged it shut.

Concerned, JR walked to her and placed a hand gently on her shoulder. In a quiet voice, he murmured, "Mia, talk to me. What's wrong?"

Her slender and petite body shuddered. He turned her around to gaze into her almond-shaped brown eyes. Tears flowed down the cheeks of her round face. He drew her into an embrace. At first, she resisted for several moments. Then she placed her forehead on his chest, wrapped her arms around his waist, and openly wept.

Neither spoke. They remained in the embrace for several minutes as she sobbed. Finally, he felt her calm. "Mia, I can't help you if you don't tell me what's wrong."

She pointed to the island separating the kitchen from the dining area. A FedEx overnight envelope lay open in the middle of the space. Concerned, he released her from his embrace and retrieved the package. Inside was a single page letter addressed to Mia. When he finished reading, he turned his attention to his wife. "When did this arrive?"

"Today, about four."

"Why didn't you call, I would have come home immediately."

She shook her head and brought her hands up to cover her face.

"Mia, I'm sorry. What do you want me to do?"

Taking a deep breath, she uncovered her eyes and straightened. "I need to find my father and let him know what's happened."

JR tilted his head to the side. "You've never tried to find him before. It's been almost forty years since he disappeared. How do you know he's still alive?"

"Thirty-nine years, and you're right. I have no idea if he's alive or dead. That's the problem. I have no memories of the man. I don't even know what he looks like. Except for a grainy picture my grandparents kept." She glared at him and crossed her arms. "At least you remember what happened to your parents."

The anguish of a few minutes ago gone, replaced by a fury he had not seen in several years, he maintained his silence.

"It's important for our son to understand his heritage. It's important to me as well."

"I understand, Mia. Where do we start?"

"We?" Her nostrils flared. She stopped, closed her eyes, and took a deep breath. Letting the breath out slowly, she said, "I'm sorry." The anger now subsiding. "I can't believe she died without reaching out to me."

"Most of the time, people don't know when they're going to die."

"I understand that. But the damn letter was so cold and impersonal. They don't mention anything about why she died. Did she get sick or have an accident? The letter tells me nothing." She hesitated for a moment. "I guess I have to go to California. I'll need to make arrangements for the body and see to her affairs."

JR held up his hand, palm toward her. "Why don't you let me do it?"

"Why?"

"Joey needs his mother with him. He doesn't need her running off to California."

She stared at him for several moments and then gave him a grim smile. "Okay."

***

"Do you have any idea where he might be?" JR packed an overnight bag for his early flight the next morning.

"No. I was only a month old when my mother returned to Texas. My grandparents told me years later, she showed up one day holding me in her arms. They knew nothing of my mother's pregnancy or of her marriage. She told them my father abandoned us and we needed a place to stay. I do remember my grandfather telling me he met him once and thought he was from northeastern China. Manchuria, they believed. Mom never talked about my father. When I asked, she would cry and remain silent."

"Do you know why?"

"Not really. I was four when she made the decision to

return to California. Her excuse was she wanted to search for him. That was pure bullshit. She joined a commune instead, and I never saw her again."

"Didn't you tell me she never responded to your letters?"

"Yes, I wrote her all during high school and college. After I graduated, I flew out to California to visit. She refused to meet with me when I got to the commune. I finally realized she wanted nothing to do with me. So, I returned the favor. I haven't spent much time thinking about her since I met you. Until that damn letter arrived today."

Tears welled in her eyes, and she grew quiet. JR went to her and hugged her. "You tried, Mia. It's not your fault she didn't want to see you. Maybe she had a reason."

"What reason? Was I a burden? Was it my fault my father abandoned us? Other women raise children on their own, why not her?"

JR calmly shook his head. "No, there must be another explanation."

"What?"

"I have no idea, but I intend to find out."

***

It was past 9 p.m. when he stepped onto the front porch of his longtime friend who lived across the street. Retired FBI agent Sean Kruger and co-owner of KKG Solutions stood waiting for him. He opened the storm door and waved his friend in. "When you called, you said you need to hire KKG Solutions?"

"Yes. I need two things. First, I need Stephanie to keep an eye on Mia while I'm gone. Next, I need to hire KKG to help me find Mia's biological father."

Stephanie Harris Kruger walked into the front room as JR spoke. "Why the sudden trip, JR?"

He held up the letter. "She received this today. The commune where her mother lived informed her in a very impersonal letter that her mother passed away two days ago."

Stephanie's hand shot to cover her mouth. "Oh no... I'll go over and check on her. Kristin and Mikey are asleep, so don't wake them." With those words, Stephanie hurried out the front door.

Kruger read the letter and handed it back to JR. "You're right, extremely impersonal, almost like it was written by a lawyer."

JR stared at the letter. "Something doesn't smell right about this, Sean. Do you still have any contacts in the San Francisco FBI office?"

Kruger raised an eyebrow. "Yeah, last I knew, Charlie Brewer was still in charge. Why?"

"Could you call him and find out if they know anything about this commune?"

"Sure. What time is your flight?"

"Six thirty or something like that. I fly into Dallas for a connecting flight to San Francisco."

"Jimmy's already out there, recruiting. Do you want any help?"

"Would he mind?"

Kruger chuckled. "He'd love to help. After I talk to Brewer, I might have some answers for you. What do you suspect?"

JR did not answer right away. He studied the letter and then said, "I don't know, but they never allowed the woman to have contact with her daughter. Now that she's dead, they suddenly need someone to come immediately out there and take care of her affairs. Something smells fishy about this, Sean."

"What kind of affairs would they need handled? She's been living in a commune for what, thirty-plus years?"

"At least. But the letter doesn't answer any questions.

Mia is confused and angry at the same time. I don't blame her. I'd be angry as well."

"When was the last time she saw her mother?"

"She was four."

Kruger remained silent for a few moments. "That's a long time."

"I know."

"This will be the first time you've traveled out of town by yourself since your incident in New York City. Are you okay with doing so?"

JR shrugged. "I'll be fine. I refuse to go east, but I'm good heading out to California. Besides, it's for Mia."

Kruger could only nod.

CHAPTER 2

Somewhere Over the Western United States

Diminski stared out the window of seat 2A on American Airline flight 417 nonstop from Dallas to San Francisco. The mountains of Colorado slipped silently underneath the Boeing 737 as it flew westward.

The landscape below sparked the memory of his first trip with Mia to a bed-and-breakfast in Boulder. He remembered her fascination with the mountains. The trip cemented their devotion to each other. Seldom apart since, this trip would be their first long-term separation. He felt an emptiness not experienced since leaving his old life in New York City. He thought back on the randomness of his life and how it led him to be with Mia. A woman he admired because of her intelligence and personal strength.

As he stared at the mountains below the plane, his thoughts drifted back to his journey.

JR Diminski was not his given name at birth. Memories of his parents had faded years ago. He didn't even have a picture of them. Two days after his sixth birthday, a poor decision by a college student who drank two too many beers at a fraternity party before driving home ended the life of JR's parents and the student. With both sets of grandparents gone, a foster family took him in. Three years later, they adopted him. He flourished as a resident in the small town in a rural part of Georgia, northeast of Atlanta. Their ten acres of land possessed an abundance of oak and walnut trees. It also provided a haven to more squirrels than his adoptive father preferred. It was there, JR learned how to hunt with a .22 rifle and assist in controlling their population.

The rural setting restricted his access to television, so he devoured books from the local small-town library. One of his favorite topics being computers.

He remembered, with fondness, how his adopted father assisted him with the gathering of fallen walnuts to sell to a local huller. The money he earned allowed him to buy a used Commodore 64 personal computer. And so began his lifelong fascination with the machines.

After graduating at the top of his high school class, he joined the Army where his natural ability with a computer led to training as a warrior in the first cyberwarfare unit. During this enlistment, he honed his skills as a marksman with both rifles and pistols. After a disagreement with his commanding officer, he left the Army and earned an undergraduate and master's degree in computer science from MIT.

College introduced him to Tony Chien and Steve Watson. The three close friends shared an apartment together and made plans for life after graduation. They formed CWZ Software. Ten years later, the company was on the cusp of becoming a leading-edge computer software company when Tony Chien made a fatal mistake.

As the leading shareholder of CWZ, Chien made the decision to sell a chunk of his shares to a large private equity company. The dream faded and the partnership broke up. Everyone in the company was let go and, for the first time, JR found himself without a purpose. After a chance meeting with the individual who owned the private equity company, JR made the decision to get even. Events escalated, and he became a fugitive accused of murder. Using his skills as a hacker, he erased the digital evidence of his former life and became JR Diminski. Now over a decade later, he had a successful marriage and business. All thanks to two men, Sean Kruger and a man he knew as Joseph. These were the two individuals who befriended him and proved him innocent of the murder charge.

With his former life behind him, he kept no secrets from Mia. Except one. He was one of the founding members of the underground computer hacktivist network known as Anonymous. When the group received unwanted attention during the Occupy Wall Street protests, his activity with the group waned. This was also the time he was in transition from his former identification to his current one. With the group back in the shadows and virtually no media coverage, he was supporting the movement again.

His reminiscing ended as the plane touched down at San Francisco International Airport. With his backpack over his shoulder and his carry-on bag in tow, he walked toward the rental car area of the airport.

Exiting the secured area, he noticed a young man in a gray suit holding a sign with his name on it. At first, he didn't recognize the man, but, as he got closer, he remembered. This was FBI Agent Tim Gonzales.

When they first met, Gonzales had been a recent graduate of the FBI Academy. JR walked up to the man. "I'm JR. You're Agent Gonzales, right?"

Gonzales grinned and shook JR's offered hand. "Yes, sir. I'm surprised you remember me. It's been a while since we met in Las Vegas during the search for Randolph Bishop."

"Sure, I remember. What brings you here?"

"Sean Kruger spoke to my boss and indicated you needed background on a local commune. Special Agent Charlie Brewer sent me to escort you to our office for a briefing. I'm your guide."

"Why would I need a guide?"

"Agent Brewer will explain."

Ten minutes later, they were driving toward the FBI offices in San Francisco. JR was quiet, not sure how having an escort would help. Gonzales glanced at his passenger and then returned his attention to the road. "I volunteered to help you while you're in the area."

"Really. Why?"

Gonzales glanced at him again. "Because of Sean Kruger. He recommended my transfer to San Francisco. I can't thank him enough, so it's the least I can do to help a friend of his."

"Sean's like that, I have a lot to thank him for as well."

JR figured the shorter man barely made the height requirements for the agency. But what he lacked in height, he probably made up for in upper body strength. The man's shoulders were wide and his hips narrow. The fabric of his gray suit seemed ready to burst from the size of his biceps. His short, coal-black hair and tanned male-model features would serve him well in the image-conscious FBI.

"Was Las Vegas the first time you met Sean Kruger?"

Gonzales nodded, not taking his eyes off the busy traffic ahead. "Yes. I really didn't think he would remember me. All I cared about, at the time, was not screwing up in front of Agent Kruger. He has a legendary reputation within the bureau. A lot of agents were bummed out when he was forced to retire due to age."

JR laughed. "Don't worry. He's still sticking his nose into things."

"Good. Do you still see him?"

"Yeah, I live across the street from him."

"I imagine that can be interesting."

"It has moments. Why the meeting at your office, Agent Gonzales?"

"Please call me Tim." He hesitated. "Uh, well, there are some things you need to know before you go out there. Agent Brewer believes you will need one or two of us agents to accompany you."

"Why?"

"I'll let Agent Brewer tell you."

They did not talk for the rest of the ride.

***

Special Agent in Charge Charlie Brewer stood as JR and Gonzales walked into his office. Coming around the desk, he extended his hand, which JR shook.

"It is nice to finally meet you, JR. Sean Kruger speaks highly of you and indicated you were instrumental in helping prevent the assassination of President Roy Griffin when he was still a senator."

"I had a small part."

"Not according to Kruger."

"He has a tendency to exaggerate at times."

Brewer motioned to a chair in front of his desk. "Please, have a seat. We can get started."

JR sat while Agent Gonzales stood by the door. After Brewer returned to his seat, he placed his arms flat on the desk and clasped his hands.

"Sean was evasive about your reasons. Why are you interested in this particular commune, JR?"

"My wife's mother joined it in the mid-eighties and never made contact with her daughter afterward. Two days ago, she received a letter from the commune stating her mother had passed away, and they demanded someone immediately come settle her affairs and make arrangements for the body."

Brewer bowed his head, slightly. "I'm sorry for your wife's loss."

"Thank you."

Clearing his throat, Brewer directed his attention to Gonzales. "Agent, would you shut the door?"

The young agent started to leave.

"Please stay, Tim."

With a nod, he shut the door and returned to his parade-rest stance.

The SAC said, "Sean asked me to tell you everything we know about the place. Some of it isn't good."

JR sat back in the chair and studied Brewer. "I suspected as much." He saw a man who appeared younger than Kruger by a few years. He was of average height and average build. While not overweight, he showed the signs of too many years behind a desk. His brown hair, which he kept short, was thinning on top. Glasses sat on a noble nose in front of green eyes.

Brewer continued. "The commune came into existence after the Summer of Love activities in the Haight-Ashbury neighborhood. By the fall of 1967, the neighborhood had deteriorated to the point most of the so-called hippies left. From county tax records, we know there were twenty original members. Those twenty members bought thirty acres of land in Sonoma County. By the summer of 1968, the population had grown to around seventy. They started as a farming community, selling their produce on the side of Route 116."

Brewer referred to his laptop screen situated to his left. "Sonoma County records indicated the original deed of trust on the property was paid off in 1976 and more land purchased. Notably, a vineyard north of the original thirty acres. In the late seventies, they opened a winery. I'm told they produced a rather well-crafted Cabernet Sauvignon. When did you say your mother-in-law joined?"

JR thought for a moment. "Somewhere around the

middle of 1989. Mia was four when she left, and her grandparents were always vague about the exact date."

Brewer returned his attention to JR. "The commune was still legit at the time. The winery made enough profit to pay off the vineyard in five years, according to county records. Through the rest of the eighties and well into the late nineties, there are no references to any violations or run-ins with the Sonoma County Sheriff's Department. That all changed in 1999."

"What changed?"

"Several female members were arrested for solicitation in San Francisco."

"Prostitution?"

Brewer nodded.

"Was Mia's mother involved?"

"Her name was Judith Ling, correct?"

"Yes."

"According to police reports, she was one of the members arrested."

JR sat back in his chair. "Really?"

Handing JR a mug shot, he said, "A woman going by that name was arrested several times between 1999 to 2002. Is that your wife's mother?"

Studying the picture, JR took a picture of it with his cell phone and sent it to Mia. "I have no idea. I've never seen a picture of her. But I've sent it to her. She'll get back to us."

"I might add, JR, the name never appears again in department records. The commune started a period of construction on newly purchased land east of the original plot. Office and retail space were built to take advantage of the increased tourist trade due to the growing number of wineries in the area. By this time, county records showed the commune to be a large corporation. The only problem was they were still classified as a nonprofit organization."

Frowning, JR tilted his head. "The research I did before I came out here didn't reveal any information like this.

How did they keep it so quiet?"

"Leadership changes occurred at the same time as their construction projects started. They formed several LLCs to cover their tracks. The commune was not on the bureau's radar until July, 2010."

"What happened in 2010?"

"A semitrailer was stopped in Las Cruces, New Mexico with over a hundred women in the back. Its destination, Mexico."

"What were the nationalities of the women?" JR suspected he knew the answer but decided to confirm.

"Mostly Vietnamese, Thai, and Cambodian."

"Kind of thought so. They got into human trafficking?"

"We couldn't prove anything at the time, but a lot of the women from the trailer were interviewed and told us where their ordeal began. After our agents cross-referenced the interviews, their conclusion named the commune as the location."

JR remained silent for several moments. Finally, he said, "What about recently?"

Brewer shook his head. "They changed their tactics. Plus, too many other issues took up our time. Since I was promoted to this position, we've had to send agents to the site almost a dozen times."

JR's phone buzzed with a text message. He looked at it and returned his attention to Brewer. "Mia believes it's her mother. But she's not sure. The woman in the picture is considerably older than she remembers."

"That's interesting."

"So, why were agents sent to the commune?"

Brewer hesitated before answering. He stared at JR for several moments. "There's circumstantial evidence the group is involved with cyber espionage."

CHAPTER 3

San Francisco, CA

"Cyber espionage? Really?"

Brewer nodded. "The proximity to Silicon Valley may be a factor."

"The commune was founded before the computer revolution."

"Yes, but remember, by then, the leadership group had changed numerous times. Profit became their prime motive. This office began to scrutinize the group closer once they appeared on our radar screen."

Brewer moved the mouse next to his right hand and clicked the left side. He read for a few moments and returned his attention back to JR.

"First, garden produce and marijuana. Second, after buying the vineyard, they produced wine. Then, prostitution and drugs. After that, they got into cybercrime: identity theft, credit card fraud, and most recently, cyber espionage."

JR shook his head slightly and did not respond for

several seconds. "I didn't fin—"

Brewer laughed. "Relax, JR. Sean briefed me on your concerns. He told me you were handy with a computer. It doesn't go beyond this room."

"Thanks. I didn't find an internet presence for the group."

"I don't doubt it. At first, our cyber team couldn't, either. They keep that fact well hidden. Let me see the address you're supposed to go to tomorrow."

JR handed him the letter.

"This is their lawyer's office. Not the commune."

JR hesitated. "Their lawyer's office?"

"Yeah, they've been run by the same individual for the last fifteen years, a lawyer."

"Huh."

"Their lawyer doesn't have any other clients."

"That's not good."

"Nope."

"From what you've told me, it sounds like they've turned into a twenty-first-century organized crime group."

Brewer nodded. "I would agree."

"Has the bureau made any arrests?"

"No, we don't have any hard evidence. Just a lot of conjecture and unsubstantiated accusations."

JR watched the second hand move on a wall clock over Brewer's left shoulder. After several moments of study, he turned his attention back to the Special Agent in Charge. "I need a path into their servers."

***

Gonzales drove JR to his hotel after the meeting with Charlie Brewer. During the first part of the ride, JR remained quiet. Before they arrived at the hotel, he turned to the young agent. "What time can you pick me up in the morning?"

"Whenever you need me. I'm assigned to you until you leave."

JR returned to staring out the car window. Eventually, he said, "The letter gave me a number to call for an appointment. I thought it a bit strange when I first read it, but now I understand. Maybe I should get a lawyer, too."

"You already have one."

JR turned to the young agent as he drove. "You're an attorney?"

Gonzales nodded. "Got my law degree at Baylor. However, about three quarters of the way through law school, I realized I didn't care for the business side of being a lawyer. So, I joined the FBI after passing the Texas Bar Exam." He glanced at JR. "It's another reason Agent Brewer wants me going with you. He wants me to hear what they have to say."

***

The next morning, Gonzales drove JR to the lawyer's office. They found Range Rovers, Audis, Teslas, Lexuses, and the occasional BMW in the parking lot surrounding the three-building complex. JR studied the three structures positioned at the tips of the triangle center court. Each building contained ten stories of steel, concrete, and glass. A typical Northern California business park.

"Is this part of the commune?"

Gonzales parked his gray Chevy Malibu in a visitor's slot. "This land was part of the original thirty acres. It used to be prime farm land fifty years ago."

As JR got out of the car, he muttered to himself, "And we wonder why the climate keeps getting hotter."

At precisely 9 a.m., JR and Gonzales were escorted to a small conference room containing a long table surrounded by eight leather office chairs. The occupant, a tall, thin man in his late sixties, wore an expensive dark-blue suit, with a white silk shirt and a charcoal-gray paisley tie. His oblong face and swept-back silver hair reminded JR of a bird of prey. He closed an open file as they entered the room.

Standing, the lawyer extended his hand. "I'm Randall Becker, Mr. Diminski, we spoke on the phone last night."

JR shook the man's hand. "Mr. Becker, this is my attorney, Tim Gonzales."

The attorney shook Gonzales' hand, but his pleasant demeanor disappeared. He turned his attention back to JR. "You didn't mention you would have an attorney with you, Mr. Diminski."

JR shrugged. "You didn't ask. Besides, your letter to my wife lacked detail as to what this meeting would entail. I thought it prudent to have representation." He smiled. "Just in case."

The attorney glared at JR and then at Gonzales. With a huff, he sat. "Very well. Let's get started."

On the table next to Becker sat a cardboard storage box with Bankers Box logos and a black pinstripe surrounding the top. The cardboard lid was off. Becker nodded at the box. "This contains all of the worldly possessions of the deceased Ms. Judy Ling. I have an inventory list you will need to sign."

He removed a sheet of paper from the open file in front of him and handed it to JR.

After glancing at the list, JR looked up. "How do I know this box contains all of her possessions?"

Becker's eyebrows rose. "Are you doubting the document?"

"As I mentioned earlier, the letter from this office to my wife was cryptic at best. This is the first correspondence she has received concerning her mother in over thirty years. There are many unanswered questions, Mr. Becker." JR stared at the attorney with a neutral expression. "Besides, the contents of the box seem a bit sparse for thirty years of a person's life."

J.C. FIELDS

"I see. Very well." He handed JR another sheet of paper. "This is the Last Will and Testament of Judy Ling. It outlines what was to be left to the co-op and what was to be given to her daughter. I have noted in the file the daughter is not present due to a medical condition and her husband is acting as her agent."

JR passed the will to Gonzales, who started reading.

The attorney continued. "As you can see from the will, there was a small estate, which she bequeathed to the co-op. Since her cottage and furnishings were supplied by the co-op, those reverted back to community property. You are welcome to examine the contents of the box and compare it to the list."

"Where is the body?"

"The remains of Judy Ling are still at the funeral home listed on the property list. She was cremated."

JR frowned. "Without contacting the next of kin?"

Becker pointed to the will. "According to her wishes."

"Was an autopsy performed?"

A shake of his head was Becker's only response.

"Why? What was the cause of death, Mr. Becker?"

"I was told she had health issues."

"What issues?"

"I was not informed."

"Why was my wife never allowed access to her mother for over thirty years?"

Caught off guard by JR's question, the attorney stared at Diminski and blinked several times. Finally, after collecting his thoughts, he said, "I have no knowledge of the personal relationship of Ms. Ling and her daughter. Therefore, I am unable to answer your question."

"Who could?"

"I beg your pardon?"

"Simple question. Who could tell me why my wife's mother refused to see her daughter for over thirty years?"

"If a resident wishes to see someone from the outside,

they are welcome to have them visit. If the resident does not wish to see someone, the community is obligated to restrict that individual's access to the member. If your wife's mother did not wish to see her daughter, then the co-op would have followed those wishes and not allowed it."

"You didn't answer my question. Who could I talk to about Judy?"

"I speak for the co-op."

"You just said you have no knowledge of the relationship between my wife and her mother."

"Correct."

"Then who would?"

"This firm speaks for the community."

"Your logic is circular, and you're not answering the question."

Becker put his elbows on the arms of the chair and made a steeple with his hands.

Gonzales spoke for the first time. "This will does not appear to be properly executed."

"I assure you, Mr. Gonzales, it was properly executed according to the laws of California."

"I tend to differ with your opinion, Counselor."

The corporate attorney only shrugged.

JR stood and reached for the box and placed the lid over the opening. He turned his attention to Becker. "Mr. Gonzales will be filing a complaint with the California Bar Association about the lack of cooperation this firm has provided. Good day, Mr. Becker."

As JR and Gonzales exited the room, Becker called after them, "You did not sign the receipt?"

JR said over his shoulder, "Sign it yourself."

***

As Gonzales drove away from the attorney's office, JR rummaged through the box. "There's nothing of value in here." He stopped and picked up a bundle of letters. All were written in Mia's beautiful handwriting. "Check that. Here are Mia's letters to her mother. They've all been opened." He picked three envelopes at random and looked inside.

"They appear well read. At least she didn't ignore the letters."

Gonzales remained silent as he drove.

JR picked up another bundle of letters, all addressed to Mia at her grandparents' home. "Huh."

Gonzales glanced at JR and then back to the road. "What?"

Holding one of the envelopes in his hand, he noted it was sealed, stamped, yet never mailed. He gently opened it and withdrew the paper inside. Judy Ling had responded to her daughter's letters. They were never mailed. He held one of the letters up. "Somebody is lying to us, Tim."

"What are those?"

"Letters from Judy to her daughter."

"You're kidding. Why did they leave those in there?"

"What do you mean, Tim?"

"JR, it seems a little dumb to leave Judy's letters in there. No one would have known she didn't write back."

"Maybe they wanted us to find them."

"Possibly. Where do the other residents live?"

"I thought you might want to check it out. We're heading there now."

JR placed the sheet of paper back into the envelope and searched the box again.

CHAPTER 4

Petaluma, CA

JR spent the second night in the hotel going through the items from the box with more scrutiny. The contents were laid out and organized next to it on the bed. Each of Judy Ling's letters was opened and read. He felt a slight touch of guilt as he read the private letters, but it passed quickly as he learned more details about Mia's mother.

The last letter he opened was different. The paper appeared new, whereas all the others were slightly yellow with age. When he unfolded the page, he found a key with a unique shape secured to the top of the sheet with tape. The only writing on the paper consisted of a series of numbers. After staring at it for several seconds, he realized the meaning of the numbers. The page was a message written in standard ASCII code.

With the page in hand, he walked to his laptop sitting on the desk. At one time in his career, the computer expert could have read the electronic text coding without help. Now, he needed the assistance of an ASCII table on the internet to translate. Fifteen minutes later, he finished. It read:

mia or jr key is to lockbox at bank with grandmother maiden name mill valley

A little vague, but he understood it. He checked the time in the lower right corner of his laptop. It was 7:08 p.m. Pacific Time, 9:08 Central Time. Mia would still be awake. She answered on the third ring.

"Hi, JR."

"How are you doing?"

"I'm okay. Stephanie's been here a lot. So has Sean." She paused. "I miss you."

"I miss you, too. What was your grandmother's maiden name?"

She hesitated for a few seconds. "Granny's maiden name was Marin. Why?"

"Before I answer, let me check something."

He did a quick Google search and found The Bank of Marin in Mill Valley. "What did your mother study at Berkeley?"

"Sociology."

"Your father?"

"I was told electrical engineering. What's going on, JR? Why all the questions?"

JR took a deep breath, dreading what he had to tell his wife. "The meeting at the attorney's office did not go well."

Silence.

"He gave me a box of your mother's possessions. In the box were all the letters you wrote to her over the years. They were open and well read. There were also just as many letters written to you. Unfortunately, they were never mailed."

Her sob could be heard through the phone.

"Mia, did you ever write to her about us?"

It took several moments before she said, "Yes. Several times. Particularly when I got pregnant with Joey. I was so happy, I had to share the news with her. I wanted her to know she was going to be a grandmother. Of course, I never heard back."

"That explains her knowledge of me." He paused. After several moments, JR said, "I didn't find a letter like that in the box. She did leave a note in ASCII code with a key taped to the letter. Apparently, it's a lock box located at the Bank of Marin in Mill Valley. I'm going there tomorrow."

"When are you coming home?"

"I was going to leave day after tomorrow. But now, I'm not sure. It depends on what I find at the bank."

"Okay."

They spoke another twenty minutes before JR said goodbye.

***

The Bank of Marin in Mill Valley occupied a small building located on a busy street surrounded by homes and apartment buildings. Accompanied by Tim Gonzales, JR presented the key, his ID, and a certificate of death to a bank vice president.

"I'm sorry for your loss, Mr. Diminski."

"Thank you." JR glanced at the woman's business cards on her desk. "Ms. Perez."

"Will you be closing the box?"

"Yes."

She referred to a card taken from a file before sitting down at her desk. "It appears that you and your wife are the only ones authorized to have access to the box. Is that correct?"

JR said, "Yes." Even though he had been unaware of the information.

Emily Perez was slender and in her mid-fifties. She studied the card and frowned. "Mr. Diminski, it appears someone tried to gain access to the box two days ago. They were denied."

JR glanced at Gonzales, who showed his FBI credentials to her. When he held up the badge and ID, JR noticed no discernable surprise from the woman.

Perez said, "If the FBI is involved, is there a question about Ms. Ling's death?"

Gonzales replied quickly. "We have reason to suspect so."

JR realized Gonzales was getting suspicious, like he was.

Perez studied the card again. "A note here on the card indicates a man named Randall Becker requested access to the box. He claimed to be Ms. Ling's attorney. But, without his name on the authorized access list, we had no other choice but to deny him access to the box."

Gonzales asked, "Has anybody else tried to gain access?"

She referred to the card again. "No."

"Ms. Perez, can you make a copy of the access card for our records?"

"Yes. I can do that while Mr. Diminski checks the box."

They all stood and entered the vault containing the lock boxes. After Perez used her key and JR finished the ritual with his, she stepped out of the vault. JR spoke first. "What are you thinking, Tim?"

"Mr. Becker lied to a federal agent. That's a felony."

JR's attention turned to the metal box as he placed it on one of the pull-out shelves amongst the lock boxes. When he opened the lid, he saw a seven-by-nine journal. The black leather cover did not display any letters, only an ornate design. A leather strap held it closed. It appeared old but well cared for. JR asked Gonzales, "Got any gloves I can use?"

The agent pulled two latex gloves out of his suit coat pocket and handed them to JR. After he pulled them on, the computer hacker picked up the book and opened it.

After thumbing through the pages and stopping every now and then for closer inspection, he looked at up at the FBI agent. "Holy shit."

"What?"

JR continued to study one page for a several moments.

"What is it, JR?"

"Without reading it more closely, this appears to be Judy Ling's diary. The story Judy's mother told Mia's grandparents about the father abandoning them was a lie."

CHAPTER 5

FBI Field Office – San Francisco, CA

JR occupied an empty cubicle, his cell phone pressed to his ear as he typed on a laptop.

Sean Kruger said, "Do you need me to come out there?"

"No. Tim Gonzales is my shadow."

Kruger laughed. "Good."

"He's a good man, Sean. He reminds me of you, quiet until he needs to say something. When he does, people listen."

"Why do you think I told the director to transfer him to San Francisco? Charlie Brewer will bring out the best in him. So, what do you think is going on?"

"No idea at the moment, but it's not passing the smell test."

"Okay."

"Tim is starting to believe the death of Mia's mom is suspicious."

"You told me that earlier. Why does he think so?"

"She left her personal journal in a lock box a long

distance from where she lived. To tell us where the diary was, she left a message written in ASCII code hidden in a bundle of letters. Why would she do that?"

No answer came from the retired FBI agent.

"You're thinking the same thing I am, aren't you?"

"I haven't said anything."

"Yeah, but you're thinking it."

More silence.

JR stood and pressed the phone tighter to his ear. "When we got to the bank, we were told the commune's lawyer tried to retrieve the journal but was denied access."

"Huh... What's your next step?"

"Brewer's team is processing the journal for fingerprints. Once he's done, I can read it more carefully."

"JR, I'm not going to tell you what to do, but be careful. Something's not right."

"I agree."

"Do you need backup?"

"I don't think so. But I would like to know more about the commune. What's Jimmy Gibbs doing right now?"

"Driving to San Francisco. He was in San Diego."

JR smiled. "Am I that predictable?"

"I'm learning how to stay ahead of you."

***

The knock on the hotel room door came at 11:13 p.m. JR glanced at the clock in the lower right-hand corner of the laptop. He stood, walked to the door, and peered through the peephole. Satisfied the late-night visitor posed no harm, he released the chain lock and dead bolt.

Jimmy Gibbs glided into the room and moved swiftly to the middle. He turned and offered his hand. "How are you, JR?"

JR shook the offered hand. "Good, Jimmy, very good. Thanks for coming."

Gibbs glanced around the room. "Sean told me you had some developments today."

JR respected the man standing in front of him. Gibbs was in his late thirties, tanned, slender, with a long brown ponytail reaching down to the middle of his back. Movie-star handsome, he wore his normal attire. An untucked wild patterned silk shirt, baggy cargo shorts, and Birkenstock sandals. His appearance masked the fact he was a retired member of SEAL Team Three and one of the owners of KKG Solutions, an up-and-coming private military contractor.

"Sandy will be here tomorrow."

JR's eyebrow rose. "Why?"

"He says he owes you. Wouldn't miss it."

"Why does he think he owes me?"

"He still can't get over the rifle shot you made that fall in the woods around Joseph's house."

JR took a deep breath as he thought about the events leading up to the end of Randolph Bishop, a serial killer on the verge of executing Sean Kruger with a pistol. Dawn cast an eerie diffused light over the wooded area. Sunrise was minutes away with most of the area in twilight. Especially within the tree line. Bishop could barely be seen standing next to a tree raising a pistol to end Kruger's life. Both he and Sandy Knoll were a hundred yards away when JR realized they would not get to Bishop in time. He stopped, dropped to a knee, took aim, and pulled the trigger. Bishop's head disappeared in a mist of blood and brain tissue as the shot from the high-powered Remington 700 found its mark.

Realizing he was staring at a spot on the wall. JR blinked several times to dissipate the mental image of that morning. "I appreciate him coming."

"So, what've you got?"

JR summarized the information known about the commune.

Gibbs sat on the edge of the bed without comment. He studied the contents of the cardboard box and the items stacked in neat organized piles.

When he finished, JR asked, "What do you think?"

"I think I need to do a little snooping around."

***

After Gibbs left the room to check into the hotel, JR did what JR did best. He employed his computer to find information. Starting with the email address from a business card taken from Becker's receptionist desk, he located the internet provider used by the attorney's office. With skills learned and honed over years of practice, JR gained access to the provider's servers. He then downloaded a program to monitor all email traffic from the attorney's office.

Afterward, he accessed the dark web via the Tor Network. He found the chat room he used years ago and gained admittance using an old *nom de guerre* from his days in New York City.

As the sun peeked over the California horizon, JR lay down for a quick nap. The information from his dark web search connected several dots of the puzzle surrounding the commune. He'd also learned more about Randall Becker. But how the information related to the death of Judy Ling, JR didn't know.

***

A knock on his door at 9 a.m. woke him from a dream about Mia. Groggy after only three hours of sleep, he stumbled to the door and placed his forehead against the cool metal. "Yeah."

"JR, it's Tim Gonzales."

He unbolted the door and stood back. The young FBI

agent blew into the room with an enthusiasm JR did not feel.

"Did I wake you?"

"No." He shuffled over to the coffee machine. It was a small Keurig unit, which JR appreciated. His coffee would be ready in less than thirty seconds.

While brown liquid filled a paper cup, JR noticed the journal in Gonzales' hand. "Whose fingerprints were on the diary?"

"Only Judy's."

"Good, then it's probably legit."

"That was the conclusion of our lab."

After a few sips of coffee, JR grimaced. But his head started to clear and he stood straighter. "Did you read any of it?"

"Just the first few pages. After that it got a little personal. I think we need to make a trip."

"To where?"

"Los Gatos."

"Why?"

"To talk to someone who knew Mia's father."

JR was fully awake now. "Who?"

"Ever hear of a small company called Apple?"

JR tilted his head. "Come on, Tim. Who?"

"Steve Wozniak."

"He left Apple in 1976."

"So, according to the diary, your wife's father knew the guy and was going to go to work for him at a new venture."

"Which one?"

"CL 9, the company that invented the first TV universal remote."

CHAPTER 6

FBI Field Office – San Francisco, CA
The Next Day

Special Agent in Charge Charlie Brewer closed the door of the small conference room and took a seat at the head of the long table. Tim Gonzales and JR sat to his right and Jimmy Gibbs and Sandy Knoll to his left. Keeping his attention to his right, he said, "Okay, you two, tell me what you learned in Los Gatos."

Gonzales said, "I have no idea what they talked about for the first hour of the meeting. JR and Wozniak were talking a language I didn't understand. Once they started talking English again, we learned the following. Mia's father's name is Chun Mao Ling. He went by Chu, or Chuy, not Chun. Second, his major in college was electrical engineering, specializing in transistor design. Third, and most importantly, Wozniak had started a new company called CL 9 and had an idea for the first universal TV remote. He needed someone who knew how to design the transistors, which Chu did. They had a deal all worked out, and Chu would be the main design engineer for Wozniak's new venture."

Brewer said, "Remind me what a transistor does, JR."

JR cleared his throat. "Computer codes, or, more specifically, computer instructions, are created by binary code. Which is a state of off or on. Off is a zero, on is a one. Transistors are the switches to create the off-or-on state. They're the guts of a computer, or any electronic device for that matter. Microchips are made with silicon and can have millions or billions of transistors embedded in them. From what Steve told me, Chu was a brilliant transistor designer. One day, he vanished. No one ever heard from him again. According to Judy Ling's diary, he was abducted by men working for Chu's father. Tim told me the only fingerprints on the journal were Judy's. Lab compared the handwriting to known samples, and they believe it is legit." He paused for a moment. "One other thing about the diary, and this bothers me. They found several pages cut out."

Gonzales took the journal from JR and opened it. "Three, toward the front. Hard to see if you're not looking for them."

Brewer asked, "Any hint to what might have been on them?"

"None. If you examine the page before and the page after, you can't detect anything missing."

"Okay, so who was Chu's father?"

Sandy Knoll said, "One of my sources at the State Department told me he was the Minister of Science and Technology for the PRC from 1988 to 2010." Sandy Knoll was a large man with light-brown hair kept short. His tanned face was lined from too many assignments in the Middle East. His wardrobe normally consisted of a dark-blue polo shirt with sleeves stretched tight over his bulging biceps. With twenty years as a retired Army special forces major, he then spent a few years as the leader of an FBI

Rapid Response Team. He clasped his hands and said, "JR found a reference to a death notice for the man posted in the winter of 2012."

Gonzales picked up the narrative. "According to the diary, Mia was one month old when Chu was abducted. Judy took her daughter and fled to Texas. The mother waited four years before she returned to search for him."

"Gentlemen, people with higher authority than I will want answers. Why do we, the FBI, need to be involved with this matter?"

The young FBI agent sat back in his chair and folded his arms before he answered. "Because, we feel Judy Ling was murdered."

"Which would be a local police problem. So, again, why should the FBI be involved?"

"We have evidence an agent of a foreign government was involved in the death of Judy Ling."

Gonzales remained quiet as he waited for Brewer to respond.

"What evidence?"

JR spoke next. "The original commune property has evolved into more of an assisted living complex. Only a few of the original members are still alive. They've had zero new members since the late nineties. Many of those members, like Judy Ling, who were longer-term residents, had nowhere else to go. So, in exchange for the stock they held in the commune corporation, they were given lifetime care. There is a possibility Judy was the last resident."

Brewer pursed his lips and leaned forward, arms on the conference table. "I thought it was a nonprofit entity."

"You can make any organization appear to be a nonprofit with the right accountants."

Brewer was quiet for several seconds. "How did you find this out and where is this leading, JR?"

"I'm getting there."

Chuckling, Brewer gave JR a crooked grin. "Kruger told

me you like to draw out your explanations. Go on."

"The commune is an unnamed gated community now. The residents who lived within its perimeter were each given a small cottage. The structure and furnishings remained the property of the corporation. It's where a lot of the profits are hidden. That's why the only personal belongings given to us were in a cardboard box. Their policy is anything of value goes back to the corporation."

Knoll took a deep breath and let it out slowly. "Sounds a little like socialism."

JR continued. "The concept of a commune is the core belief of communism. All property is communal. However, the commune Judy Ling chose is a little dysfunctional. It probably wasn't at the beginning when she joined, but it is now. There was a core membership that adhered to the deep-rooted philosophy of shared resources. Those members have either died or moved away. The group leading it today are extreme capitalistic. Their leader is Randall Becker."

Brewer said, "Despite the fact you haven't answered the original question, I will ask another. How did Becker get involved?"

JR shook his head. "Don't know. The name Randall Becker doesn't appear anywhere on the list of members. But, that's not unusual in a loosely organized group like the original commune. But his name does appear in the nonprofit organizational paperwork on file with the state."

Gibbs spoke up for the first time. "When was that?"

"June of 1997."

Gonzales referred to a file laying in front of him. "He didn't earn his law degree until he was forty-four in December of '96. He's never been in private practice, either, has he?"

"No." JR handed Brewer a piece of paper. "Not that I could find. As you can see in this screen shot of the original company org chart, he's always been the lawyer for the nonprofit."

Knoll doodled on a notepad in front of him. "My guess would be he was a member of the commune at one time. Probably in a position of leadership."

Everyone around the table nodded, except Brewer. He turned back to JR. "This is a wonderful story. But you still have not answered the initial question of why the FBI should be involved."

JR displayed a grim smile. "Because Judy Ling got serious about finding Mia's father after being told she was going to be a grandmother. It took her five years, but she finally secured an appointment with the San Francisco office of the Consulate General of the People's Republic of China. There are also records of an envoy visiting her cottage on numerous occasions a few weeks before her death. There are no references to those visits in her diary."

Brewer took a deep breath. "Kruger said you loved to drag explanations out, JR. Where is this leading?"

"Judy Ling was found dead several hours after her last visit from an emissary of the consulate's office."

"And…"

"That particular individual left the United States on a flight to China four hours later."

"What was the cause of death?"

Gonzales answered, "We don't know. The body was hurriedly cremated. No autopsy."

Sitting back in his chair, Brewer took a deep breath. "Okay, you have my attention."

JR tapped the file in front of him with a finger. "I can't find any references to a man with Mia's father's name. I'm speculating here, but I think he has become an extremely important person within the Chinese government. His father was, and the fact someone is willing to kill to keep him from being found gives the theory credibility."

"What's next?"

"Find Mia's father."

"How?"

JR inclined his head toward Gibbs and Knoll. "With a little help from my friends."

Brewer drummed his fingers on the conference table. "I don't think I want to know any more details. Sean Kruger speaks highly of all of you. I trust him. Do what you need to do. But don't get caught."

All three men stood. JR said, "Goes without saying."

CHAPTER 7

Sonoma County, CA

Retired Army Major Sandy Knoll kept his attention on traffic ahead of the rented black Chevy Tahoe. With the meeting at the FBI field office over, Knoll headed for their hotel. Jimmy Gibbs sat in the passenger seat staring out the side window. The only sound inside the SUV, the radio tuned to a local jazz station.

"What do you think, Major?"

"I agree with Gonzales. Mia's mom was murdered."

"Without a body or eye witness, it's going to be tough to prove."

Knoll nodded, and the two men fell into silence again. After several minutes, Gibbs turned his attention away from the window.

"Unless someone checks out Judy Ling's cabin and finds evidence."

"Who would that someone be, Jimmy?"

"I would need to change clothes and wait until dark."

"Agreed."

"How do we know which one was hers?"

Leaning forward in his seat and keeping his eyes on the road, Knoll pulled a folded piece of paper from his back jean pocket. He handed it to Jimmy. "JR gave this to me as we were leaving the meeting."

Gibbs unfolded the paper and appeared to study it. It was a printed copy of a PDF file for the lease agreement between Judy Ling and the co-op designating the address of the cottage she would call home. A map on the document clearly identified where the house could be found. "He's scary sometimes, Major."

Knoll smiled. "Yes, he can be sometimes. Glad he's on our side."

"No shit."

***

A light mist swirled from low-hanging clouds, leaving everything damp. The combination of an overcast sky and being a few minutes past midnight plunged the rural road in Sonoma County into total darkness. A large SUV slowed to a crawl as one of the passenger doors opened. A figure exited and shut the door. As soon as the man disappeared into the tree line next to the road, the vehicle accelerated away.

Gone were the colorful shirt and baggy shorts from earlier in the day. The slim figure wore black shoes, black jeans, a black long-sleeved T-shirt, black watch cap, and black face paint. He wore night vision goggles attached to a stabilizing harness resting on his head. Strapped to his right ankle was a Sig Sauer P226 and on his left, a Fairbairn-Sykes combat knife. A slim black rucksack clung to his back. With the practice from years of clandestine activities, Jimmy Gibbs melded into the trees surrounding the commune's residential area.

He encountered his first obstacle, a ten-foot wrought

iron fence, twenty yards from the road. He checked to make sure there were no security cameras close to his location. Satisfied none existed, he scaled the fence with ease. Now inside the compound, he headed for the cabin recently occupied by the late Judy Ling. From the backpack, he extracted a small GPS unit with the cottage coordinates programmed in.

Once on the residential roads, his night goggles became unnecessary due to streetlights placed every half block. The brightness of the surrounding neighborhood slowed his progress as he kept to the shadows and away from being illuminated. Each of the cabins in this section of the community were spaced fifty-to seventy-five yards apart.

When he drew closer to Judy Ling's cottage, headlights slowly approached his location on the asphalt road. The vehicle would occasionally stop, and a spotlight would shine on one of the small homes. Once the light extinguished, the car would move forward to the next cottage and the process repeated. Gibbs waited patiently until the car drove past the cabin where he hid.

Moving forward carefully, he came to the house diagonally across from Judy's. Keeping a low profile, he scurried across the road and blended into the darkness.

Identical in construction, the only difference between each building was the number on the front wall next to the door. A square front porch covered by an awning adorned each dwelling, along with a large window to the right of the door and a smaller one to the left. As he approached the rear of the house, he mused how the builder must have received a huge discount on the vinyl siding. Each of the cottages appeared the same color in the light from the streetlamps. It made all the homes of equal stature; no one had a nicer home than their neighbor. Chuckling, he thought about the irony of everyone having the same thing in a community designed for nonconformists.

A small concrete patio identified the rear entrance. He

found it locked. Holding a small Maglite, from his backpack, in his teeth, he used a slender metal tool from his back jeans pocket. After inserting it into the lock, he gained entry twenty seconds later.

With the door shut, he stood in the total darkness of the interior and listened for any movement in the small house. He detected a faint musty smell. Lowering his night vision googles, he surveyed the small kitchen. Paint cans, brushes, a small ladder, and tarps were arranged neatly on the floor. Apparently, the supplies were staged for a refresh to start later. Next to the painting supplies, he found several shipping cartons and spools of coax cables. Gibbs kneeled next to them. With the use of the goggles, he could read clearly. Descriptions on the side of three of the boxes revealed the contents. He frowned and withdrew his cell phone. The camera was a military version of the civilian model. It took detailed pictures with a small concentrated flash. After snapping several photos of the boxes, he stood.

Moving into the main living area, he found it empty. No furniture. He assumed the contents were removed for the remodel. Or to hide evidence of a struggle.

In a short hall on his right, something on the wall caught his attention. The green hue seen through the night vision goggles did not allow color determination, but from past experience, it appeared to be a blood splatter. He took a picture of the smear with his cell phone and walked farther into the hall. On his left appeared a small bathroom and a bedroom to the right. Inside the bedroom more smears and several dark handprints on the walls. Taking the backpack off, he removed a small box containing razor blades and a bundle of plastic tubes. Scraping samples from each of the five handprints, a fresh tube and blade were used for each smear. He then took a picture of each one and labeled the tube in the same order as the camera shot. These he returned to his backpack.

As he withdrew from the bedroom, additional stains

could be seen on the carpet. Snapping a picture, he used another tube and blade to cut fibers from the stains.

Stopping in the living room, he glanced out the front window. The vehicle with the spotlight was back and he heard voices outside. Quietly, he retreated to the kitchen and peered out the back door window. Carefully, he opened the rear exit and as he left, the click of a doorknob and the squeak of hinges could be heard as the front entry opened.

Keeping the NVGs down, he ran toward a small creek fifty yards from Judy's cabin. Gibbs reached it in less than six seconds. Sliding into the water, he returned his attention back to the house.

Overhead lights came on in the cabin as two figures appeared in the windows. One of the men opened the back door and stepped out on the patio. Gibbs removed the goggles and watched. The newcomer shined a flashlight over the backyard and then yelled at his companion inside the house, in Mandarin.

Being fluent in French, Spanish, Arabic, and Mandarin, Gibbs knew the man on the patio had told his companion the back door was unlocked.

As soon as the man on the patio disappeared back inside the house, Gibbs climbed out of the stream. His next destination would be his extraction point for Knoll to pick him up. As he moved closer to the asphalt road, more vehicles approached at high speed. Withdrawing into the shadows of the houses, two small SUVs sped past his location. No emergency lights or sirens, just moving fast.

Taking refuge in one of the cabins would be unwise. Keeping to the shadows and using the goggles, he maintained an advantage over anyone searching for him. He could see them. They would not see him.

He glanced at his digital watch. His infiltration of the gated community was lasting longer than planned or anticipated. As he moved closer to his extraction spot, more vehicles converged on his location. Having maintained radio silence since leaving the Tahoe, he tapped the small radio bud in his right ear. "Alpha."

"Go, Bravo."

"Too many guests. Changing party location."

"Agreed."

"Use Delta."

"On my way."

When he arrived at the Delta location, a white Ford Escape blocked his access to the fence. One man stood outside the vehicle speaking Mandarin on a cell phone.

Keeping to the shadows, he made a wide circle around the area. He approached the figure from the rear, but, when he was ten feet away, the man suddenly turned. They stared at each other in the dim light from the SUV interior for a brief second. The guard still held his cell phone in one hand. With the other hand, he withdrew a weapon from a holster. He wasn't fast enough.

Gibbs was on him in half a second, immobilizing his gun arm and rendering him unconscious with a choke hold. Relieving the cell phone from the man's other hand, he stared at the face for a few seconds and then rushed to his extraction point.

***

Knoll watched as Gibbs slipped into the Tahoe. "We're not paying you to take a swim, Jimmy."

"I got hot. How many vehicles converged on the place, Major?" Gibbs turned the cell phone over and removed the back cover.

"I counted twenty, but more were coming."

With practiced hands, Gibbs removed the cell phone battery. "Any particular direction?"

Knoll said, "It seemed like from everywhere." Glancing over at his partner, Knoll asked, "What are you doing?"

"Something JR taught me."

"What else did you find?"

Gibbs was silent for several moments. "Not sure, but I think there was a struggle in the house. I found what appeared to be bloody handprints. But we won't know for sure until they're analyzed. I managed to get several samples. The furniture was gone, and they had supplies ready to paint the place."

Knoll stole a quick glance at Gibbs. "They're going to cover up the evidence."

"Yeah, I would agree." He remained silent for a few moments. "When is JR leaving?"

"He's on a noon flight to Dallas. Why?"

"There were some boxes and cables stacked in the house next to the painting supplies. I didn't recognize them, so I took a few pictures. JR needs to see them."

Knoll glanced at the clock on the dash. "Let's wake him."

***

JR sipped on a cup of coffee, his eyes barely focusing. "What time is it?"

Knoll smiled. "Early."

"No shit." JR stared at his laptop as it downloaded pictures from Gibbs' cell phone. When the series of photos appeared on his screen, he squinted at them for several moments. Tilting his head, he zoomed in on the writing. After several more moments, he said, "Huh…"

"What?"

"I haven't seen these for a while. It's old technology."

Knoll rolled his eyes and sighed. "What are they, JR?"

Gibbs chuckled.

"Well, when you think about it, this accounts for why I couldn't find a trace of them."

Knoll took a deep breath and let it out slowly. "JR, what are you saying?"

Looking up at the large man, JR pointed to the boxes and cables. "Someone is setting up an internet access point, all hardwired, nothing wireless."

Gibbs frowned, understanding where JR was heading. "Everyone I ran into last night spoke fluent Mandarin. My guess it's their native language, plus they appeared the part." He paused for a few moments and reached into his back jean pocket for the cell phone he had taken in the early hours of the morning. The small plastic Ziplock baggie held three separate pieces. He handed it to JR.

JR stared at it for several moments. "Where did this come from?"

"One of the guys fluent in Mandarin."

"That's interesting."

Knoll crossed his arms over his broad chest. "JR, what do you think is going on in those cabins?"

"Well, these boxes contain servers." He pointed at the image on his laptop. "They were originally manufactured by a Japanese firm with zero scruples about exporting to China. I'd have to tear one apart, but I would bet they've been repurposed in China and shipped here."

Knoll tilted his head slightly to the left. "Why?"

"The pieces of the puzzle are coming together. My guess is they've been altered to be hidden from the Clearnet."

Knoll frowned. "In English, what the hell does that mean?"

"There are two internets, the Clearnet and the Darknet. The Darknet is accessible with the TOR browser and basically makes the computer using it invisible. These cabins are being used for a specific purpose."

"What purpose?"

"The Chinese government's hacking of the United States may not be originating from inside China. It may be hiding in plain sight right here in our own country."

Knoll reached for his cell phone.

CHAPTER 8

Petaluma, CA

Randall Becker listened as the caller informed him of the early morning invasion at the residential compound. His shoulder pressed the cell phone against his left ear, leaving his hands free to access his laptop. He remained silent as the events were described. When the caller finished his narrative, Becker stopped typing on the computer and took the phone in his left hand.

"Are you saying the missing cell phone hasn't been found?"

"Yes." The caller's English, while excellent, could not hide how his native Mandarin influenced his pronunciations.

"And?"

"It is not within the confines of the compound."

"Very disappointing. Surely, you've tried to locate it on its network."

"Whoever took it probably removed the battery."

"I see." Becker paused for a few moments. "What about

the Ling woman's cottage?"

"Painted, carpet ripped out and replaced. The house is now empty. Except for the equipment."

The clock in the bottom right corner of his laptop, showed the time to be a little after 9 a.m. "Impressive." Becker paused a few moments. "Who did the incursion?"

"We don't know. Whoever did it was good, very good. Evidence suggests military rather than law enforcement."

"CIA?"

"Possibly."

"What did they see in the house?"

"Paint cans, tarps, bloodstains, and equipment boxes."

"Most disappointing."

"Any instructions?"

"Yes. Shut down the project for a few days. Whoever did this will be unable to use any evidence they found in court due to it being an unlawful search. However, if, let's say the FBI returns with search warrants, we'll know who did it. If warrants are not served within a few days, resume operations. In the meantime, get the equipment out and store it somewhere."

"Very good."

The call ended.

Randall Becker stood and walked over to a credenza containing a small Keurig machine. He popped a dark-roast pod into the unit and waited for his cup to fill. Taking the steaming coffee back to his desk, he resumed working on his laptop. Closing the current document, he opened a web browser.

A Google Maps search brought up a diagram version of the southwest side of the town where Mia Ling-Diminski lived. Switching to the satellite version, he scrolled until the image converted to street level. The home was located in a neighborhood of newer houses. Becker used the mouse to travel the streets of the surrounding area. An elementary school appeared on a street several blocks away, but no commercial buildings were within a mile of her dwelling. Returning the image to the street in front of the address, he stared at the screen for several minutes.

Picking up the handset of his desk phone, he punched in a number. The call was answered on the third ring.

"Yes."

"It's Becker."

"Yeah."

"I need you to take a trip."

"Where?"

"Missouri."

"When?"

"Tomorrow. Stop by my office later, and I'll give you the details."

***

JR stared out the rear passenger window of the Tahoe. "I've rescheduled my flight for early tomorrow."

Knoll steered the truck into the parking lot of the FBI San Francisco field office. "We should have a preliminary analysis of Jimmy's scrapings when we get into the office. How do we prove it's Mia's mother's blood?"

JR kept his attention focused on the parking lot. "Mia had a complete blood and DNA workup after we found out she was pregnant five years ago. I have the information on my computer."

Knoll stole a quick glance at JR. "Really."

JR nodded.

Gibbs laughed. "Damn, JR, you think of everything."

"Uh... No. I should've contacted her mother years ago."

As Knoll parked the truck, silence descended upon the interior.

***

"From preliminary tests, the sample scrapings Jimmy

provided are indeed human blood. Furthermore, the blood-type antigens from those samples indicate a positive correlation to the individual in the detailed DNA workup you gave me a few hours ago. But, until a complete workup is finalized, a verifiable match is not possible."

Knoll stood in front of the forensic tech's desk and frowned. "In English, Debbie."

Debbie Sandoval was in her mid-forties, dark hair cut short, black blocky glasses in front of droopy hazel eyes, and thirty pounds overweight. She took a deep breath and rolled her eyes.

"I can't say positively until we can get the full DNA analysis on the scrapings, but I would say there is a strong possibility these two individuals are mother and daughter."

"That's what I needed to hear. Thanks."

Returning to the conference room five minutes later, he saw JR hunched over his laptop and Jimmy Gibbs leaning back in a chair talking on his cell phone. Gibbs ended the call when Knoll walked in.

"What'd they find?"

"Final tests aren't complete, but the blood you found in the cottage was probably Judy's."

JR said, "Now what?"

Knoll shook his head. "Don't know. We can't use the evidence in court." He gave Gibbs a half grin. "Your search wasn't exactly legal."

Gibbs stood and leaned against the table. "Doesn't matter. That was Gonzales on the phone. There's been a ton of activity this morning at the compound. They have the place under surveillance and saw a pickup with rolls of carpet and three Hispanic gentlemen go through the gate at 6 a.m. The same truck, without the rolls of carpet, left around eight thirty."

"They've probably painted the walls by now, too." JR closed the laptop. "No point wasting our time on it anymore."

Knoll stood in the door of the conference room. "Yeah, I'd say you're right."

***

"I have a tendency to agree with your assessment, Sandy." Brewer sat in a chair across from Knoll in the conference room. Gibbs was standing by a window, and JR sat next to Knoll. "Serving a search warrant would tip our hand. My guess is they don't know who conducted the incursion last night. Let's keep it that way. Gives us an edge."

Knoll nodded.

Brewer turned to JR, who had yet to say anything. "Have you been able to find anything about who's running the show over there?"

JR pursed his lips as he turned a paper coffee cup two turns to the right and then two turns to the left.

Brewer tilted his head slightly. "Want to tell us what you're thinking?"

The cup stopped turning and JR said, "The cell phone Jimmy brought out is basically a satellite phone made by Huawei. Which means, they aren't using any of the major carriers, so the servers are invisible to me. Plus, the SIMM card is of a design I've never seen before."

Brewer frowned. "A cell phone that is also a satellite phone."

"Yes. But something else is bugging me."

"What?"

"This all started because Judy Ling began searching for Mia's father. What is so important about keeping his identity secret that it cost Judy her life?"

Gibbs pushed himself away from the wall and sat at the table. He took a deep breath and said, "Because his knowing Judy and Mia are alive could cause problems for someone's plans. Someone very powerful."

Everyone turned to Gibbs. JR spoke first. "What makes you say that?"

"I don't have any proof, but what I saw at the compound convinced me something wasn't right."

Brewer tapped his fingers on the conference table. "What did you see?"

"It's what I didn't see. Every single house was the same. Not a bit of diversity, no personal touches visible on any of the cabins. Very institutional and impersonal. The place reminded me of a prison."

Knoll scowled. "It was night, Jimmy."

"Yeah, it was. But there was enough racket with all the cars speeding up and down the road trying to find me, it should have disturbed somebody. It didn't. Not one single porch light came on, or, for that matter, an interior light. Nothing."

Brewer frowned. "Maybe whoever lives in those cabins knew not to be too curious."

JR stood up suddenly. "I have to get to the airport."

Knoll stood, too. "Why?"

"I didn't think of it before. My visit to Randall Becker's office and the raid happening the same night could put Mia in danger."

Gibbs followed Knoll as they rushed out of the conference room behind JR.

As they drove toward the airport, Knoll placed a call on his cell phone. The voice on the phone listened as Knoll ordered the company plane to pick them up as quickly as possible. He ended the call and immediately made another. It was answered by a familiar voice on the fourth ring.

"Sandy, how are you?" Joseph Kincaid's voice was cheery.

Knoll's voice was not. "Fine, sir. We may have a situation and need your help."

CHAPTER 9

Southwest Missouri

Joseph Kincaid sat at the kitchen table of JR Diminski's house just outside the southwest city limits of a medium-size city in Southwest Missouri. After taking a sip of coffee, he watched Mia Ling-Diminski put plates in the dishwasher.

"Everything's fine, Joseph. JR's being paranoid. You know him. He gets carried away with his conspiracy theories."

"Yes, he has in the past been overly distrustful of our government's intentions. But, from what I was told, he may have good reason to be cautious this time."

Joseph was a tall, slender gentleman whose normal uniform consisted of a white Oxford dress shirt, neatly pressed khaki Dockers, navy blazer, scuffed brown loafers, and bold, colorful socks. His snow-white mustache and goatee enhanced his remarkable resemblance to the actor Morgan Freeman. No one knew exactly how old Joseph was, but Mia guessed mid-to-late seventies. She knew he, at one time, worked for the CIA during the Vietnam War. He also used to own a home security company and maintained close ties with an ex-president of the United States. Beyond those facts, she possessed little knowledge of his past. All she needed to know was that Joseph had befriended her and JR during a desperate time in their lives. He was JR's best man at their wedding and the namesake for their five-year-old son.

Mia chuckled. "Yes. He still dreams about black helicopters."

The older man's smile lacked mirth. "Have you seen any strange cars driving by the house in the last few days?"

"No, but it would be hard to tell with all the high-school-age kids living in the neighborhood, they have friends over all the time."

Joseph took a sip of his coffee. "I think it would be prudent for you and Joey to stay with Mary and me until we determine who killed your mother."

Mia stopped loading the dishwasher and turned to Joseph. "My mother was murdered?"

"Yes."

"JR didn't mention anything about it when I talked to him this morning."

"Sandy Knoll told me."

Mia stared at a spot on the wall and sat down across from Joseph. "Why?"

"They don't know. But JR believes it has something to do with your father. Judy tried to find him through the Chinese Consulate's office in San Francisco. Apparently, that may have led to her death."

A tear slid down her cheek as she clasped her hands together and studied the tabletop.

"Mia, JR will tell you more when he returns home. The KKG company plane is en route to pick them up. In the meantime, I believe it would help everyone sleep better if you and Joey stayed with Mary and me tonight."

She nodded slightly. "Okay."

"Why don't you pack a few things, and I'll drive you."

She stood and left the kitchen.

Joseph reached into an inside breast pocket of his blazer and retrieved his cell phone. He pressed a speed dial and waited. The call was answered on the fourth ring. "Mia is going to my property tonight."

"Thank you, Joseph. That makes me feel better. We won't arrive until late tonight. So, I'll head to your house after we land."

"Do you want us to install the cameras?"

After a few moments of silence, JR replied, "Yes. I'll just have to live with them."

"You'll be fine." After the call ended, Joseph stood to see if he could assist Mia.

***

As Joseph placed Mia's overnight bag in the back of his black Range Rover, a van parked on the street in front of the house. Lettering on the sides of the van indicated it belonged to a company called Ozarks Security. Two men stepped out of the vehicle. Both were trim, muscular, and wearing blue coveralls. They had a military bearing about them. Joseph walked over to greet them. Mia watched as the men shook hands with her friend and then point to several spots on the house. Joseph conversed with the men for several minutes before he returned to the Range Rover.

After he sat behind the wheel, Mia turned to him. "Friends of yours?"

Joseph smiled and said, "Yes, I've worked with them a few times."

She continued to stare at him.

He started the SUV and looked over his shoulder as he backed out of the driveway. "I sold my home security company to them when I started working for the president."

"What are they going to do to my house, Joseph?"
"Nothing you will ever notice."

***

The first drive-by occurred at three the next morning.
Motion-sensor cameras secured in various areas of the
front, sides, and rear of the Diminski home recorded the
entire incident. A black Chevy Equinox passed the house
moving west and not a minute later headed east. It slowed
on the second pass and parked two homes east of the
Diminski residence. A figure dressed in black was caught
by the various cameras as it walked around the home. This
individual could be seen stopping at each window and
touching it toward the bottom. The cameras then captured
an image of the person placing a small box behind a large
shrub in the front yard.

Afterward, the intruder returned to the SUV and drove
it out of camera range.

***

JR and his friends arrived in Springfield at 12:16 a.m.
Sandy Knoll headed toward Stockton where he lived.
Jimmy Gibbs drove JR's vehicle parked at the airport to
Joseph's Christian County home.

Joseph's property was a sprawling parcel of land five
miles south of Sparta, Missouri and a half mile west of
Fairview Road. To the east, Bull Creek ran through the
front part of the property. Trees were the main feature of
the twenty acres behind the modern log house. Access to
the home was difficult by anything other than a four-wheel-
drive truck or SUV.

Few individuals, outside of Joseph's friends and family,
knew about the house. Joseph considered JR and Mia part
of his immediate family.

As JR exited their all-wheel-drive Honda CRV, he could see Mia standing on the well-lit wraparound front deck. JR always marveled at the elegance and beauty of the structure. He never tired of visiting. The presence of Mia at the entrance added to the beauty of the place. When he got to the porch, they embraced and held on to each other longer than normal.

***

JR sat on a stool at the breakfast bar watching a video of the first drive-by on Joseph's laptop. "Why is he touching the windows?"

Joseph handed JR a small transparent disc. "They appear to be very sophisticated sound pickups that transmit any conversation in the room to the box hidden in the shrub. The box is a burst transmitter."

While JR examined the small disk, Joseph continued. "These little things rival some of the CIA's most advanced equipment. If you didn't know they were there, you wouldn't see them."

"Huh..." was all JR could say.

Finally, after studying the object, he looked at Joseph.

"Any detailed images of the SUV?"

"One good image of the license plate. It's a Hertz rental."

"Do we know who rented it?"

Gibbs chuckled. "Waiting for you, dude."

JR turned his attention to Gibbs. "Right." He opened the lid to the laptop. When it booted up, his fingers danced on the keyboard. Five minutes later, he straightened on the stool and took a deep breath. "It was rented last night and returned this morning. Credit card was a corporate American Express owned by a company called Oriental Imports, based in San Francisco. Driver's license used by the renter is fake. No such person in the California

Department of Motor Vehicle database."

Joseph grinned. "That's the JR I know and love. Anything on the company?"

"Yeah, according to the California Secretary of State's office, it's a subsidiary of a holding company based in Hong Kong. Guess who's listed as a board member for the holding company?"

Gibbs said, "Randall Becker."

"Yep."

Joseph raised an eyebrow. "Who's Randall Becker?"

Typing again, JR pointed to the screen. "That is Randall Becker."

Leaning over JR's shoulder, Joseph saw a headshot from the California Bar Association. "A lawyer?"

"Uh-huh." JR typed some more. "He's the attorney I met with in San Francisco about Judy's will. His only client is the company formed by the commune. Which, by the way, is no longer a commune. It's still classified as a nonprofit organization, but it owns a lot of property and commercial developments."

"How does it keep nonprofit status?"

Gibbs answered the question. "They operate a housing community for aging commune members. It's where Judy Ling was living when she was murdered."

Mia had been sitting at the kitchen table quietly. With the mention of her mother's name, she said, "I've been reading my mother's journal. My mom and dad were scared of his father. Do we know anything about him?"

Joseph nodded at his wife, Mary Lawson. She said, "I spoke to an old friend at the State Department. Mia's grandfather was the Chinese Minister of Defense until 2010. He died in 2012. His name was Ling Mao Yin."

JR asked, "Ling is the family name?"

"Yes. Apparently, Mia's father Americanized his name to Chun Mao Ling. My friend in the State Department could not find any references to a person by that name.

However, in a State Department summary after his death, there is mention of Yin having a son. No name was given."

Joseph said, "I checked with one of my contacts at the farm. The only reference they have to Yin's son is from a memo dated November, 1994. Apparently, he was doing sensitive research for the Ministry of Defense."

JR had turned his attention back to his laptop. "Did the memo mention a name?"

"Yes, Ling Mao, nothing more."

Typing as fast as he could, JR was quiet for several minutes. "Huh…"

Joseph rolled his eyes. "What?"

Looking up from his laptop, JR said, "It seems the reason I could never find anything about Mia's father was I was using the wrong name." He cast his gaze on Mia. "Ling Mao is the reason China is gaining a leadership role in manufacturing of microchips. He's a reclusive figure, rarely appears in public. But, from what little I can find, he's the reason China is gaining on the United States in innovative chip designs."

CHAPTER 10

Later That Same Day

JR placed his hand on his wife's shoulder. "Mia, we can't go home right now. Our house is bugged. You heard what Joseph said."

"Yes, but Joey's getting restless. We need some of his things so he'll feel more at home."

"And so are you."

She placed her hand on his cheek. "Yes. I feel like a fish out of water here. Nothing to do but sit around and worry."

"What do you need?"

"I didn't bring my laptop, so I can't work on any of the projects Jodie needs help with. Plus, I need to swing by the library and pick up some books for Joey."

"Let me talk to Jimmy. Maybe he knows a way for us to get in and out of town without being seen."

"Thank you, JR."

***

JR opened the passenger door for Mia to enter their Honda CR-V. When she was comfortable and put on her seat belt, he closed her door and walked to the driver's side. He glanced around the parking lot behind his office building. Jimmy Gibbs sat in a dark-gray Ford Explorer several rows back. Using a prearranged signal of having both hands on the steering wheel, Jimmy told JR the parking lot was clear. JR rubbed his chin, acknowledging he understood, as he opened the driver's side door.

The drive back to Joseph's place in Christian County took around thirty minutes, depending on traffic, from the city limits of Springfield. Twenty minutes later, they were driving east on Highway 14 past the eastern edge of Ozark, Missouri when JR noticed, in his side-view mirror, Jimmy's dark-gray Explorer followed about a quarter of a mile behind. Then an older black Chevy Tahoe passed Jimmy's vehicle at a high rate of speed. Concerned, he checked the road ahead and saw a tractor-trailer rig in the westbound lane of Hwy14. As distance between the Honda and semi decreased, the Tahoe veered toward the shoulder of the highway. A quick glance in the rearview mirror showed Jimmy's Explorer closing the gap.

As the paths of the semi and the Honda merged, the Tahoe drew alongside the Honda on the right and slammed into the side of the SUV. Anticipating something like this, JR attempted to counter steer, but the nearly three-ton mass of the Tahoe compared to the one-and-a-half-ton mass of the Honda, made this move unsuccessful. The Honda veered into the path of the nearly forty-ton truck.

***

Homer Hopkins, a thirty-year veteran of driving over-the-road tractor-trailer rigs, watched the drama unfold in the opposite lane. A man of average height and slightly overweight, he wore his hair short, making it easier to keep clean on long over-the-road trips. He always kept an unlit cigar clamped in his teeth when he drove. He never smoked them. He liked the aroma. During those thirty years, his safety record with A&B Freightlines revealed he had two-and-a-half-million accident-free miles. A record for the company. A plaque awarded to him by his supervisor for this feat was proudly displayed in the den of his home in Ava, Missouri.

His empty rig headed west on Missouri Highway 14 toward Ozark, MO. The drama in front of him played out as the black Tahoe veered to the left onto the shoulder of the highway next to the Honda. One of the reasons Homer Hopkins had two-and-a-half-million accident-free miles came from his anticipation of what stupid drivers were about to do. With reflexes honed by thirty years of driving, his mind's eye saw the Honda being forced into his lane seconds before it happened. Steering the big-rig toward the shoulder of the road, the Honda flashed past the cab of his truck, avoiding a horrendous head-on collision. Unfortunately, the empty trailer had not cleared the road when the Honda struck its back wheels.

***

Accelerating away from the incident, the driver of the Tahoe glanced into his rearview mirror. His restricted view showed the Honda skidding toward the shoulder of the highway in a violent spin, the front of the vehicle destroyed beyond recognition. Returning his attention to the front window of the Tahoe, he sped toward the east.

***

Jimmy Gibbs made a call to 911 as the Explorer skidded

to a stop next to the damaged Honda CR-V. Steeling himself for what he would find in the crumpled vehicle, he rushed toward the passenger side where the damage seemed less severe. A quick glance into the interior of the Honda revealed, to his surprise, not as much damage as he feared. All the airbags had performed as designed.

The driver's side of the vehicle appeared to have the heaviest damage. As designed, the collision pushed the engine under the Honda and not into the passenger compartment. Mia's door opened with some reluctance. Her eyes were closed when he felt her neck. His experience as the medic for his SEAL Team paid off as he quickly found a strong pulse. Relieved she was alive, he glanced over at JR. He appeared dazed. A deep cut above his eye bled profusely. JR wiped the blood with the back of his hand and reached for Mia with the other.

"She's okay, JR. Don't move."

JR appraised Gibbs with a faraway expression. He sat back, leaned his head against the head rest, and closed his eyes. In the distance, the wail of sirens could be heard as first responders rushed to the scene.

***

The driver parked the Tahoe in the parking lot of a large box store next to a dirty white 2005 Ford F-150. He exited the Tahoe and walked into the store where he purchased a pack of cigarettes and a one-liter bottle of Coke. Keeping his head away from the security cameras, he paid cash for his purchase. He then returned to the lot and got into the pickup. He backed out of the parking slot and drove the short distance to US 65 and Highway 14. Turning north on 65, he settled back to put as many miles as possible between him and the accident.

***

As Gibbs watched the firemen use their Jaws of Life to extract JR from the wreckage, he stood next to the semi driver. "How did you know to steer to your right?"

Homer Hopkins glanced at Gibbs. "You ever drive a rig over the road?"

Gibbs shook his head.

"I've been doing it for thirty years. You see a lot and learn to anticipate the consequences of drivers doing stupid things. The guy in the Tahoe was being stupid."

"He did it on purpose."

Hopkins appraised Gibbs. "How do you know?"

"I just know."

Hopkins said, "Shiiiitttt."

As a medivac helicopter hovered in preparation to land on the highway, both Hopkins and Gibbs flinched.

Hopkins noticed Gibbs' reaction. "You act like you were in the military."

Gibbs nodded. "Navy."

The semi driver chuckled. "I won't hold that against you. I was Army."

Gibbs watched the EMTs load Mia into the air ambulance. As soon as the doors shut, the rotors spooled up for takeoff. As the copter rose and turned toward Springfield, he turned to Hopkins. "Did you see the driver?"

"Yeah."

"Can you describe him?"

"Only got a glimpse. I was in 'Nam during the evacuation of Saigon. I'll never forget what they look like."

"What do you mean?"

"I was only eighteen at the time. First deployment. I remember the panic and desperation of the citizens as Charlie encircled Saigon."

Gibbs let Hopkins reminisce.

"The driver of the Tahoe looked like a native of Saigon."

Taking his eyes off the extraction of JR, he turned to Hopkins. "He did?"

"Yup."

Gibbs reached for his cell phone.

***

Sean Kruger arrived at the hospital's emergency room waiting area and found Joseph talking on his cell phone. When Joseph saw him, he ended the call and walked toward his old friend.

Kruger asked, "What happened?"

"JR and Mia were forced into the path of a semi by a Chevy Tahoe. Highway Patrol found it thirty minutes ago in a Walmart parking lot in Ozark. Damage on the left side of the vehicle matches paint color of JR's Honda. Allen Boone called me and said the Highway Patrol would run an analysis on the paint to confirm."

"What about the driver?"

"The store has a security camera trained on the parking lot. Quality isn't good, but it shows the driver of the Tahoe parking the truck and walking into the store. He then returns and gets into a white Ford F-150 parked next to the Tahoe. Picture quality is poor, and the license plate of the Ford is obscured with dirt."

Kruger said nothing as he listened.

"The Tahoe was stolen off a car lot in Republic a day ago. Jimmy was following them, keeping an eye out for this type of thing. He's not sure where the Tahoe came from and blames himself for it happening."

"How are they?"

"Banged up a bit, but otherwise fine. JR bought the Honda for Mia five years ago when they learned she was pregnant. At the time, it ranked among the safest SUVs to drive, by several automotive groups. The vehicle has automatic emergency braking, which helped slow it down considerably. Plus, the driver of the semi anticipated what was going to happen. They were lucky. JR has a bad cut over his left eye. Mia had her seat belt on and all the airbags deployed. She's okay, just shaken up. The Honda's totaled, but it did the job of protecting them. If the truck driver hadn't been aware of the situation, the outcome would have been a lot different, and we would be gathering at a different place." He paused. "One other thing."

"What?"

"Jimmy was talking to the driver of the semi. He got a glimpse of the person in the Tahoe."

"Yeah…"

"Probably, Chinese."

"Did JR stir something up when he was in California?"

"Apparently. He said the commune didn't pass the smell test. Plus, Jimmy had a midnight excursion into Mia's mother's house."

"And?"

"Everyone he encountered during his intrusion spoke fluent Mandarin and looked the part."

Kruger was silent for several moments. "When can I see them?"

"I was waiting for you. Follow me."

CHAPTER 11

San Francisco, CA / Springfield, MO

Randall Becker held his cell phone tight to his ear with his left hand. His eyes were closed as he pinched the bridge of his nose. "So, you didn't see the bodies. You just assumed they died in the accident. Is that what you're telling me?"

"No one could have survived a head-on with a semi. No one."

"But you have no proof."

"There was someone following them, I thought it best not to stick around. Besides, I saw the car hit the truck head-on. Trust me. No one got out of it alive."

Becker reverted to silence. As a lawyer, he wanted undeniable proof. He found the speculation by the caller irritating. The conversation taxed his patience. "Very well. Where are you?"

There was a moment of hesitation on the call. "Uhh...about ten miles west of a town called Lebanon on I-44."

Becker's laptop displayed a map of Missouri. "Good,

you're heading toward St. Louis. Drive to Lambert International Airport. We'll arrange for your flight. In the meantime, don't go over the speed limit."

"Wasn't planning on it."

After the call ended, Becker stood and walked around his desk toward the door of his office. He stopped at the receptionist's desk. "I've a lunch meeting at eleven, I'll be back midafternoon."

She smiled. "Do you want me to forward your calls?"

"No, that won't be necessary today."

Arriving at his Jaguar F-Type coupe, he sat behind the wheel without starting the car. Gripping the steering wheel with both hands, he clenched his jaw as he tried to steady his rapid breathing. Closing his eyes, he concentrated on taking deep regular breaths. Finally, his anger subsided, and he could think clearly. He started the car and drove out of the parking lot. He touched the In-Control screen and searched for a contact number. When he found it, the car made the call. It was answered on the third ring.

"Is our problem handled in Missouri?"

Becker replied, "Not sure. Our associate who made the trip screwed up, again. He let the intruder get away the other night at the residence compound and now can't confirm his assignment was complete in Missouri."

"Most disappointing."

"Yes, indeed, disappointing."

"What are your plans?"

"I believe we need to let this particular associate go. His performance has been subpar."

"Where is he?"

"Driving to Lambert International in St. Louis."

"Hmmm. Did you call me so that I can arrange his termination?"

"As your attorney, I am here to consult. How you handle personnel issues are up to you. But I would offer counsel it is time to terminate his association. Immediately."

The individual on the other end of the conversation laughed. The baritone voice reverberated in the small confines of the Jaguar's interior. "Becker, you are a piece of work. You want all the benefits, but will not get your hands dirty. Amazing."

Becker said nothing. This was not the first time he was accused of this by his employer, and it would not be the last.

"Very well. I will handle the situation. Tell him to wait near the Frontier ticket counter. Someone will meet him with his flight information."

"Consider it done."

The call ended, and Becker called the driver.

***

Kruger stood at the foot of JR's hospital bed. Joseph knew the right individual who pulled the necessary strings for the couple to be in the same room. Folding his arms, the retired FBI agent said, "I've seen you look better."

"That bad?"

"Depends on your definition of bad."

"Mia is okay. That's all that matters." He glanced over at Mia in the next bed. She smiled.

Kruger took on a serious demeanor. "What happened?"

"Guess I pissed off somebody in California."

"How?"

JR shrugged. "You know me. I can get cranky sometimes."

"I'm serious. How?"

"Something's not right with the commune, Sean. Their lawyer's hiding something. From what Jimmy found in Judy's house, they're converting the residential compound. And it appears to be concerning computers."

"What?"

"Without seeing the actual equipment, I can't say for

sure."

"Can you guess?"

"Yeah, I can guess."

Kruger rolled his eyes. "What, JR?"

"I believe they are converting the houses within the community to be remote workstations."

Tilting his head to the side, Kruger frowned. "Workstations?"

"Yeah, workstations."

"For what?"

Taking a deep breath, JR grimaced and grabbed his side. "Shouldn't do that." Taking a shallower breath, he continued. "Once again, I'm guessing here, but it makes sense."

"Would you please spit it out, JR?"

"I have no proof, but I think someone is setting up hubs to conduct hacking incursions into targets within the United States."

"That's a serious charge. What makes you think that?"

"The pictures of the equipment Jimmy obtained. I traced the serial numbers on one of the boxes back to the manufacturer. It's a specialized server used for internet access. My guess would be they've been modified."

"Are you sure?"

"No. Like I said, it's a guess."

"How would you know for sure?"

"I would have to have access to one of the hubs."

Jimmy Gibbs sat in the corner of the room, his new mission the protection of Mia and JR. He spoke for the first time. "A repeat of the other night?"

JR nodded. "Only I would have to be the one doing the intrusion."

Gibbs gave him a mischievous grin. "Sneaking two into the compound will be challenging."

Kruger said, "No way."

Standing, Gibbs strolled over to where Kruger stood.

"Not if I cause a distraction."

"How?"

Looking at JR, Gibbs said, "Want to tell him?"

"The cell phone Jimmy retrieved from the compound revealed they have a vibrant IT department. One of the best I've ever encountered. As soon as they knew the phone was missing, all of their security protocols changed. Once I turned it on again, it became a seven-ounce bundle of inert plastic and nonfunctioning circuit boards. The internal memory chips were wiped clean. I was impressed."

"You're not telling us how you plan to cause a disruption."

"I'm getting there."

Joseph chuckled, Kruger rolled his eyes, and Mia shook her head slightly.

JR continued. "I hacked into Becker's email service."

Kruger crossed his arms. "Go on."

"It seems our Mr. Randall Becker opened an email he should have ignored. My initial low opinion of the man declined a bit more. He keeps his attorney laptop strictly for his legal business for the corporation. That's what it is now. A corporation."

Joseph straightened in his chair. "Who owns it?"

JR gave him a grim smile. "Public records show it owned by the commune. Once you get past the public veneer, it's a front for the People's Republic of China."

Standing, Joseph walked closer to JR's bed. "Can you prove it?"

JR did not answer right away. Finally, he said, "My source is good, but inadmissible in court."

"Who is it?"

"Can't tell you."

"JR?"

"Really, I can't tell you, because I have no idea who the source is. When I was active in Anonymous, this person was always our go-to person for information."

"Are they still active?"

"In Anonymous, yes. Very much so."

"Would they be willing to help you?"

"I'd have to reach out to see. If they are, we might have a way to disrupt Becker's plans."

Joseph frowned. "You keep referring to this person as they, why?"

"I have no idea if they are male or female."

Gibbs said, "Why does the Chinese government want to stay hidden behind a corporation?"

JR shrugged. "No one seems to know. I can guess, but I can't prove it. That's why I need to get access to one of their hubs."

Kruger started pacing. "I have an idea." The retired FBI agent crossed the room and then reversed course.

"That's good because I don't have a clue how to do it."

"We have to get you and Mia out of harm's way."

"Okay."

Kruger stopped pacing and turned to Joseph. "Has the hospital released the condition of Mia and JR?"

Joseph said, "No, all they are saying is they've been admitted without revealing medical status."

"Good."

JR asked, "What are you thinking, Sean?"

"Do you have anyone who can take over your business for a while?"

"Yeah, Jodie and Alexia."

"Good."

Joseph picked up on Kruger's train of thought. "Are you suggesting what I'm thinking?"

Kruger grinned. "Yeah, I am."

JR asked, "Would someone like to enlighten Mia and me? After all, we're the ones you're talking about?"

"JR, what do you do best?"

"Computer security."

"I know that." Kruger paused for a second. "But what do

you do equally as well?"

"I'm not following you, Sean."

"You know how to create a new identity for someone."

"I'm not doing that again."

Kruger shook his head. "No, this is only temporary. They killed Mia's mother and tried to do the same to Mia. They're afraid of something, and the only way they will be satisfied is if Mia is dead."

Gibbs chuckled. "I like it."

JR shot him a quick glance. "What? I'm not following any of this?"

Kruger folded his arms. "You're usually quicker on the uptake, JR. The hospital will state Mia died due to complications of the accident. You will then take a long leave of absence from your company to grieve and return her to Austin."

"I'm not going to hide, Sean. Never again."

"No, you're not going to hide. You're going to become someone else and infiltrate the commune's corporation."

JR stared at Kruger for several moments. As a smile grew on his face, he said, "I like it."

***

The driver glanced at the clock on his cell phone for the third time in as many minutes. The area around the Frontier ticket counter at Lambert International Airport was busy. Becker's instructions to wait in the area for someone to meet him with flight information made him nervous. One person sitting alone in this busy area with travelers coming and going, without luggage, would eventually draw unwanted attention. He glanced at his cell phone again. One hour. His wait was rapidly extending into a second hour.

When the clock on his cell phone indicated he had been waiting for sixty-five minutes, he made the decision to leave. As he was about to stand, a tall, lanky individual sat down next to him. The man was dressed in a dark business suit with an open-collar white shirt. Dark wraparound sunglasses hid his eyes. The driver noticed the newcomer's pockmarked cheeks. The man did not look at the driver.

"Relax. You're starting to draw attention to yourself with your fidgeting." He spoke English with a slight British accent.

Being cautious, the driver said, "Excuse me. I am waiting for my wife to join me."

The newcomer chuckled. "Becker sent me."

The driver relaxed. "Give me the ticket. I want to get out of here as quickly as possible."

"You will. But we can't let you take a plane right now."

"Why?"

The newcomer had still not looked at the driver. "The Missouri Highway Patrol has a security video of you coming out of a Walmart in a place called Ozark. It shows how you disposed of the Tahoe and transferred to the pickup. Very sloppy."

The driver stared at the side of the newcomer's head. "They can't trace the truck. The license plate was stolen."

Turning to the driver, the newcomer faced him and snarled. "They found the truck in long-term parking fifteen minutes ago. They're already searching the airport for you."

The driver said nothing.

"Becker's not pleased with your performance. You lost your cell phone the other night. Now you've screwed this assignment up."

Silence was the driver's only response again. He felt pressure on his thigh next to the newcomer. He glanced down and saw the man's fist against his leg. "What was that?"

"Your reward."

"I don't understand."

"No, I don't suppose you do."

The man in the business suit stood and walked out of the terminal. The driver started to stand, but he couldn't feel his legs. The numbness spread upward toward his chest, and a dark wet stain spread around his crotch. He smelled urine. When the numbness reached his chest, his ability to breathe stopped. He tried to scream, but without the use of his lungs, no air passed through his vocal cords. The realization he was dying was his last conscious thought.

A woman standing next to his seat looked down at the now-dead man and started screaming.

CHAPTER 12

Southwest Missouri

A two-year-old Toyota Camry parked in front of the house at 11 a.m. With the majority of the residents at work or school, the street remained quiet. The professionally dressed young woman stepped out of the car and scrutinized the well-kept home. She went to the trunk of her car, unlocked it with her key fob, and opened it.

Reaching in, she removed a large metal sign from a local real estate company. With some difficulty, she managed to drive the two sharp prongs at the bottom of the sign into the neatly mowed yard close to the sidewalk. With this task fulfilled, she returned to the trunk and removed an object resembling a large padlock. This she placed on the front door of the home and then returned to her Toyota.

Sean and Stephanie Kruger watched from across the street from a window in his office. They observed the woman placing the For-Sale sign in the Diminskis' yard. Kruger placed his arm around his wife as the woman in the Camry drove off.

Stephanie put her head on his shoulder. "How long do they have to play this little charade?"

"As long as needed."

"What if someone actually tries to buy the house?"

Kruger chuckled. "It will suddenly be under contract, pending financing."

Stephanie Harris Kruger patted her husband's chest and said, "Good."

***

The obituary appeared the next day, only online, not in the print version of the local newspaper. It was a summary of a young wife and mother whose life and promising future had been cut short by a tragic traffic accident. It explained how she was proceeded in death by her mother and maternal grandparents. It spoke of a loving husband and son and how she would be missed by friends and family. A local service for the newly departed young woman was not mentioned. Interment would be in her home town of Austin, Texas. The picture accompanying the online article was of a woman who vaguely resembled the actual person the obituary highlighted.

The grieving husband's company placed a notification on their website telling visitors the CEO would be taking a leave of absence for personal reasons. His longtime assistant and current President, Jodi Roberson, would assume his duties until further notice.

***

Only the husband, a tall muscular minister sporting short sandy hair, an attendant from the funeral home, and a slender man, who wore his long hair in a ponytail attended the service in Austin, Texas. The slender individual identified himself to the funeral home as the husband's brother. After the service, JR Diminski walked the one hundred feet to his rented gray Ford Focus parked on an access road in the cemetery and promptly melded into obscurity.

As soon as JR's car drove off, a man in a rented Chevrolet Malibu put his binoculars down on the seat next to him, started the car, and headed back to the airport. His report would state he saw the body being buried.

***

At 2 a.m. the day after the funeral, a black Jeep Wrangler parked on the street several houses to the west of the Diminski's home. A figure dressed in black dashed around the home removing small objects from the windows and a small box buried next to a shrub in the front of the house. The figure returned to the Jeep and drove off.

Pictures of the figure were taken at each window by motion-sensitive cameras. The images were downloaded to a laptop hidden in a hall closet and emailed to another laptop in Christian County thirty miles to the south of the house.

***

As the sun peeked over the tree line in Christian County, the supposedly grieving husband and the supposedly dead wife sat in the breakfast nook of Joseph's modern log cabin. Their five-year-old son remained asleep in his temporary bedroom. Both had an arm around the other, holding on for support. Both reviewed images of a person removing the sound sensors from the windows of their home.

Joseph stood behind them, sipping a cup of coffee. "I would say your ruse worked."

JR nodded as he concentrated on the images. At the end

of the video loop, he said, "For now."

Mia said, "What do you mean, for now, JR?"

"It means, we can't go back home yet. I need to find out why they killed your mother and why they tried to kill us. There's a reason they don't want your father found."

Kruger entered the kitchen. "I just got an email from the Highway Patrol. There was a body found in the ticketing area of Lambert Field."

Joseph turned to the retired FBI agent. "Oh?"

Kruger continued. "They found a Ford F-150 in a long-term parking lot with the same license plate as the one in the supermarket security video." He held the cell phone up for Joseph to see. On the phone was the image of a man, his face frozen in a death mask of horror. "They wanted to know if any of us recognize him."

Joseph replied, "No."

Kruger held the phone so JR and Mia could see. Both shook their heads.

Turning the phone so he could see the image again, he said, "I took a chance and sent the picture to Jimmy."

Joseph's eyebrows shot up. "Why?"

"Basically, on a hunch. It was a good hunch. Jimmy identified him as the guy he took the cell phone from during his incursion."

JR pursed his lips. "They're tying up loose ends."

"Yeah, I would agree." Looking at his friend, Kruger said, "Why would they send this guy to take out you two?"

Moving over to the sink, Joseph poured out is now cold coffee. "A good question." Reaching for the carafe in the Cuisinart coffee maker, he poured another cup. Turning, he leaned back on the kitchen counter. "A question that has a dire implication."

"What's that?" Mia sat straighter in her chair.

"Let's assume they sent the now-deceased man here to take care of business with no intention of allowing him to return to California."

Kruger nodded. "Yeah, punishment for allowing his phone to be stolen."

"Possibly. The implications of getting him out of California are more disturbing. I am now more concerned about your plan, JR, than I was before. These people are not playing games. They're dangerous and have no qualms about killing people."

Joseph turned to Kruger. "Did your contact with the Highway Patrol mention anything about finding identification on the body?"

"Such that it was. Driver's license was phony and a credit card issued by a bank in Atlanta. They're following up on it as we speak." Kruger turned to JR. "If you had the card number and the bank, could you get the information?"

JR pursed his lips. "Maybe."

"I kind of thought so. I asked Boone for it, and this is what he gave me." He handed the piece of paper to JR.

The computer expert studied the page for a few minutes. He then returned his attention to the laptop and started typing again. Ten minutes later, he stopped and stared at the screen. "The card was issued by a small bank north of Atlanta, The First Bank of Fair Oaks." He paused for a few moments as he switched to another screen. "It's really more of a debit card. There's a balance of five thousand dollars. If a charge is made, the balance is reimbursed automatically from a bank in the Caymans." He typed furiously for half a minute and then leaned back in his chair. "Huh."

Joseph viewed the screen over JR's shoulder. "What?"

JR pointed at the image. "Apparently, the account in the Cayman's is owned by a company in China."

Turning to his friend, Kruger asked, "Where?"

"Shenzhen."

A soft whistle rose from Kruger and Joseph.

Mia glanced at JR then at Joseph and Kruger. "What am I missing here?"

Her husband answered, "Shenzhen is the closest thing

China has to Silicon Valley. Most of their most advanced tech companies are located there."

Kruger asked, "Can you pinpoint which company controls the account?"

"Not at the moment. My guess is it will be a shell company anyway. It'll take time to dig any deeper."

The conversation waned for several moments. Kruger broke the silence. "How's your new identification coming?"

JR stood and went to the coffeepot. "Everything will be in place by tomorrow."

Joseph's brow furrowed. "I'm still opposed to this."

"I'm not crazy about it myself. But I can't think of a better way. With the help of Sandy and Jimmy, it should work."

"I hope so."

***

An hour later, Mia fixed Joey breakfast, and JR returned to the bedroom they used at Joseph's cabin. With the young boy fed and now watching television, Mia asked, "When do you think you'll be leaving?"

He was sitting at a small desk next to the bed. "Early in the morning. The FedEx package is supposed to be delivered to Sean's house by noon."

"What's in it?"

"New passport and driver's license."

"Your hacker friends?"

"Yeah."

She took a deep breath and let it out slowly. "How long do you think you'll be gone?"

"Not sure. Sandy returned to San Francisco over the weekend, and Jimmy leaves today. I'll get there around noon Pacific Time tomorrow. We'll see how it goes."

She frowned. "Please be careful."

"I will. I'm flying with Sean on the corporate jet tomorrow."

She folded her arms. "Is that supposed to make me feel better?"

He stood and went to her. They embraced and did not let go for a long time.

CHAPTER 13

30,000 Feet Above the Western United States

The Rocky Mountains slipped silently below the HA-420 HondaJet as JR studied the cumulonimbus clouds forming on the western side of the mountain range. While not a superstitious man, he hoped the appearance of the thunderstorm did not foreshadow ominous events in San Francisco.

He turned to the only other passenger in the jet. "Have you seen Charlie Brewer lately?"

Kruger shook his head. "I've spoken to him on the phone numerous times, but I've not been to San Francisco since I retired."

JR returned to staring down at the Rocky Mountains.

"Do you think your disguise will work, JR?"

"Don't know. I haven't worn my hair this short since grade school. I'll look ridiculous in the blocky glasses and blue contacts. Did I mention the contacts hurt?"

"Several times. Where did you come up with the name Harry Mudd?"

"I wish I could say I stole it from an episode of *Star Trek*, but I can't. A long time ago, I thought I might need to disappear again. I secured a passport and Virginia driver's license from a source on the internet. I opened a bank account under the name and tied it to an American Express card. Harry has a stellar credit rating."

"Who was the source?"

With a chuckle, JR said, "Alexia. The thin version. I personally think she used the name a few times during the time she lived in Mexico before we smuggled her out."

Kruger chuckled. "She was a little skinny in those days. Are you glad she works with you now?"

"More than glad. She's a fantastic partner. I'm sure Jimmy's glad we brought her out as well."

Except for the drone of the jet engines, silence returned to the plane's interior.

"Okay, Harry Mudd, what do I need to know about your background if asked?"

"Not much. He's a professor and a computer consultant with a doctorate in artificial intelligence. If anyone checks his credentials at Carnegie Mellon's School of Computer Science, my face, name, and academic successes will be readily available. As will my graduate records. I was able to digitally implant them last night."

"What if they get really curious and go back further?"

"Harry's secondary school records will be available at a large high school in Norfolk. Articles of incorporation of the company he supposedly owns are available from the Virginia Secretary of State's office. He has a successful computer consulting company with a dynamic website. The website was designed and will be maintained by Alexia. Everything on it is bogus, but should pass a cursory examination." He regarded his friend. "Anyone who accesses the site will get a stealthy virus downloaded without their knowledge."

"Sounds like you've thought of everything."

"I somehow doubt it. Alexia is on standby and can help at a moment's notice. She's worried about Jimmy, and I think this is her way of keeping track of him."

With the conversation returning to silence, JR leaned his head back and closed his eyes. Even though he knew Mia and Joey were safe staying with Joseph and Mary, he felt a tightness in his chest and a longing to touch her. Tears welled in his closed eyes. A feeling of emptiness overwhelmed him as he realized he would not feel whole until they were together again.

Somewhere over southern Utah, he fell asleep, waking as they touched down in San Francisco. Momentarily disoriented, the plane taxied to its hanger and his dream of Mia dissipated. Now fully awake, he realized it was time to get serious.

Parked next to the rented hangar near the FBO office, a black Denali with tinted windows waited. After he and Kruger deplaned, they threw their overnight bag into the vehicle. Kruger sat up front, and he slid into the back seat where Jimmy Gibbs waited. Before the door was completely closed, the driver sped ahead toward the airport exit.

Sandy Knoll drove, his light-brown hair longer than normal. Dark aviator sunglasses hid his eyes, and his biceps stretched the fabric of a dark-blue polo shirt.

Jimmy Gibbs displayed his normal grin and asked, "Nice flight?"

JR looked at his friend. "Better than flying on a commercial airline."

"Amen to that. I'll never forget flying halfway around the world in a C5 Super Galaxy. My back still hurts thinking about those flights."

Sandy chuckled. "No shit."

"Fill me in on what's going on here?"

Sandy kept his eyes on the road as he answered. "We've got Becker under 24-7 surveillance. Charlie Brewer's assigned the Gonzales kid to us full time, plus we've got a group of our guys wandering around keeping their eyes on things."

JR furrowed his brow. "We might spook Becker if he sees too many people following him."

Sandy shook his head. "He'll never see our guys."

Gibbs turned to JR. "Are you really going to use the name Harold Mudd?"

"Yes."

Knoll chuckled. "Maybe we should call you, Dirty Harry, JR. You have talents far beyond being a computer geek."

Kruger turned in his seat and motioned toward his friend. "While I didn't see it personally, I've been to the location where this computer geek took down a target with an eight-hundred-yard shot in one attempt." He paused for a second. "After not firing a rifle for ten years."

Keeping his gaze out the side window, JR's face grew crimson. "It actually took two shots. I missed the first time."

Sandy glanced in the rearview mirror. "One, two shots, who cares? You're a far better marksman than me."

JR shrugged. "Didn't know it was a contest."

Both Kruger and Knoll laughed. With a grin, Gibbs said, "JR, it's always a contest."

***

"So, what's your first step, JR?" Charlie Brewer and Gonzales stood inside JR's hotel room. Kruger leaned against the wall while Knoll and Gibbs stood by the window.

"I've been trying to hack into their computer system ever since Jimmy brought the cell phone out. It's one of the most impregnable firewalls I've ever experienced. So, that's our first step, getting access to their servers."

Brewer folded his arms. "How?"

JR took a deep breath. "Subterfuge."

"You didn't answer my question. How?"

"You sure you want to know?"

Brewer nodded.

"By creating a situation where they will want to check my background."

Turning his attention to Kruger, the FBI supervisor said, "You told me he liked to drag out explanations." He turned back to JR. "If you want my support, JR, you need to tell me exactly what you plan."

"Very well. I'm interviewing to be an artificial intelligence consultant for them. They'll want to check my background. Once they visit a website we created for this very purpose, their system will be infected, and I'll have a back door for access."

"I've heard a lot about AI recently. Do you know how they're planning to use it?"

"No, but artificial intelligence has a lot of applications besides the ones the entertainment industry is having a stroke about."

"What if they don't check your background?"

"Oh, they will. Computer people love to check the credentials of rivals. They have a need to know if the other person is smarter than they are. It's ingrained into their psyche."

Brewer stared at JR for several moments. The wrinkles on his forehead grew more pronounced. "What if they don't want to interview you?"

"They already do. My appointment's tomorrow."

The San Francisco SAC's eyes widened slightly. "How did you…"

JR raised his hand, palm toward the FBI supervisor. "You'll just have to trust me on this one. I won't tell you."

***

"I'm going in with you," Knoll stated more as a fact than a suggestion.

JR glanced over at the big man. "Why?"

"No questions. I'm going with you."

"Again, why?"

"In case something goes sideways."

"What could go sideways? It's a ruse to get them to check my website."

"What if you're recognized?"

JR's brow furrowed. "I've thought about that. Becker would be the only one who would know my face. He's not supposed to be there."

"What if he is?"

Taking a deep breath, JR said, "Let's hope my disguise holds."

"Kind of what I thought. You haven't thought this through. I'm going with you."

"What's your role?"

"I'm your assistant."

Raising his eyebrows, JR asked, "To an interview?"

"Then I'm your bodyguard."

JR chuckled. "Fine. I'll think of some way to explain your presence." He stared ahead as Knoll drove the busy streets of San Francisco heading toward the meeting. The only sound in the interior of the GMC Denali was the hum of the trucks' tires on pavement and the din of traffic.

Five minutes later, JR turned to the big man. "Thanks, Sandy. The more I think about it, the better I like the idea."

CHAPTER 14

Sonoma, CA

Randall Becker's cell phone vibrated. He chose to ignore it. The sound stopped and, twenty seconds later, it commenced again. He glanced at the caller ID. The call was from an international number, one he recognized. Debating whether to answer the call, he decided not to. The noise stopped and the phone went silent. Exactly one minute later, the same caller tried again. Taking a deep breath, he accepted the call.

"This is Randall."

"Why are you ignoring my calls?"

"I beg your pardon?"

"You're ignoring my calls."

The lawyer took a deep breath. "I have a few other tasks on my desk besides answering the phone."

"Whatever. Is the problem in Missouri resolved?"

"Yes."

"How?"

"The funeral was observed by one of our associates."

"Was the body identified?"

"It was taken directly to a funeral home."

"Did anyone see the body?"

Becker closed his eyes, his voice rising an octave. "From what I was told, a funeral service did not occur, just an interment. The casket was never open."

"Settle down, Becker. Where was the burial?"

"Austin, Texas. One of our associates observed the service."

Silence radiated from the cell phone. Finally, Becker heard, "Who attended?"

"Someone from the funeral home, a minister, the husband, and his brother."

The caller did not speak for a long time. Finally, Becker heard, "There is no record of the husband having a brother."

"I'm reporting what I was told."

"Where is he?"

"Who?"

"The husband."

Pinching the bridge of his nose, Becker said, "Unknown. He disappeared right after the service and has not returned to the home. Which is for sale, by the way. Website at his company indicates he is taking a leave of absence. For personal reasons."

"I am not hearing definitive answers from you. Is the daughter dead?"

"Yes."

"But the husband is not."

"Correct."

"Why?"

Becker took a deep breath. "I am not in a position to answer."

"Until the husband is dead, this matter is not over. Understood?"

"Yes."

"Good."

The call ended.

Becker put the phone down and leaned back in his chair. Taking a deep breath, he let it out slowly and closed his eyes. When he opened them, he stood and left his office.

***

The three buildings of the complex made a triangle. In the middle, the architects designed a courtyard for the office workers to relax and enjoy fresh air. At any given time, individuals could be seen sitting on one of the many concrete benches. Some contemplated cell phones. A few walked on an asphalt path that meandered around and through the green space. There even were a few holdouts huddled together smoking. And on occasion, individuals walked fast, with purpose, from one building to the next. Randall Becker was one of the latter individuals. His destination, the corporate IT department.

***

Using his ID badge, he entered the southernmost building via the rear door used primarily for maintenance and by technicians. He climbed the emergency stairwell to the third floor and burst through entrances into a large area dominated by rows of computer servers. Turning left, he followed the open area surrounding the server banks until he came to a closed door. The sign on the door was simple. One word indicated who occupied the office. It read, *Director*. He knocked once and opened the door without waiting for a response.

The man sitting at the cluttered desk was staring at a large video monitor as he clicked away on a keyboard. He was a large man: broad chest, protruding gut, bald, bearded, and thick wire-rim glasses in front of brown eyes. His weight a product of too many years sitting in front of a computer. But he was one of the best IT directors in the tech-savvy Northern California region. He did not look at Becker or acknowledge the attorney's presence.

Becker stood impatiently in front of the desk, allowing the man to finish his current task.

After several minutes, the man at the desk stopped typing and stared at the monitor for several more moments. Only then did he turn his attention to Becker.

"What do you want, Becker?"

"Have you made any progress in finding Diminski?"

Ethan Matheson shook his head. "Nope, not a trace. He's a ghost. At least he is on the internet. One day he's everywhere, the next…" He shrugged.

"That's unacceptable, Ethan."

"It may be unacceptable to you, Becker, but it is what it is."

"How can he just disappear? Everyone leaves a digital trace."

Crossing his arms, Matheson tilted his head slightly. "Not if you know how."

"What does that mean?"

"It means what it means. If you're an IT guy, and Diminski is a very good IT guy—maybe one of the best—you know how to disappear on the internet."

Becker stood in front of the desk, his hands on his hips as he glared at the IT director. His eyes narrowed and he said through clenched teeth, "Keep searching."

"Goes without saying."

"What about your other project?"

"Which one? I've got more than a few on my desk."

"The search for an AI consultant."

"We've had a few interviews. In fact, I have another one this afternoon."

"And?"

The big man shrugged again. "Don't know. He's a

professor on the East Coast. I don't know much about him, but his references are excellent. We'll just have to see."

"Don't forget the AI project is at the top of your priority list, Ethan."

"How can I forget? You send me ten emails a day about it."

Becker turned to leave but stopped. He faced Matheson again and leaned forward, palms on the desk. "Why do you think Diminski disappeared?"

Matheson didn't answer immediately. He chuckled and locked his stare on Becker. "Do you want a guess?"

"Yes."

"If my wife had died suddenly, I'd disappear, too."

Becker straightened. "Not the answer I needed. Keep searching."

"Whatever."

***

Sean Kruger sat on one of the concrete benches in the courtyard of the three buildings. Gibbs sat next to him. The retired FBI agent nudged his friend in the ribs. "There's Becker."

"He appears pissed."

"I agree, he does." He observed the attorney until he disappeared into one of the buildings. "How long before JR's appointment?"

Gibbs glanced at his cell phone he had been pretending to read. "About three hours."

"Who's on the lawyer's car?"

"Rick Evans and Bobby Garcia."

"Good. I like those guys. Make sure they know Becker is on the move."

Pressing the send icon, Gibbs brought the cell phone to his ear.

The call was answered on the first ring. "Yeah."

"Heads-up. You might have to take a drive."

"Got it."

The call ended. Gibbs said, "Now what?"

"We position ourselves in case Sandy and JR need assistance."

Standing, Gibbs said, "I'm going to meet Sandy and JR at the hotel. You got this?"

Kruger said, "Yeah, I'm good. Let Rick and Bobby know I'll be joining them in a few minutes. What are they in?"

"Gray Toyota RAV4. There are so many of them out here, they're practically invisible."

Kruger chuckled.

CHAPTER 15

San Francisco, CA

JR stared into a mirror as he attached a fake dark-brown mustache and goatee. The goatee featured gray hairs randomly on both corners of the chin rendering the facial hair prosthetic realistic. Gibbs was leaning against the bathroom doorframe as JR worked. "Damn, that looks real."

"Two years ago, I started working with a movie studio. They were getting hacked on a regular basis and their movies released early on the web." He chuckled. "I stopped the hacking, and they've been one of my best word-of-mouth clients ever since. Before I came out here, I called the CEO and asked for help with changing my appearance. He sent a limo with two makeup artists over this morning as consultants. He never asked why, he just did it."

When he was done, he turned toward Gibbs. "What do you think?"

"To be honest with you, with the short hair, glasses, and the chin hair, I wouldn't have recognized you if I hadn't seen you put it on."

"Then I believe I am ready for the interview."

"You never told us how this interview came about?"

"Before they wiped the cell phone, I was able to locate where their servers are."

"Yeah?"

"They're in one of the buildings adjacent to the attorney's office. With a little digging, I found out they had put out an SRFP on several academic websites."

"What's an SRFP?"

"Standard request for proposal."

"You put all this together in that short a time?"

JR grew quiet for a few moments. "No, the Harold Mudd persona was prepared a long time ago during a period of time I thought I might have to disappear again. The crisis passed, and I've kept him around for safekeeping." JR grinned. "He has a perfect credit score."

Gibbs chuckled.

Walking back into his hotel room from the bathroom, JR started placing files in a backpack. Gibbs now leaned against a wall next to the room's entrance. When a knock could be heard at the room's door, Gibbs turned and glanced through the peephole then opened the door. Sandy Knoll walked in and glanced at JR.

"Damn, JR, that's a good disguise."

Diminski gave Knoll a grim smile. "Let's hope so."

***

JR, in the disguise of Harold Mudd, was escorted into the conference room where Ethan Matheson sat in front of an open laptop. When JR entered, Matheson stood and extended his hand.

"Dr. Mudd, I'm Ethan Matheson. It's nice to finally meet you."

Shaking the offered hand, JR spoke with a slight English

accent he had perfected years ago when he was deep into the hacktivist movement. "Likewise, Dr. Matheson."

"Are you from England?"

"No, born in Cambridge, actually, parents moved to Oxford to teach when I was three. We moved back when I was eighteen. Can't quite rid myself of the accent." He chuckled. "And you?"

"Oh, nothing quite so continental. I'm from Oakland."

"Ahh."

He gestured toward one of the chairs surrounding the conference table. "Please, make yourself comfortable. I'm anxious to discuss the consultant position we have open."

"Very good. That's why I'm here."

JR kept eye contact with Matheson as both men sat. The larger man moved his laptop to his right.

Matheson spoke first. "We're looking for an individual to consult with our IT department. This person must be on the cutting edge of AI research. Our plans are to integrate AI into several protocols to enhance their efficiency. I've reviewed several of your papers on the subject. I must say they are most impressive, Dr. Mudd."

JR dipped his head slightly. "Thank you." His eye contact remained locked on Matheson.

"Are you still doing research?"

"Yes, mostly for the government, very hush-hush, you know. Mustn't discuss."

"Ahh..." Matheson checked the screen on his laptop for a few moments. "Are you in a position to consult with other firms?"

"Depends on the application. What did you have in mind?"

Matheson proceeded to tell him.

The interview lasted more than two hours. Toward the end, JR was beginning to put the pieces together, understanding what the eventual project would entail.

A sudden knock on the door of the conference room

distracted the two men from their conversation. Without waiting for an answer, in walked Randall Becker.

***

Sandy Knoll sat in the lobby of the IT department reading a magazine and listening to JR's interview with Matheson through a wireless earbud. A cell phone in JR's backpack acted as the transmitter.

A disturbance in the lobby drew his attention. Randall Becker charged through the area and headed straight for the conference room. Knoll stood and followed.

***

JR's stomach knotted, but he kept his face neutral.

Matheson appeared annoyed but stood anyway, as did JR.

"I apologize for the intrusion, gentlemen, but I wanted a chance to meet Dr. Mudd."

Matheson's nostrils flared as he glared at Becker. "Ahh, of course. Dr. Mudd, this is Randall Becker, our corporate attorney and general manager."

Becker walked around the table and offered his hand. "Nice to meet you."

JR shook the offered hand but did not respond.

Tilting his head slightly to the left, Becker stared at JR. "Have we met before?"

"Doubtful. This is my first trip to the West Coast."

"Ahh, what do you think so far?"

"The palm trees are interesting."

The attorney folded his arms and studied JR's face. "You do remind me of someone. You're sure we've never met?"

"I get that a lot, I must have a common face."

"Yes, maybe that's it. Anyway, don't let me disturb you,

I wanted to meet you, Dr. Mudd. I'll be going."

JR's expression remained neutral as he fought the tightness in his chest. When Becker left, JR remained standing. He glanced at his watch. "Unfortunately, I should be going. I have a late flight back to the East Coast. Do you have any additional questions for me, Dr. Matheson?"

Matheson pressed his lips together. "No, I believe we covered the topics needed. Once again, I apologize for the intrusion."

Raising his hand, JR said, "Think nothing of it."

"If we decide to offer a contract, when would you be available?"

JR pursed his lips and stroked his fake goatee. "I'm afraid I would need a month to rearrange other commitments."

"Good. That would work well with our timetable as well."

"Excellent."

Matheson offered his hand, and JR shook it. "Expect to hear from us by the end of the week."

"Very good. I'll look forward to your call."

JR exited the conference room and glanced at Knoll who stood nearby. The big man fell into step beside him as they made their way to the building's front entrance.

When they were outside, Knoll asked, "How'd it go?"

"We may have a problem."

***

Becker returned to his office and locked the door. After accessing the computer on his desk, he did a Google search for Harry Mudd, PhD. When he clicked on the website, a program downloaded and buried itself within the laptop's BIOS firmware.

After he browsed through the site, he settled on a picture of the professor. He studied it for a few moments and then went to the man's bio page. Five minutes later, he picked up his phone and called the head of the IT department.

"Matheson."

"Is Dr. Mudd still there?"

"No, he left right after your intrusion."

"Whatever. Did you offer him the position?"

"Not yet. I didn't think you wanted to be involved with this decision, Becker?"

"I didn't, but now I am."

"Okay."

"Under no circumstances are you to hire that man."

"That's ridiculous. He's the most qualified of any of the candidates."

The lawyer raised his voice. "Doesn't matter. Do not hire him."

"Becker, I am tired of you interfering with this department. I'm taking this up with the board."

"I speak for the board."

"Not what the chairman says."

Becker did not reply.

Matheson continued. "I had a chat with him several weeks ago about your constant micromanaging of this department. He agrees with me. Your lack of IT experience disqualifies you from making decisions about my team or myself. I, my team, and this department are off-limits to you."

"We'll see." He slammed the receiver back on its cradle.

CHAPTER 16

San Francisco

Knoll leaned against a wall in JR's hotel room, his arms crossed. He watched the computer hacker pack his bag as he prepared to check out. Jimmy Gibbs searched the hotel room for anything JR might have unknowingly forgotten. Knoll spoke first. "When are you two going into the residence compound?"

JR looked up. "Tomorrow night. I'm leaving this hotel in case Becker suspects anything. If they check with the hotel, my story of leaving tonight will hold up. I hope. Sean is meeting us there. He's talking to Charlie Brewer right now."

"About?"

"He didn't say."

Gibbs appeared out of the bathroom. "Do you know if they took the bait and checked your website?"

"Not yet."

Knoll frowned. "Becker didn't appear too happy when he left the conference room."

"He told me I seemed familiar to him. I think he suspects something."

"You think you're burned?"

"Let's put it this way. Harry Mudd won't be taking the consulting position."

Walking over to the window, Gibbs stared out. "What's next, JR?"

"I still need to get inside the company computers."

Knoll said, "Thought that's what your virus was supposed to help with."

"Matheson's no dummy. They'll find the virus and will trace it back to Mudd's website. I underestimated their capabilities."

"What makes you say that?"

Taking a deep breath, JR straightened. "From what Matheson described during our meeting, it's my belief they are working on taking hacking to a new level using artificial intelligence."

Jimmy stopped searching. "Why would AI take hacking to a new level?"

JR formed his answer in layman's terms. "Cyber hacking is a trial-and-error function. Most hackers try various methods to find holes and vulnerable pathways into secure servers. Once they are successful, someone comes up with a method to stop them. With AI doing the hacking, the time required to find an entry with trial and error would be reduced to microseconds versus the hours or days. Plus, AI would learn with each success. Safeguards, no matter how sophisticated, would be overcome in a matter of minutes versus the months or even years it takes human hackers."

Knoll frowned. "So, no matter what our government does, if the Chinese use AI, they can hack any server they want, whenever they want."

JR pursed his lips and said, "Kind of, it's more complicated than that, but, yeah, it's a good way to visualize the problem."

Gibbs displayed a puzzled expression. "I get all this, but why are Americans helping the Chinese with hacking our government?"

Staring at his cell phone, JR smiled. "Let's move to your hotel, I now have a path into their computers. Then, maybe I can answer your question, Jimmy."

***

By a little after 12 a.m., JR rubbed his fatigued eyes and stood. His neck and back were stiff from too many hours sitting in his new hotel room's uncomfortable desk chair. However, the hours spent doing so revealed grim facts concerning the true purpose of Ethan Matheson's project. He checked the time on his cell phone and hesitated for only a moment about calling Kruger at this late hour. He pressed the buttons and sent the call. His friend answered on the fifth ring.

"Yeah, what is it, JR?" Kruger's voice sounded husky with sleep.

"Got a problem."

His friend did not answer immediately. "Must be serious, you only call in the middle of the night when it is. Talk to me."

JR took a deep breath and slowly let it out. "We started on this little sojourn trying to find Mia's father. Right?"

"Yes."

"Then they tried to kill Mia and me. Right?"

"Again, yes."

"After rummaging around in their computer after you guys left the room, I think I found the reason they killed Mia's mom and tried to kill us."

"Spit it out, JR."

"Bear with me, Sean, I'm getting there. Remember in the last election all the accusations of the Russian's hacking our election?"

"Yeah, Washington wasted millions of dollars with special prosecutors and congressional hearings without a definitive answer. Why?"

"What the Russians did was a prank compared to what I've found."

Kruger did not comment for several moments. "Okay, talk to me."

"Despite being retired, you still have connections within the FBI and the government. Correct?"

"Depends. What did you find?"

"The commune is now a cover for a group sponsored by the Chinese government with plans to manipulate elections. They also have plans to attack crucial infrastructure, like utilities and telecommunication systems."

"How?"

"I wasn't able to put it together until a few minutes ago. The artificial intelligence experts they're interviewing specialize in how AI learns. Think about it for a moment. If an AI system can be taught to hack a computer, it makes human hackers obsolete. The advantage of an AI system doing the hacking is the speed at which it can gain access. Plus, it can then learn how to defeat any counter measures an IT department implements. This is very scary stuff, Sean."

"So, how do you know this?"

"Like I said, I'm in their computer system. Very sophisticated firewalls. I've never seen anything like them."

"Okay. What does that mean?"

"It's more or less hacker proof."

"So, how did you get in?"

"Deception."

"Okay, I won't ask for details. Now what?"

"Their system is extremely sophisticated. They will eventually find the code I downloaded. I'm surprised they haven't already. I doubt I'll still have access by morning."

"How are you going to monitor them?"

"By changing our plans on what I need to accomplish tomorrow night."

"Not following you, JR."

"When Jimmy made his incursion into the residential compound, he stumbled onto a key component of their plan. The hacking is being done domestically, not overseas."

"Okay. Can you prove it?"

"Not at the moment. Jimmy and I have to get into one of the cabins tomorrow night and turn one of their hacking stations into an access point for me. It's the only way I can do it without their system knowing about it."

"Okay. What do you need from me?"

"The FBI needs to know about these activities."

"I'm not an agent anymore, JR."

"You still have contact with Ryan Clark, correct?"

"Yes."

"You have to convince him about this problem."

"He'll need proof."

"I know. I'm going to get it for him."

Kruger did not say anything for a long time. Finally, he said, "JR, I'm not going to tell you not to do this, but Mia and Joey need you. Let Jimmy and Sandy handle it."

"I can't tell them how to do it until I see the equipment. This is a hands-on problem, Sean." Kruger let out a long breath. "How long before they start to implement the hacking?"

"I can't say for sure. But they're getting close."

"Okay, keep me posted. My flight out is at nine in the morning. I'll talk with Joseph and get ready to meet with Ryan as soon as you get the evidence."

"Thank you, Sean."

The call ended, and JR sat on the edge of the bed, his mind racing. After fifteen minutes of staring blankly at his laptop, a plan coalesced in his thoughts. He went back to his computer and hacked into the American Airlines website to make sure a boarding pass for Harold Mudd had been scanned at San Francisco International that evening. With that accomplished, he typed out two emails. After he sent them, he went to the bathroom to get ready for bed.

Matheson's firewall was strong, but not strong enough to fight off the maelstrom he had initiated against it.

CHAPTER 17

San Francisco, CA

Ethan Matheson awoke to the sounds of his cell phone playing the opening stanza of Wagner's *Flight of the Valkyries*. The clock indicated it was 2:07 a.m. He accepted the call in a groggy voice.

"Yeah."

A panicked voice said in a thick Chinese accent, "Sir, we have a breach."

Matheson sat up, immediately alert. His still-sleeping wife stirred but did not wake. He walked out of their bedroom before answering.

"How bad?"

"Bad. It opened a gaping hole in our firewalls. We can't tell if anyone gained access to the system, but it would have allowed a massive breach."

"Where did it come from?"

"We've traced it to a website you and Mr. Becker accessed yesterday."

Matheson frowned. The only website he had accessed

was Harold Mudd's. "Are you sure, not an email?"

"Positive, sir. We believe the code was attached to a JPEG image."

"Where is the website located?"

"Cincinnati."

The IT manager paced back and forth in the darkened hallway outside the bedroom. "Cincinnati? What's in Cincinnati?"

"Servers for a company hosting websites. They have over ten thousand of them, sir."

"Very well. I'll be there in twenty minutes."

"Thank you, sir."

Matheson ended the call and walked back to his bedroom and straight to the bathroom. His wife stirred and mumbled something. He walked over and kissed her. "I've got to go in. There's a problem with the computers."

She mumbled something else and he kissed her forehead. From other events like this, he knew she would not remember his leaving. He would need to leave a note.

***

By 6:06 a.m., the foreign computer code was deleted from their system. Matheson scrolled through the virus on an isolated computer. He marveled at the simplicity of the code and how vicious it could have been. He looked up at the technician standing next to him. "The code opened a hole in our firewall. Are you sure no incursion occurred?"

The technician said, "Yes, sir." He was a twenty-something with thick glasses, almond-shaped eyes, and coal-black hair. Matheson knew him only as Tim. He was sure his real name was more difficult to pronounce.

"No evidence of an incursion could be found."

"Good. Okay. Make sure we are prepared for any additional attacks like this."

The young man bowed slightly and left the office.

Dreading the next call he had to make, Matheson dialed the cell phone number of Randall Becker. The call was answered on the third ring."

"Is there a problem, Matheson?"

"There was. It has been resolved."

"Enlighten me."

"We found a malicious computer code on our system last night."

Becker's voice grew loud. "I was told that was impossible."

Not wishing to debate the attorney, Matheson said, "It came from an infected website."

Becker did not respond right away. "Let me guess. Harold Mudd's website."

"That is the conclusion of our staff."

"I accessed it after I met him."

"As did I. It was a trap. You said when you met him you thought you recognized him."

"I thought I did. I realized later I was mistaken. Where is he?"

Matheson realized Becker was lying his ass off. But it would be impossible to prove it. He said, "I called his hotel. He checked out yesterday after our interview."

"What about airlines, did you check them?"

"Yes, he boarded a plane at eight last night."

"Then he's gone?"

"Yes."

Becker's voice grew loud again. "What damage was done?"

"None. The code was isolated and removed from our system. I'm told there were no other incursions."

"I see. Keep me informed."

"Yes, sir."

The call ended, and Matheson returned to studying the code. The feeling Becker was less than truthful nagged at the back of his mind. He decided it was time to put his resume out and find something less stressful. Another thought nagged at him. He wondered if he should find a good attorney.

***

Randall Becker placed his cell phone back on his nightstand. He now knew why Dr. Harold Mudd looked so familiar. He realized halfway through the phone call who Mudd actually was. The husband of Judy Ling's daughter. This was a direct attack on their system. He picked up the cell phone again and dialed a number. It was answered on the second ring.

"Yes."

"Has your team seen the husband since the funeral?"

The man with the pockmarked face said, "Per your instructions, we stopped surveillance on the house."

Becker screamed, "Find him."

"Why?"

"Because that's what you get paid to do. You are tasked with providing security for this company. He's a threat, just like the daughter."

Becker pressed the cell phone to his ear but did not hear a response. Realizing the man might have hung up, he said, "Are you there?"

"Yes, be careful who you order around, Becker. I don't work for you."

"You are paid to protect this company, do your job."

"Very well, we'll have to pick up the trail again."

"See that you do."

***

"Why do we need to wait another night, JR?" Jimmy Gibbs stood with his arms folded. Knoll stood behind him, displaying a slight grin.

JR looked up at the ex-SEAL from the laptop he worked on. "Because, we need a diversion, and it will take that long to set one up."

Gibbs took a deep breath. "What kind of diversion? Fireworks on the street?"

Shaking his head, JR said, "Nothing that obvious. I have to set up a cyberattack on their computer system. It has to be vicious enough they won't see me corrupting one of their access points."

Knoll laughed. "Jimmy, I've seen some of JR's diversions firsthand. Trust him."

Gibbs pursed his lips. "What if the diversion points to our intrusion?"

"It won't."

"How can you be so sure?"

"Because when I get it properly set up, it will appear millions of computers are trying to hack into the commune's servers. I'm leaking information on the Dark Net, giving anyone who might be interested instructions on how to circumvent the firewall. I learned how their firewall structure works. It's clever, but not impregnable. I've asked for help from a group of hacktivists I used to be associated with. I've given them a noble cause and a reason they should attack the servers."

"Are you talking about Anonymous?"

"Maybe." JR grinned slightly. "I used to be involved with them before I left New York City."

Gibbs chuckled. "What's the noble cause?"

Sighing, JR continued to type on his laptop. Finally, he stopped and directed his attention to Gibbs. "I told them the group was trying to subvert democratic elections around the globe."

"I thought they were only interested in the US system."

"So far. But if you project out, they could use the same procedures around the globe."

Knoll laughed out loud. "Well played, JR."

Gibbs chuckled. "I was told to expect the unexpected from you."

***

The video started with a revolving skeletal globe and music. The image of a slender figure dressed in a hooded robe and a Guy Fawkes mask faded in as the globe faded out. The electronically altered voice with a slight British accent stated, "Greetings world, we are Anonymous."

The progress bar at the bottom of the screen showed the presentation was six minutes and twenty-two seconds in length.

Sitting back in his chair, JR watched the video just posted to *YouTube* as the figure described the mission of the group. Gibbs and Knoll stood behind him.

Knoll said, "Do they always make a political statement?"

JR replied, "Generally, after they give us the sermon, they will hint at an action plan. However, it will be unspecific at best."

The trio watched the video as a computer constantly altered the appearance of the speaker. With thirty seconds left in the video, they heard, "Forces of a known entity are subverting democratic elections across the globe. We at Anonymous will not let this continue. We will take action against this entity in the near future. We are back. We are Legion. We do not forgive. We do not forget. Expect us."

Knoll laughed. "That wasn't an unspecific or vague plan, it was nonexistent."

"Fairly typical for them. No point in advertising what you're going to do." The image went dark. JR glanced at the time at the lower right-hand side of the laptop. "It's four in the afternoon here in California and 12:00 a.m. Greenwich Mean Time. The attacks against the servers will start in six hours. We need to be in position to enter the residential compound a little after midnight."

Knoll nodded. "What kind of attacks will they be, JR?"

"At first, they'll be like fish nibbling on your feet, then the attacks will get more aggressive. As a rule, the night crew of any IT department is small and the least experienced of their team. They might not even see the first incursions. Once the attacks start penetrating the firewall, they'll be too busy to notice us subverting one of their access points." He paused for a few moments. "At least, that's the theory."

Both Gibbs and Knoll frowned.

CHAPTER 18

San Francisco, CA

The first malicious attack on the commune's computer occurred at 10:04 p.m. Due to their stealthy nature, the probes did not attract the attention of the night technicians. More aggressive attacks started at 11:36 p.m. and lasted until after midnight. Once again, these went unnoticed by the night IT team. Finally, at 12:21 a.m., the commune's computers were hit with a two-prong attack. First, a nasty virus infected the operating system with a countdown clock for its eventual shutdown. Second, numerous key data files and programs were encrypted with a ransom demand of one million dollars per file. Once this occurred, the hackers' demand reached thirty million dollars for the encryption key.

At one minute after one in the morning, the countdown clock reached zero, and the operating system froze. The result caused the microchips on the system's main motherboard to be inert nonfunctioning silicon wafers.

For the second time in two nights, a late-night phone

call interrupted Ethan Matheson's sleep. He arrived at the office at 2:34 a.m. to start his damage assessment. As each minute passed, he forced himself to breathe, swallow the bile rising in the back of his throat, and question why he continued to work for Randall Becker.

***

Jimmy Gibbs, dressed all in black, studied one of the surveillance cameras on the fence surrounding the residence compound through binoculars. He took his eyes away from the device and looked at JR standing next to him. "How long?"

JR, dressed exactly the same, checked the clock on his cell phone. "Any time now. When the camera's power light goes off, their system will have shut down."

Gibbs returned to observing the camera. They stood at the northwest corner of the residential compound within a tree line. Across the access road and fifty yards from their position stood a fence restricting access to the property. Darkness blanketed this section of the property due to the nearest streetlight being a quarter of a mile away. Sandy Knoll had deposited them a half mile from the front entrance. Using night vision googles, they negotiated their way through fields and wooded areas to the spot they now occupied.

Keeping his eye on the camera, Gibbs asked, "Where is the first house located from our point of entry?"

"North 100 yards. From what I saw on Google Earth, it is fairly isolated. The rest of the cabins are on different streets."

"Will it have what you need?"

"Don't know."

Gibbs glanced at JR. "You don't know?"

"Nope."

"Geez." Finally, after several moments, Gibbs replied,

"Whatever, dude. This better not be a wild goose chase."

"It won't be."

Returning his eyes to the binoculars, he concentrated on the camera's power light. Thirty seconds later, it went dark. "Bingo, light blinked off. Ready?"

"Yeah."

After replacing the binoculars into a side pocket of his tactical pants, Gibbs flipped the night goggles down, bent over slightly, and emerged from the foliage of their hiding spot at a dead run, JR close behind. He snipped the chain links of the fence next to a steel post then pulled the metal fabric back. JR slipped through the opening, followed by Gibbs. The retired SEAL returned the links to their original position and zip-tied it at the bottom. If someone drove by the incursion spot, it would be invisible in the darkness.

Fifteen minutes later, they stood at the back entrance to a small cabin at the end of a cul-de-sac. Gibbs whispered, "You sure this place is unoccupied?"

Through his night vision googles, JR observed the area around the building. "Most of the cabins are well maintained. Grass regularly mowed, landscape tended to, and knickknacks on the front porch. This place doesn't appear that way. I would guess it's abandoned."

"I agree." He pulled a small tool from one of his utility pant side pockets and inserted it into the lock. Twenty seconds later, they both stood inside. Gibbs went immediately to a panel in the kitchen, opened it, and peered inside. All the lights were out. "Security system is off. We're good."

"How did you know it was there?"

"Saw a wire on several windows and the door we used. Started looking for the panel as we entered. We got lucky it was in the kitchen. How long do you need?"

JR moved from room to room searching for a computer station in the unfurnished house. "It shouldn't take long. I need at least ten minutes, no more, with each computer."

Frowning, Gibbs scrutinized the kitchen as JR moved toward the bedrooms. Both kept their night vision goggles in place. As he checked under the sink, he heard JR from the back of the house.

"Found it."

Rushing toward the sound of JR's voice, he located him in a back bedroom. In the eerie image provided by the goggles, he saw JR sitting at a small desk staring at a computer screen.

The seated figure said, "Flip your goggles up."

Gibbs complied.

Holding a Maglite in his teeth, he turned it on and the screen lit up. Checking the back of the unit, JR said, "Nice, an all-in-one system."

"What do you mean?"

"The computer is integrated into the back of the screen. It eliminates having more than two pieces of equipment. Easier to move." JR continued, "See if you can locate a Wi-Fi unit. This thing's totally wireless."

Gibbs turned and rushed out of the bedroom.

JR waited as the computer finished its start-up routine. When it finished, he got to work.

When Gibbs returned to the room, he saw JR typing furiously on the keyboard.

"It's in the garage on a shelf."

JR turned to Gibbs. "Any lights blinking?"

"No, all were solid. The light labeled internet was red."

"Great. We're good for the moment."

"What do you mean, for the moment?"

"Computer talk, don't worry."

"JR…"

"We're good, Jimmy. This won't take long."

***

The next two houses were completed in less time than

the first. They found each laid out similar with the computer station in a back bedroom and the Wi-Fi unit in the garage. These houses were also vacant. JR wondered how many of the cabins were actually being lived in by former commune members.

As they entered the final house, JR said, "I'm beginning to think none of these houses are occupied."

"I was wondering the same thing, JR."

"It would be interesting to see how many residents moved out on their…"

"What, JR?"

"I think I know why Mia's mother was killed."

"Why?"

"She was the last resident and they were tired of waiting."

Gibbs did not respond as he picked the lock on the next house.

Two hours after gaining access to the compound, they entered the last house. Repeating the same steps, he used in the other cabins, JR completed the download of his program. Gibbs watched from the doorway.

"You mentioned Mia's mom. After I broke into her house and all the security guys converged on it, I wondered why none of the neighbors reacted."

JR turned. "Because those houses were already vacant."

"Yeah. Explains a lot."

Returning his attention to the computer he mumbled, "Yes, it sure does."

Five minutes later, he stood and said, "We know they will suspect a reason for the attack on their computer system."

Gibbs said, "That makes sense."

"We'll leave a crumb for them to find on this computer. They won't find anything on the other systems."

"I won't ask how you do that."

"It's not that difficult, but it's hard to explain."

"Okay, what exactly did you do to the other ones?"

"I wrote a program many years ago to record keystrokes. Once the keystrokes are recorded, the file is emailed to a nondescript account. Since the file is never saved to the hard drive, there is no residual data."

"Was that the program that got you in trouble in New York City?"

"Yeah. They never found the program. I got caught by a security camera."

Gibbs chuckled.

"Beginner's mistake." He continued to type. "This program is an improvement on the old one."

"So, what are you doing on this one you haven't done on the others?"

"It will be a subtle difference. I'm leaving an additional program on this one they can find. It will be difficult to do, but it should satisfy their curiosity about the attack." He stopped typing and shut the computer down. He switched off his Maglite and flipped his night vision goggles down. JR said, "Done, you ready to get out of here?"

"Yeah, it'll be dawn in a few hours. We need to be long gone before then."

JR stood. "Let's go."

As they walked through the front room, a searchlight flashed through the front picture window on the walls. Both men had to flip their goggles up to keep from being blinded.

Startled, JR said, "What the hell was that?"

Gibbs froze. "Security. Same thing happened the last time I was in this place. Our plans just changed. Let's hurry."

Both men scurried to the back door. Jimmy asked, "Want me to leave the door unlocked?"

"No, let's not make it too obvious. They'll find the program eventually."

Gibbs locked the door and both men faded into the

darkness of night.

Twenty minutes later, they arrived at the extraction location. Gibbs pulled out his binoculars and checked the security cameras. "Uh-oh."

"What?"

"Power light's on."

"Not good."

"Thought you said the security system would be down for the count."

"It should be. Everything is tied to their computer system." JR checked the nearest camera. "Unless..." He pulled his cell phone out and checked for an open Wi-Fi signal. "Huh."

"Do you want to enlighten me?"

"Their system is still down." He glanced back up at the camera. "I'll bet they have their security set up to operate on a backup power system that takes over when the computer is down."

"It would have been nice to know before."

"Yes, it would have."

***

Gibbs noticed JR still staring in the direction of the camera. During the short time he had been around JR, he knew this meant the man was thinking when he grew quiet and stared off into the distance.

After several minutes, Gibbs asked, "Got any ideas?"

"Yeah. How did you get out the last time you were in the compound?"

"Over the fence."

"That's what they'll expect this time. Let's go back to the last cabin."

A few minutes later, they knelt in the darkness behind a cluster of Oregon grape bushes. The foliage was located in the yard next to the last house they entered and a dozen or so yards from the access road.

Gibbs checked his watch. "We need to hurry. It'll start getting light soon. Let's try not to be crouching behind these bushes when that occurs."

"Not planning on it."

"What've you got in mind?"

"Let's wait for the next security vehicle to drive by."

"And?"

"I'm going to stop it. They'll see one intruder. You, on the other hand, will still be invisible in this bush."

"That's a good idea, JR."

They waited in silence for the next five minutes. Gibbs asked, "So, we're just gonna drive out of here?"

"That's the current plan. Any other ideas?"

"What if there are two men in the vehicle?"

JR chuckled. "Thought you were a SEAL."

"I was."

"What was your motto?"

"The only easy day was yesterday."

"I was Army. Our motto was, improvise, adapt, overcome. Since yesterday was our easy day, today we will improvise, adapt, and overcome."

Gibbs chuckled. "Got it."

Ten minutes later, headlights approached their location. JR stood and prepared to leave their hiding spot.

The car advanced on their location leisurely, a spotlight illuminating cabins as it drove down the street. This gave JR an idea. When the car was at the house next to their location, he broke cover and ran toward the street. The searchlight twisted toward him and the car sped forward. Now caught in the full glare of the headlights and spotlight, he stood still in the middle of the road. The car screeched to a halt, and the driver's door flew open.

Gibbs broke cover as the man in the car yelled, "Hey, you, get on the ground." He pointed a pistol at JR.

Standing with his arms out away from his body, JR

stayed quiet and did not move.

The security guard stayed behind the open car door and kept his weapon trained on JR. "Get on the grou—"

The man's sentence remained unfinished as Gibbs disarmed and rendered him unconscious. JR dashed for the passenger side of the vehicle. Gibbs dragged the guard toward the bushes, left him well covered, and returned to the vehicle. He retrieved the dropped weapon and slid in behind the steering wheel. The white Ford Escape accelerated down the street.

"How do I get out of here, JR?"

"Working on it."

CHAPTER 19

Sonoma, CA

"Am I to understand, Matheson, our computer system is being held hostage?" Randall Becker stood over the desk of Ethan Matheson. His clenched jaw and furrowed brow gave him the appearance of a caricature Ichabod Crane rather than a high-paid attorney. Becker's displeasure of being called into the office at half past three in the morning was on full display.

"That's the size of it."

"Explain."

"We have thirty key data files frozen by ransomware. Plus, our operating system has been compromised by an incredibly malicious virus, the likes of which I've never seen. I'm not positive, but I believe there is a strong possibility we will physically have to rebuild several of the servers."

"How much do they want for ransom? Who are these people?"

"I have no idea who they are." He took a breath and

considered Becker for a moment. "The email stated they would give us the keys to the encryptions for thirty million dollars."

Becker glared at Matheson. With his voice barely above a whisper, he said, "Thirty million dollars?"

"Yes."

"Is there a way around this without paying the money?"

Matheson nodded.

"Then, what is it? Why haven't you started doing it?"

"We have to resort to the last system backup we performed and then go to the last data backup."

"Then do it." Becker folded his arms across his chest. "Why haven't you started?"

Taking a deep breath, Matheson let it out slowly. "Because of your constant penny-pinching of this department, we've been short on staff. The last system backup was six months ago. We'll have to rebuild the system starting from there. All the files from the data backups will have to be loaded. The last one is a week old. We were scheduled to do a backup in the morning. Our—" He hesitated and gave Becker a crooked grin. "Your plan will be set back at least a couple of weeks, probably longer. Our lack of proper staffing will prolong the amount of time it takes to recover. And that's if we can get the parts. We need to rebuild the servers."

Becker scowled at the director of the IT department, his eyes wide and his mouth agape. "Two weeks?"

"At least, maybe longer. They knew exactly when and where to attack us."

"Again, who are they, Dr. Matheson?"

"Like, I told you. I don't know."

Standing straight, Becker growled. "Find out." He turned and walked out of Matheson's office.

Matheson leaned back in his chair and stared at the ceiling. He closed his eyes and mumbled, "I'm getting too old to put up with that asshole."

***

Sandy Knoll checked the clock on the Denali's dashboard for the second time in less than a minute. JR and Gibbs were going on two and a half hours inside the compound. Not good. They were forty-five minutes past due for extraction. Parked in a Walmart parking lot a mile from the compound, he was amazed at the number of customers the big-box retailer attracted at three o'clock in the morning. The activity within the parking lot helped mask the solitary figure waiting in his vehicle.

The seconds ticked by as his concern intensified with each passing minute. At 3:39 a.m., a white Ford Escort appeared and parked next to the large SUV. With his hand resting on a Glock 21 on the passenger seat, Knoll kept his eyes on the newly arrived car.

Gibbs emerged from the driver's side at the same moment JR exited from the passenger door. After his partners slipped into the Denali, Knoll eased the truck away from its parking slot.

He glanced at Gibbs. "What happened."

Gibbs, who occupied the seat next to Knoll, used his thumb to motion toward JR. He said, "Army in the back seat told me to improvise, adapt, overcome."

Knoll chuckled. "Yeah, I've had to do that a few times. Call Stewart. We'll be at the airport in thirty minutes."

"Got it."

***

The HA-420 HondaJet sat outside a hangar on the tarmac near the airport's FBO. A Phillips 66 fuel truck parked beside it topped off the tanks in preparation for the flight back to Missouri. The corporate pilot for KKG Solutions, Stewart Barnett, walked around the plane doing his preflight inspection. When the truck pulled away, the pilot walked up the airstairs and prepared the plane for takeoff.

Knoll parked the rented GMC Denali next to the HondaJet. While Gibbs and JR unloaded their luggage and equipment into the private plane, the big man walked up the airstairs to check with Barnett.

The pilot turned as Knoll entered the cabin.

"Hey, Major. We're ready when you guys are."

"We'll need a circuitous route back to Springfield, Stewart."

"Figured. Already have the flight plan filed. We're headed to Tijuana International Airport. From there, we kind of disappear off the grid." He smiled as he said it.

Returning the smile, Knoll said, "I'll return the Denali to the rental area and then let's get the hell out of here."

"You got it, Major."

***

FBI Director Ryan Clark listened without comment as Kruger summarized the situation in California. When he finished, Clark remained silent for a few moments. Finally, he leaned forward and placed his elbows on his desk and made a steeple with his hands.

"Coming from anyone, other than yourself, I'd dismiss this information as hearsay."

"I'm afraid it isn't."

"What did Charlie Brewer say?"

"That's why I'm here. He suggested I take it up with you. You and I have a shared history, while you and he don't."

Clark tapped his lips with his fingers. "How long does JR think the commune's computers will be down?"

"Depends on the supply chain. If parts are available, they can get it working pretty quick. Restoring the system from backup will take at least a week or two. At least, that's JR's assessment."

"What the hell did he do to it?"

"Ryan, he didn't do a thing. All he did was supply the information to the group called Anonymous on how to get it done."

The director buried his face in his hands. "Don't tell me those guys are back."

"According to JR, they never left. They didn't have a noble cause to pursue."

"Sean, you and I both know that until we have admissible evidence this corporation is being run by the Chinese government and interfering with elections, all on US soil, the bureau's hands are tied."

"I'm aware of that, Ryan. At least, now they're on your radar."

"Okay, we can at least put this Randall Becker under more scrutiny. I'll talk to Brewer about it."

"He's got an up-and-coming agent working for him you might want to keep an eye on."

Clark raised an eyebrow.

"His name is Tim Gonzales. I might recruit him to come work for KKG someday."

"He's that good?"

Kruger nodded. "Reminds me of you when you first joined the bureau."

"Keep your hands off him, Sean."

The retired FBI profiler shrugged. "For now."

"Okay, tell me more about this missing Chinese electrical engineer."

"From what JR can determine, he keeps a low profile but seems to be pretty high up in the PRC government hierarchy."

"His name?"

"Ling Mao Chun. He's the son of Ling Mao Yin, who was the Minister of Defense until his death in 2012. Joseph's wife, Mary, confirmed it with one of her contacts at the State Department. They told her Yin had a son. That's how JR found him. He keeps a low profile and stays out of any media spotlight. We do know he was doing research in 1994 for the PRC Defense Department. JR couldn't find a reference for him after that."

"What kind of research?"

"He studied at Berkeley as an electrical engineer. After graduation, he was recruited to design computer chips here in the States. Then he disappeared. JR believes he's working on next generation AI chips."

"JR is normally right. Why is this just now coming to light, Sean?"

"When I spoke to JR this morning, he indicated the commune where Mia's mom lived has been abandoned. No residents live there anymore. He thinks they killed her to get her out of the neighborhood. They are setting up the computer stations in the bungalows."

"Any evidence?"

"A little. Blood found in her house confirmed it was Mia's mother who was assaulted there. But the evidence was obtained illegally and they've sanitized the house since."

Clark furrowed his brow. "Does Charlie have all of this info?"

"He does."

"I don't need to remind you that you are no longer associated with the FBI, do I, Sean?"

"Very much aware of it. That's why I'm talking to you. Something is going on at the commune and I don't want it swept under the rug."

"Now that I'm aware of the situation, it won't be. I promise." He leaned back in his chair. "Are you going to help JR find Mia's father?"

"As soon as he can get a lead on where he might be, yeah."

"Keep me apprised of your progress."

PART TWO

The Manchurian

CHAPTER 20

Sonoma, CA
The Following Week

Ling Mao Chun sat in a chair across from Randall Becker, his expression hiding the inner fury he felt toward the man. However, he allowed his voice to project a menacing growl. "I thought you told me on the phone the project would be back on track in a week."

"That was the assessment of our IT director."

"Where is he now?"

"He resigned two days after the incident."

"And you allowed him to? Is that what I am hearing from you, Mr. Becker?"

"Unlike China, we cannot force individuals to stay in a job they do not want."

"How much does he know?"

Taking a deep breath, Becker let it out slowly. "He signed a confidentiality agreement. We will sue him if he discloses details about the company."

"So, he knows the details."

"Not the final phase."

Ling drummed his fingers on the arm of the chair. "What is the new projected timeline for getting the project back on track?"

Becker blinked several times. A drop of perspiration formed at his hairline and ran down his temple. "At least another six weeks. They are having trouble with the supply chain on certain circuit boards."

Leaning forward, Ling slammed his palm down on Becker's desk. "Unacceptable." He paused for only a moment. "That is the second disappointment you have achieved, Mr. Becker. Failing to get rid of the husband and now an inexcusable delay in our project. We pay you way too much money for this level of deficiency in your performance. Is my meaning clear?"

"Very."

Standing, Ling exited the office without another word.

Staring at the unclosed door to his office, Becker's hands shook, and he gasped for air as he tried to steady himself. After a few minutes, he regained control of his breathing and stood. He shut his office door and then went to the window behind his desk.

After five minutes of gazing out the window, he turned, sat, and started making phone calls.

***

With the lack of progress in finding any references to Ling Mao since their trip to California, JR returned to his daily routine. This included meeting with clients via Zoom conferences and working with them on their computer security problems.

The time approached three in the afternoon when an email arrived. He read the message and then opened the attached file. The contents made him stand and exit his office.

Over a year ago, an LLC comprised of Kruger, Sandy Knoll, JR and his wife Mia, plus, Jimmy Gibbs and his wife Alexia, purchased the building holding the offices of KKG and JR's computer company. Those two entities now leased the space from the LLC. According to their accountant, the arrangement gave everyone a legal tax break. Something to do with depreciation or something like that. Kruger didn't care. All he cared about was not going home in the evenings smelling like jet fuel anymore.

The office still featured two floors. The first floor held JR's administration staff, numerous meeting rooms and a secure, climate-controlled room for the servers used by the two companies. The top floor held a secure conference room, offices for the three principals of KKG Solutions and workplaces for JR and his co-owner, Alexia Gibbs, Jimmy's wife.

Alexia, a former hacker from Europe, handled clients from overseas and took over JR's duties during his absence.

JR stood outside Kruger's office and rapped on the doorframe. "Got a minute?"

Looking up, he waved his friend inside. Unlike most visits from JR, the computer expert shut the door.

"What's wrong?"

"I got a weird email from out of the blue."

"Okay." He waited for a response. When none came, he said, "About?"

"Remember Ethan Matheson?"

"Yeah, what about him?"

"He sent me a file containing the locations of every workstation within the network of the commune."

"Huh."

"My thoughts exactly. We only scratched the surface of their network."

Kruger frowned. "I'm not following you, JR."

"They not only have the site in San Francisco but others throughout the world."

"How many?"

"At least one on each of the populated continents."

"Six?"

JR nodded. "All controlled out of the San Francisco headquarters."

The retired FBI agent did not respond.

"Sean, this is bigger than we suspected."

"Do you trust this Matheson person?"

"He resigned as their IT director. I believe there's a chance we can."

Kruger leaned forward. "How did he learn your email address?"

"Any email sent to the address I gave as Harry Mudd's, gets forwarded directly to me."

"Could he trace it?"

"He could, but I doubt he would think to do so."

"Why?"

"Because he addressed the email to Mudd."

"JR, are they still shut down?"

"Yes."

"When do you think they'll be back up?"

"It'll be a while. Every time they test the system, they get attacked again. Plus, without an IT director who knows what he or she is doing, they'll never get back up."

"Do you think this Matheson would be willing to talk to the FBI about what's going on there?"

"Don't know. What are you thinking?"

"Director Clark won't authorize a raid on the place without evidence. Since Matheson no longer works there, maybe he'd be willing to testify against them."

JR considered Kruger for several moments. "That's a hell of an idea, Sean. How do we make that happen?"

"We can't. But Charlie Brewer can."

JR pointed to the phone on Kruger's desk. "Call him."

***

FBI Special Agent in Charge Charles Brewer listened as Kruger summarized his meeting with Director Clark and the email JR received. When he finished, Brewer did not respond for several moments.

"So, Ethan Matheson resigned right after Anonymous attacked the commune's computer system?"

"Yes."

"And JR received an email from him."

"In a sense, yes."

"Can JR forward the email to me?"

"He just walked back to his office to do so."

"What does, in a sense, mean, Sean?"

"It was sent to the email of someone Matheson thought JR might have been when they met."

"We're dancing around legal ambiguity here."

"Not really, Charlie. It was common knowledge Matheson worked for Becker as his IT director. All you have to do is send someone to interview him and see if he's cooperative."

"On what pretense?"

"Agent Gonzales was with JR when he met with Becker. Have him follow up on the death of Judy Ling." Kruger paused. "The commune still hasn't released her ashes to JR."

"Didn't know that."

"A case could be made she was murdered and they are trying to conceal evidence by not handing over the urn."

Brewer tilted his head. "Sean, you can get DNA from the pulverized teeth and bones from a cremated individual. But who's to say the ashes are actually Judy Ling's."

"Charlie, I'm aware of that."

"What's the real reason we should talk to him?"

"He knows what's going on in those cabins. He might not know the whole story, but he might be willing to give you enough info so the FBI can get a search warrant and raid the place."

"And JR believes they are being used to interfere with elections?"

"JR believes they are setting them up to do more than interfere with elections. He feels these stations could be used to hack utilities and other infrastructure. They are heavy into AI, and Matheson is the one who set up their programs. He quit for a reason, Charlie. The FBI needs to know why he quit."

"It's a good thing I like you, Sean. Otherwise, I would have hung up a long time ago."

"You also miss me."

"That is still up for debate."

Kruger chuckled.

"Okay, make sure JR gets that email to me. I'll send Gonzales to talk to him."

"Don't let him go alone, Charlie. These guys don't have a problem with leaving dead bodies behind."

"Maybe I should tag along."

"I think that would be an excellent idea."

CHAPTER 21

San Francisco Area

Ethan Matheson pulled into the driveway of his Mill Valley, California home. He noticed the black Chevrolet Suburban parked at the curb in front. As soon as he parked, two men from the vehicle approached him.

The younger man said, "Dr. Ethan Matheson?"

"Yes."

Holding his ID so Matheson could see it, Tim Gonzales said, "FBI, sir. Can we have a few moments of your time?"

The older of the two men stood slightly behind the agent, his hand on a gun attached to his belt and normally hidden by his suit coat.

"Is this about Twin Peaks Commune Co-op Incorporated?"

The young FBI agent raised an eyebrow. He then said, "Yes, sir."

Matheson took a deep breath and looked away. "We are being watched, Agent." He returned his gaze to the two FBI agents. "You will need to arrest me and take me somewhere safe. Otherwise, you guys just signed my death warrant."

Gonzales turned to Charlie Brewer. "Your call, sir."

Brewer tilted his head. "Very well, place handcuffs on Dr. Matheson. Do not arrest him. We'll take him to the office and see what he has to say."

***

Forty-five minutes later, Matheson sat at a conference table sipping bitter coffee out of a Styrofoam cup, the handcuffs gone.

Gonzales sat across from him, Brewer at the head of the table. The younger agent said, "Who's watching your house, Dr. Matheson?"

"You saw the For-Sale sign across the street?"

"Yes."

"Four men, all Chinese, entered the house a little after midnight this morning. The only reason I know is I'm not sleeping well right now. I happened to be staring out the front window when they broke in."

Brewer asked, "Why aren't you sleeping well, Ethan? May I call you Ethan?"

The former IT director nodded. "Same reason those four guys moved into the house. Because of what Twin Peaks is up to. I'm worried about what they might do. I'm glad I sent my wife to her sister's place in LA earlier this week. At least she'll be safe there."

"That's good to know. You mentioned Twin Peaks earlier at your house. What is it?"

"That's the official name of the company Becker manages."

Gonzales asked, "So the commune is now called Twin Peaks? Tell us about it."

Taking a deep breath, Matheson stared at his clasped hands on the table. "How much time ya got?"

"We have all the time you need, sir."

"They call him the Manchurian."

Gonzales stopped taking notes and asked, "Who are 'they', Ethan?"

"Becker and other members of his management team."

"Who is he?"

"He's the one designing, manufacturing, and supplying the computer chips for the AI research project. I've only met him once, when I interviewed for the position of IT director."

Brewer asked, "How long did you work there?"

"Six years. Before that, I worked for IBM in their research department. My background is with artificial intelligence. One of the reasons I was hired by Twin Peaks."

"Why is artificial intelligence so important to them, Ethan?"

The computer expert took a deep breath and looked at the ceiling. "It's complicated. The term stretches back to the late 1950s, when everyone thought machines would eventually think for themselves. The problem was computer processing would not advance enough for much progress to be made until the early part of the 2000s. I don't want to get into the weeds with this, but let's put it this way: AI could lead to self-learning computers. That's what Twin Peaks is all about. Building fast computers that learn and learn fast."

The younger FBI agent leaned forward on the conference table. "Are you telling us they are developing more advanced AI at Twin Peaks?"

Matheson gave the two agents a grim smile. "Not developing, developed. The Manchurian discovered a new chip technology that has taken AI to the next level. They are also experimenting with quantum computing. Fascinating stuff."

"Then why'd you quit?"

"Uh—it's complicated."

Brewer gave the man a smile. "We're not going anywhere. Let's hear it."

"I ran across some emails that disturbed me. It took me several days to make the decision, but my conscience got the better of me. My conscience is why I'm not sleeping well."

Gonzales made a note and then asked, "What was so disturbing about the emails?"

"They discussed the need to have several individuals killed to shut them up."

The San Francisco SAC raised an eyebrow. "Who have they had killed, Ethan?"

"Judy Ling and a few other names I didn't recognize."

"You have proof?"

"No, only the emails. Which I can't access any longer."

"Who ordered her death?" This from Gonzales.

"The Manchurian." A tear leaked from Matheson's eye. "I discovered that he was Judy's husband."

Taking his cell phone out of his suit coat pocket, Brewer stood and said, "I'm going for coffee. Do you want a refresh?"

Matheson shook his head.

"Agent Gonzales, let's give Dr. Matheson a few moments."

The younger agent stood and followed Brewer out of the conference room.

***

Kruger answered his cell phone on the second ring. "What've you learned, Charlie?"

"A lot, but the only evidence, at this point, is his testimony. Ask JR what he knows about artificial intelligence and something called quantum computing."

"He's not coming into the office today."

"Is there any way you can arrange a conference call with him today?"

"I'm sure it can be arranged. When?"

"We're placing Ethan Matheson in protective custody. He knows more than we thought. Before we question him further, I need to know more about artificial intelligence and this quantum thing."

"Got it. Let me call you back."

"Thanks, Sean."

The call ended, and Kruger sent a text message. Not thirty seconds later, his phone rang.

"JR, where are you?"

"Joseph's, why?"

"Charlie Brewer wants a conference call with us. They have Ethan Matheson in protective custody."

"Shit."

Kruger continued. "He also asked about artificial intelligence and quantum computing. Know anything about them?"

"A little."

"And?"

"It's the next step in AI development."

"Uh, JR, didn't you mention something about the commune using AI in their hacking?"

"If the commune is developing AI and combining it with quantum computing, we have a bigger problem than we thought. I'll head toward the office. It will be safer for us to make the call from the conference room. I can mask our location from there."

"Okay. See you in forty minutes."

***

JR connected the Bluetooth speakerphone to his laptop. He sat at the head of the table, to his right sat Kruger, Alexia Gibbs sat to his left. The speakerphone in the middle. "Ready to call Charlie?"

Kruger nodded.

Brewer answered the phone on the second ring. "Sean?"

"Yes, sir."

"Is JR with you?"

"Sitting next to me."

"Good. I don't recognize the area code you're calling from."

"That's being done on purpose, sir."

No one in California spoke for a brief moment. "Is that necessary?"

"JR feels it is."

"Okay, Gonzales just left to get Matheson in here. I need JR to ask some questions."

JR said, "Am I Harry Mudd or JR?"

With a chuckle, Brewer said, "JR, my guess is he already knows it was you as Mudd."

"If you say so."

The sound of scooting chairs and a door closing came through the speaker. Then they heard, "This is Ethan Matheson. Am I speaking to Dr. Mudd?"

"I'm afraid I have misled you on my real identity, Ethan. My name is JR Diminski."

"Thank gawd. I thought I was going crazy when I interviewed Mudd. He reminded me of you. We met at Black Hat several years ago. It's a pleasure to finally speak with you, JR. How are you?"

"Apparently, better than you."

"Yes, I seem to have chosen poorly when I accepted the job with Twin Peaks."

Kruger frowned. "Twin Peaks? What's that?"

Brewer answered, "That's the official name of the corporation the commune evolved into."

JR frowned and typed furiously on his laptop. Kruger pressed the mute button on the phone and looked over at Alexia with a questioning expression.

She said, "JR has apparently heard of them."

"Have you?"

"Oh yes. Cutting edge research on the utilization of AI and quantum computers."

"Huh." Kruger took the speakerphone off mute.

Raising his head, JR asked, "Uh, Ethan, why was that name not mentioned when Mudd interviewed for the job?"

"They like to keep the name under wraps as much as possible. Have you heard of them?"

"Yes. They're the ones developing ways to make quantum computers cheaper and more sustainable."

"Didn't know the company was that well-known. Does the name Ling Mao Chun mean anything to you?"

JR's head jerked back. "Yes. My wife believes it was the name of her father."

"Is she related to Judy Ling?"

"Yes, she was her mother."

A quiet fell over the conference room. Finally, Matheson said, "The emails I had access to mentioned Judy had a daughter who's now a politician. Is your wife a politician?"

Kruger's attention turned to JR, who shrugged. Alexia worked the keyboard on the laptop in front of her. JR finally said, "No. What's the politician's name?"

"I never could find it. I told these FBI agents that I quit after I found emails outlining the real purpose of Twin Peaks. Who are you married to, JR?"

"Her name was Mia Ling."

"What happened to her?"

Kruger and JR exchanged glances. The retired FBI agent nodded slightly.

"They tried to kill her and myself. They failed."

"I'm glad to hear they failed."

"Ethan, what is Twin Peaks really doing out there?"

"Developing quantum computers to advance artificial intelligence beyond its current state."

Kruger asked, "Dr. Matheson, why did you ask if JR was married to a politician?"

"From the emails I read, they've already been successful in manipulating an election here in California. In fact, they've—" The phone went silent.

"What's going on, Charlie?" This question from Kruger.

Brewer answered, "It appears Dr. Matheson suddenly figured out what Twin Peaks' purpose is."

Kruger said, "Why, what's going on?"

"He just turned pale as a ghost."

***

No one spoke on the conference call for several minutes. Finally, Matheson said, "Oh my gawd. What have I done?"

Brewer said, "Talk to us, Ethan. What did you realize?"

"I'm so dense. I was more worried about my own safety. I didn't think it through."

"What?"

"The emails mentioned a daughter of Chun who is now a politician. No names, only that she's in Washington DC. California was a test, which apparently worked. The reason they made everyone move out of the cottages was to set up more workstations. They're going to manipulate a national election."

The SAC tapped a pen on the table. "Doctor, we need those emails as evidence. We can't issue search warrants on the testimony of an ex-employee. Particularly one who left under duress."

Matheson gave the FBI supervisor a grim expression. "They're behind a firewall no one can penetrate without the proper authorization."

Directing his attention to the conference phone, Brewer said, "JR?"

After a lengthy pause, they heard, "I don't know. I can try. But their system is down for an unknown period of time. It could be days or weeks before they have it restored."

"Okay, I can take what we have to the California Attorney General and see what she says."

The call ended five minutes later.

***

Kruger turned his attention to JR who gave him a grin. The retired FBI agent said, "I take it you weren't quite truthful about your chances."

JR shrugged. "I wasn't going to say anything in front of Matheson. Who's to say he isn't running interference for Twin Peaks?"

Alexia said, "I've got a list of Congress members from California. Of the fifty-two individuals from the state in Congress, seventeen are women. If we assume the individual Matheson is referring to is of Pacific Rim ancestry, that narrows it down to five individuals. Four of them are in the House, one is a senator."

Tapping his finger to his lips, Kruger said, "Any with the last name of Ling?"

"No, sorry."

"I seriously doubt they would be that obvious." JR paused. "I think Alexia and I need to do a deep dive on all five women. Maybe she and I can find some irregularities in the election results."

Kruger stood. "Keep me posted. If you do find anything, we need to get it to Brewer."

After the retired FBI agent left the room, Alexia turned her attention to JR. "Did you know Mia might have a sister out there?"

"No. But then again, she had no contact with her mother after the age of four." He pursed his lips. "How can we assume the woman isn't a full sister. Her mother might have reconnected with Ling and had another child." He stopped. "I just realized something. Maybe that's why she didn't want contact with Mia."

"I hope that's not the case. I think finding out she has a sister she didn't know about would be devastating for Mia."

"I agree, Alexia."

CHAPTER 22

Washington, DC

Emily Soon, California's junior senator to the US Congress, smiled as she escorted the mayor of Fresno, California out of her office. She said her goodbyes and then returned to her desk. Before she sat, her assistant handed her a note.

"Emily, your uncle called. He said it wasn't an emergency, but he did consider it urgent."

"Thanks, Susan, I'll return it from here. Would you mind shutting the door on your way out?"

"Not at all."

As soon as the assistant left and shut the door, Emily picked up the phone to return the call. The code word uncle and urgent in the message caused her pulse to quicken. She did not have a real uncle, but a man in California who worked for her father would be the individual she would talk to. Normally a message from this person did not correspond to good news.

It was answered on the first ring.

The fake uncle said, "Can you talk?"

"Yes."

"We may have a slight problem."

She did not respond.

"Ethan Matheson, the IT director has disappeared. We think the FBI has him secluded somewhere. I need you to find him."

"That might be difficult. The FBI has a tendency to lie to Congress."

"You're on the Judiciary Committee, aren't you?"

The senator from California said, "That doesn't mean they'll tell us the truth. The current FBI director is very by the book when he deals with us."

The person on the other end did not speak for several moments. Finally, he said, "Nevertheless, we need to know where they have him. He knows the circumstances surrounding your election. It would be in your, and our, best interest if we can find him."

"Think about that for a minute. If I start getting nosy about this guy and he ends up dead, the bureau might start looking into why I got involved. Something we don't need at the moment."

The man's voice grew harsh. "Then use your imagination, Senator. If Matheson starts talking, the FBI will be knocking on your door anyway."

"Why does the FBI have him in custody?"

"He quit, and they took him into custody two days later."

"When did this happen?"

"Yesterday morning."

"You fool. He's already talked. They'll have offered him a deal by now."

"For your sake, I hope not."

The call ended without another word from her so-called uncle. She replaced the receiver and drummed her fingers on her desk. She pressed the intercom button and said,

"Susan, could you find Jeff and send him in?"

"Sure. Last I knew he was in his office. I'll find him."

"Thanks."

She took a deep breath and let it out slowly.

***

JR studied the image on his computer monitor. It was the official photograph of the junior US senator from the state of California, Emily Soon. Except for the hair color, he could be looking at a picture of Mia. He sent the picture to a printer and retrieved it.

He googled the name and found her Wikipedia page. The woman's birthday was five years after Mia's. It listed her age as thirty-four. The realization that Judy Ling, Mia's mother, probably had another child with her husband seemed to be confirmed. After scanning the Wikipedia page, he stood, left his office, and headed straight to Kruger's. When the retired FBI agent saw him, he waved JR in.

"What've you got?"

JR laid the picture on his friend's desk and then folded his arms.

Picking it up, he studied the photo for a few moments. "Let me guess. This isn't Mia."

"No. The woman's name is Emily Soon. She's the junior US senator from the state of California."

Still examining the image, Kruger tilted his head. "Do you know when she was born?"

"Five years, two months, and seventeen days after Mia."

"Where'd you find the information?"

"Her Wikipedia pages."

Kruger chuckled. "Really."

"Uh-huh."

"That's not like you, JR. Taking the easy way out."

"You'd be surprised how often the information found

there is helpful."

"Did it identify the woman's parents?"

"No, but I haven't spent a lot of time researching her background. The mere fact she resembles Mia and was born five years later is indicative that Judy found her husband and they had another child. Although, until I can confirm the information, I'm not going to tell Mia."

"Do you realize the ramifications of this, JR?"

"Unfortunately, I do. However, proving it might be problematic. I'm going to enlist the help of Alexia to do a deep dive on the senator. If there's more out there, she'll find it."

After handing the photo back to JR, Kruger said, "Think back on how you changed your identity. Her whole biography could be false."

"I'd almost forgotten about that." He pursed his lips. "Have you ever heard of a movie called *The Manchurian Candidate*?"

Kruger nodded. "Which one?"

The computer hacker frowned. "What do you mean, which one?"

"There's the original and then the remake. The original is from 1962 and the other from 2004. Both have to do with brainwashing and trying to create an undercover candidate seeking high office in the US government."

"I only know about the one from 2004. But, you're right, it has to do with brainwashing."

"Okay. Your point?"

"What if there's no brainwashing involved here? This could be a long-range plan to get an individual, whose allegiance is to another government, elected to high office here in the US."

"JR, if that's the case, and they're using AI, every piece of public information about her could be false and hard to disprove." He paused for a second. "Or, it could be a coincidence she bears a resemblance to Mia."

"Right, Sean, you being a person who believes in coincidence."

The retired FBI agent gave JR a crooked smile. "Okay, you caught me."

Tapping the picture, JR continued. "This woman is Mia's sister, of that, I'm sure."

"Then why would they want to kill Mia?"

"Destroy the DNA that could prove who this Soon woman really is."

Kruger stared at his friend for an extended period of time. He picked up his cell phone and made a call.

***

Jeffery Wainstein entered the senator's office after one quick knock. "You wanted to see me, Emily?"

"Yes, shut the door."

Wainstein raised an eyebrow. "Okay, what's going on?"

"I got a disturbing phone call from a constituent. She is reporting that a man named Ethan Matheson is being held by the FBI against his will."

"Who's the constituent?"

"She doesn't want to get involved but felt someone should know. So, she called me."

"How do you know this person isn't a crackpot?"

"Jeffery, who's the senator here? Me or you?"

"You, of course."

"Then as my chief of staff, it is your responsibility to do as I request. I am asking you to check into this matter."

He folded his arms.

"Well?"

"Yes, you are my boss. But inquiring into the internal business of the FBI could be fraught with problems."

"Not for someone with the number of contacts you maintain in this town. That's why I hired you. You get shit done when no one else can."

Giving her a slight smile, he said, "What did this Ethan Matheson supposedly do to be arrested by the FBI?"

"She didn't know. They just showed up at his house and arrested him."

"When?"

"Two days ago. He hasn't been seen since."

"Where?"

"Mill Valley. It's a suburb of San Francisco."

"I'm familiar with it, Senator. What exactly do you want me to do?"

"Find out where he is being held and why."

"Yes, ma'am." Wainstein turned and exited the office.

CHAPTER 23

Southwest Missouri
The Next Day

Alexia Gibbs took her notes to the conference room next to JR's office. When she sat down, she appraised the two men sitting across the table from her. "I find it remarkable how the two of you get us involved in so many improbable situations."

Kruger gave her a grin. "I take it you discovered something."

"The proper word would be somethings."

"Okay, tell us."

Taking several sheets of paper out of the file she brought, she laid them on the table, facing the two men. "The picture on the right is a PDF of a birth certificate on file with the California Department of Public Health. Note the date and the names of the parents."

Picking up the document, Kruger studied it. "Six months after her birth. The parents' last name is Soon."

"Correct. That is the official birth certificate one can

obtain with the right fee and all the other hoops you have to jump through to obtain one." She laid another sheet of paper on the table. "This is the one hidden behind a rather sturdy firewall of the state of California."

After reading the document, Kruger said, "Well, well. Chu Ling and Judy Ling. Can anyone obtain this file?"

Alexia shook her head. "For all practical purposes, that document doesn't exist." She smiled. "Unless you know where to find it."

"How'd you find it?"

Alexia shrugged. "Trade secret."

Kruger turned his attention to JR who was now studying the page with the original birth certificate. He glanced at Kruger. "That's why she's my partner in the company, Sean." He put the document on the conference table and tapped it. "Obviously, someone hacked into the California Department of Public Health's files, created a new birth certificate, and hid the original one."

Alexia picked up the narrative. "More than hid. They changed the file name and linked it to a death certificate."

"Far more efficient than the way I did it. Even if you suspect the one for Soon is a forgery, someone could point to the original certificate and the death certificate to disprove the accusation. Basically, the only way to prove Emily Soon isn't who she says she is, is through DNA?"

Kruger said, "In a court of law, yes. Full siblings share 50 percent DNA."

JR clasped his hands. "Then our next step is to get DNA from Senator Soon."

"I doubt she would be willing to offer a sample voluntarily. So, we'd have to do it surreptitiously."

"Any ideas how to do that?" This from Alexia.

With a sly smile, Kruger nodded his head.

***

An old friend of Kruger's answered the phone. "Science and Technology, this is Charlie."

"Still answering your own phone, aren't you?"

He recognized the voice immediately. "Hey, Sean. How're you doing?"

"I'm good. How's the executive assistant director for the Science and Technology Branch?"

"Well, other than I'm in over my head, thanks to you, I'm doing great."

"Whatever, Charlie. How's the family?"

"Oldest will be starting middle school in the fall."

"Middle school? You're kidding. How's that possible?"

"Yeah, shocking isn't it." He paused. "Time's passing quick, Sean. Michele and I will have been married twelve years this fall."

"Really? Twelve years? I didn't realize."

"I take it you have a question."

"Yeah. How hard is it to get a DNA sample from a sitting senator?"

Charlie Craft chuckled. "In this hypersensitive Congress, I would call it impossible. They don't trust the FBI, and we don't trust them. But for you, I could probably figure out a way to get it done. Which senator?"

"Emily Soon."

After several long moments, Craft replied, "She's on the Judiciary Committee and one of the FBI's loudest critics. She believes we overstep our authority all the time. So, getting it voluntarily would probably not occur."

"What about medical records? You know, for identification purposes in case of a disaster."

"It would take a court order, and I doubt that would even work. Why do you need a DNA sample from her, Sean?"

"Proof."

"Proof of what?"

"Proof Emily Soon is not who she says she is."

Craft hesitated before he asked, "Who is she?"

"That's what we are trying to determine. We have circumstantial evidence that her election may have been assisted by a foreign government. She could be a clear and present danger to the United States."

"Sean, you know I can't do this on an official basis. However, if you can get her DNA, I can arrange for an analysis. Whose DNA would I be comparing it to?"

"Don't worry about that. I'll get you the sample."

Charlie's response became slow and deliberate. "I don't mind helping you, Sean. But I need to know who this Soon woman is supposed to be?"

"We think she's Mia Diminski's sister."

"I thought Mia was an only child."

"So did she, Charlie. It's a lot more complicated than that. Can we count on your help?"

"Sure. I owe JR more than I can ever pay back. When can you get the samples to me?"

"Let me get back to you, Charlie. At least, we have a starting point."

***

The flight to Washington DC would occur the following day. Kruger stood in his office placing his computer in his backpack when JR came to the door.

"I need to go with you, Sean."

"Nope." Kruger turned. "Not a good idea. You're in mourning, remember? Besides, Sandy, Jimmy, and I can handle it."

"I'm the one who started this, I should be involved."

Giving his friend a reassuring smile, Kruger said, "JR, we can't let Senator Soon know what we are trying to accomplish."

"How would she possibly know who I am?"

Shaking his head, Kruger stopped packing. "At this point, JR, we can't assume the senator isn't aware of who you are and that you are married to her sister. If that is the case, your presence would jeopardize what we need to accomplish."

"When you put it that way, I would have to agree. Okay, what can I do from here?"

Jimmy Gibbs stuck his head into Kruger's office. "Everything is ready for our flight in the morning. Wheels up at six thirty."

When Kruger saw the retired SEAL, he almost laughed. Gibbs stood there in his normal silk shirt and khaki cargo shorts, but his hair had been drastically trimmed. He no longer sported a ponytail. "What the hell did you do?"

"It's my new disguise. Distinguished millennial business man. How do you like it?"

JR wrinkled his nose. "I don't."

Kruger crossed his arms and said, "It'll have to grow on me."

"Hey, guys, I even bought a suit for this trip. If I'm going to hobnob with senators as an owner of KKG, I'll need to look the part. Besides, Alexia thinks I'm sexy with my hair short."

"There you go." Kruger turned to JR. "Do you have the DNA sample from Mia?"

"I'll meet you guys at the airport in the morning. The sample will be on dry ice in an insulated thermos." He crossed his arms. "Just how do you anticipate stealing a sample of DNA from the senator without her knowing?"

Gibbs said, "It's more of a logistical problem than anything. Getting close to the senator, I'm told, is difficult. She always has two bodyguards with her. Usually, within ten feet or less." He held up what appeared to be a ChapStick tube. "If I can get her in a packed elevator or a crowded room, I can use this on the inside of her arm. It will extract blood and skin cells, and the subject won't feel a thing."

Kruger took the small tube from Jimmy and examined it. "The problem is getting close enough without her bodyguards suspecting anything."

"Might need a few days to figure it out, Sean." Gibbs turned toward JR. He said, "Unless you can hack into her office computers and steal her itinerary."

With a shrug, JR held up a flash drive. "Her schedule for the next two weeks is on here. But you'll see she is scheduled to attend a reception this coming Friday night."

Taking the small device, Kruger asked, "Who's the reception for, JR?"

With a devious grin, he said, "Veterans Administration." He turned to Jimmy. "You retired as a chief petty officer, didn't you, Jimmy?"

"Yeah."

"Take your dress blues. From what I've learned about her, she doesn't like officers. But she has a thing for high-ranking enlisted men. You, Sean, and Sandy will have invitations waiting at the reception table."

Gibbs frowned. "How did you manage that?"

"You three own one of the top defense contracting firms in the country. Getting an invitation for all of you only took a phone call. No hacking. The invitations are legit."

"Huh. Guess we're going to the reception Friday."

CHAPTER 24

Washington, DC
Friday Night

Kruger leaned against a column halfway up a staircase leading to the second floor of the ballroom. A bottled beer held in his right hand remained untasted as he followed the progress of Emily Soon through the packed crowd milling around below him.

His presence at the reception, so far, remained unnoticed since no one had approached him to engage in small talk. He found this fact comforting. His reluctance to engage in meaningless banter at these types of functions had served him well during his tenure with the FBI. But avoiding social gatherings during his career more than likely contributed to not being offered any meaningful promotions. A fact he still held no regrets about.

Sandy Knoll stepped up next to him and asked, "What's our girl doing?"

"Working the floor. Quite effectively, I might add."

"I noticed that as well."

Nodding toward the crowd, Kruger said, "The two behind her are keeping their distance, so far. Big dudes. Have you seen them?"

"Yeah. They have a military air about them."

Turning his gaze on Knoll, Kruger frowned. "Is that a problem?"

"Not for me or Jimmy."

Kruger returned his attention to the crowd below. "Have you made any contacts tonight?"

Knoll gave Kruger a thumbs-up gesture. "Yeah, a couple of good ones."

"Good. Make sure you and Jimmy contact them again in case someone questions why you're here."

"Goes without saying."

"I know, but I don't want the senator to suspect our real purpose for being here."

Turning, Knoll scanned the crowd for the location of the senator. When he found her, he said, "When do we start this little exercise?"

"As soon as you two are ready."

"Then let's get started. Where will you be?"

"I'll move toward the main exit. As soon as you have the sample, get it to me, and I'll leave. Charlie told me to drop it off at his place. If you two can pull this off without raising any suspicions, stick around for a while. See what transpires."

"Got it. Meet you back at the hotel.'"

Kruger headed down the stairs to situate himself close to the main exit.

***

Jimmy Gibbs, sporting shorter hair and wearing his dress blues, drew the attention of several women at the reception. Their attempts to draw him into conversation ended with a polite but subtle display of his wedding ring.

Most got the hint, except a rather persistent blonde in her mid-thirties who insisted on engaging him in a discussion about her conquests of other special forces members.

"I've known several SEALs, James. You're different."

He smiled politely, glanced at her, and then returned his attention to the gathering. When he caught sight of the senator, he said, "How so?"

"At this time of the evening, most would have asked me if I'd like to find someplace a little more private."

"I like crowds."

"Yes, but it is hardly a convenient way to get to know each other better."

He saw Knoll approaching and turned to the woman. "I don't mean to be rude, but I am very married, happily I might add, and don't feel the need to know you better. Excuse me. I have to go." He turned and worked his way through the crowd to where Knoll stood waiting.

When he reached the big man, Knoll said, "Pretty lady. Making plans?"

"She was. I chose not to." He scanned the room again and caught sight of Emily Soon. "When are we doing this?"

"Sean's waiting at the front exit. I'll run interference with the bodyguards. How long do you need to get the sample?"

"All I need to do is to brush past her. She shouldn't feel a thing."

"Then, let's get this done."

The two men worked their way through the crowd toward the location where the senator stood. She appeared to be chatting with three men in suits. Her bodyguards, five feet behind, made sure no one approached from the rear.

Moving perpendicular to the space between the senator and the two men, Knoll would be closer to the bodyguards, and Gibbs would brush against the woman.

The whole incident took less than twenty seconds from beginning to end.

As they moved toward the senator, one of the large men behind her attempted to block Knoll's path with an outstretched arm.

"Sorry, sir, this…"

Knoll growled at him. "You sure you want to touch me?" While the guard was big, he looked up at the slightly taller, more muscular ex-Army Ranger.

While this confrontation drew the attention of both the senator's protectors, Gibbs, using Knoll as a shield, quickly touched the small needle to an exposed part of Soon's arm. Just as fast, he returned it to his pocket and kept on walking, leaving Knoll to contend with the men.

When the senator turned to see what was occurring behind her, she could be seen rubbing a spot on her arm. "What's going on back here?"

The one who stopped Knoll said, "We were making sure no one got to close to you, Senator Soon."

She frowned. "Do you see the tan beret this gentleman is wearing?"

Both men said, "Yes, ma'am", in unison.

"Obviously, you don't know what it means. He is an Army Ranger. Let him pass, Greg."

"Yes, ma'am."

The senator peered up at Knoll. "Sorry, Major, they were doing their job."

"No problem." He dipped his head once to her and strolled away.

The senator returned to her discussion with the three men still standing in front of her.

***

As Knoll approached Gibbs, the big man asked, "Did you get it?"

"Already in Sean's hands and on its way to Charlie."

"Good." He returned his attention to the crowd. "We

need to mingle a while longer. I don't think we'll hear anything additional from the senator's goons, but you never know."

"Do you think they suspect anything?"

"I don't see how. Their eyes were focused on me the whole time. I doubt they even saw you."

"Well, it would be hard to prove anything since the device isn't even on the premises."

Knoll turned to survey the crowd. "I saw a general I need to follow up with. What are you gonna do?"

"Stay away from the woman who's trying to get me into bed."

With a chuckle, Knoll said, "Then come with me." They both headed toward a group of officers.

***

Kruger handed the small tube to Charlie Craft. They stood on the younger man's front porch. "Sorry it's so late, Charlie."

"I'd invite you in, Sean, but everyone's asleep."

"Best no one know I was here."

"You're probably right."

"How long before we know the results?"

"I should have preliminary results by midmorning. I have time already scheduled on the machine."

Kruger offered his hand. As they shook, he said, "Thanks, Charlie. I owe you one."

"No, you don't. After all you did for me over the years, I'll be in your debt forever."

The retired FBI agent placed his hands on Charlie's shoulder and said, "I don't see it that way. Just pay it forward with someone you think will benefit from your guidance."

"Already doing that."

"Good. Take care my friend. Call me when you know

something."

***

Kruger heard the knock at a quarter to midnight. When he opened the door, Knoll and Gibbs slipped into his room.

Gibbs said, "Does Charlie have the sample?"

"Yes. We should know something by midmorning."

Knoll chuckled. "We're glad you didn't stick around, Sean."

"What happened?"

"One of the senator's guards saw a little blood on her arm and freaked out. He hunted me down and demanded to know what I had done."

With a laugh, Gibbs said, "Sandy and I were talking to a couple of four-stars when the goon confronted him."

"I can't wait to hear how this turned out." Kruger folded his arms.

"You'll love this," Knoll continued the story, "One of the generals we're working with on a contract stepped in front of the man and demanded to know what was going on. The guy pointed at me and said I attacked the senator. The general folded his arms and glared at him. He then said, 'Did you see Major Knoll touch the senator?' The guy told him no. The general then leaned in to his face and yelled, 'Then, how the hell did he attack her?'"

Taking up the narrative, Gibbs said, "The guy glared at the general for at least fifteen seconds, shook his head, and walked away."

Kruger asked, "What about security cameras, Sandy?"

"Didn't think about it."

Kruger remained quiet for several moments. "Gentlemen, we need to leave tomorrow, early. I want to be a long way from DC if someone checks the videos."

Gibbs said, "I think that's the appropriate move, considering."

"Can either one of you find out who owns the facility we were at tonight?"

The big man said, "It's a Hilton property."

Pulling his cell phone out of his pocket, Kruger sent a text message. His phone vibrated a minute later.

"What kind of trouble did you three get into?"

"Thanks for the vote of confidence, JR. I need you to see if you can hack into the security system at the reception venue."

"What happened?"

"One of the senator's guards spotted blood on her arm, and they freaked out. They confronted Sandy, but he didn't touch her. I need you to see if you can make the image of Jimmy brushing by the senator disappear."

"I'll call you back."

"Thanks, JR. We're leaving early in the morning."

"I'll still call."

CHAPTER 25

Southwest Missouri

From scrutinizing the various security camera angles displayed on the computer screen, only one revealed an important image. It showed Jimmy Gibbs walking next to Sandy Knoll as they passed between Senator Soon and her bodyguards. While JR knew what transpired, he saw no evidence of it occurring on this or any of the other camera videos. While someone could infer the incident happened at this moment, JR doubted it would provide any proof.

The other reveal uncovered by watching the various video feeds several times was a meeting between Randall Becker and Senator Soon. To anyone unfamiliar with the identity of Becker, the meeting could only be described as a typical encounter at any social gathering.

JR found several images of the meeting. One view showed them conversing for a short period and then quickly moving on to other interactions. A second view reviewed the transfer of an object from Becker to the senator, the identity of the object impossible to determine from the camera angle.

The final video viewed by JR revealed Becker taking what appeared to be an SD card from his pants pocket. A few moments later, from the same camera, he saw the senator slip the small device into her clutch bag. He could not find an image of the two individuals actually exchanging the object.

Instead of making the decision for his friend, JR placed a call to Kruger's cell phone.

***

Glancing at the digital clock on the hotel nightstand, the retired FBI agent answered, "What'd you find?"

"The news is not all bad."

"JR, it's three in the morning. Just tell me what you found."

"I didn't find a single image of Jimmy brushing against the senator."

"Well, that's good news. What's the bad?"

"There was a meeting between Randall Becker and Senator Soon."

Kruger did not respond right away. Finally, he said, "What else?"

"He gave her an SD Card. Not on any screenshot I can find, but there is a shot of him removing the object from his pocket and then one of her placing the object in her clutch bag. Nothing else."

"Huh. Interesting."

"The only conclusion I can come up with is, whatever he gave her had to be so sensitive they couldn't afford to send it electronically. It had to be delivered by hand by someone high up in the organization."

"That would be a fair assumption, JR. Why Becker? Wouldn't he draw a lot of attention being in Washington, DC?"

"Not if he's a regular there."

"Explain."

"He meets with attorneys based in DC on a regular basis."

"Lobbyist?"

"That would be my guess. I don't know for sure."

"Okay, JR, I think everyone here needs to leave earlier than we planned. I'll let you know our ETA when we get in the air."

"Okay." JR hesitated. "Uh, Sean?"

"Yeah."

"If Emily Soon is Mia's sister, what then?"

"I don't know, JR. If she is, we need to understand how they are utilizing her position. Plus, how deep the group has penetrated our government. Then we need to find proof."

"Then what?"

"We take our proof to the FBI."

***

Midmorning

Charlie Craft read the result of the DNA sibling test. The samples revealed the two test subjects were daughters of the same biological mother and father. He quickly cleared away any residual evidence of the test and stored the results in one of several secure evidence safes in his office. Copies of the result were then placed in a FedEx envelope. He left the office for the short trip to a drop-off station frequented by those in his office.

Before arriving, he dialed a number on his cell phone. A familiar voice answered.

"What'd you learn, Charlie?"

"The two women are sisters, Sean. They share the same parents."

Kruger did not respond immediately. Finally, he asked,

"Okay, where are the results?"

"In a FedEx envelope. I'm on my way to drop it off. Where do you want me to send it?"

"Not JR's office."

"I didn't think so."

"Let me think for a second."

As Charlie drove, he heard muffled voices in the background.

Kruger came back on. "Send it to Joseph's place in Christian County."

"Do they deliver to him? His house is a long way from an urban setting."

"Yes."

"Uh, Sean, you sure? He has ties to Washington, DC."

"Damn, your right."

"I'm using the return address of Michele's aunt who lives in Baltimore."

"Okay. Send it to Stephanie, at the university." He recited the address. "Use her maiden name, Harris. She started using it several years ago after a suspect in one of my FBI investigations tracked us down through the school."

"Got it. I kind of remember the event."

"Thanks, Charlie."

"If you need the original test, it's in the evidence safe in my office."

"Let's hope we don't need it. Thanks again, Charlie."

The call ended, and Charlie Craft continued on to the FedEx drop-off station.

***

By noon, Kruger and team were back in their office building. Alexia joined them in the conference room, as did JR.

"Charlie is overnighting the DNA evidence." Kruger

regarded each person at the table. "I don't have a good feeling about what to expect if Twin Peaks learns we have proof Emily Soon is not who she says she is."

JR drummed his fingers on the conference table. "With the info Alexia found on the birth certificates and now the DNA, why not give it to the FBI?"

Kruger stood and looked out the window for several moments, his hands behind his back. Finally, he turned. "We could. But she can claim she never knew who her real father and mother were. My guess is she'll have access to phony adoption papers somewhere. We need more hard evidence this is a conspiracy."

"Like what, Sean?" Jimmy tilted his head. "You were with the FBI. What would you have needed to take the case higher up the ladder?"

Returning to stare out the window, he pursed his lips but said nothing. No one spoke as they kept their attention on Kruger.

Sandy Knoll asked, "What about the Matheson character? Doesn't Charlie Brewer have him on ice in California?"

Turning around, Kruger turned his attention to his friend. "I forgot about him, Sandy. Time to give Brewer a call."

***

"Good to hear from you, Sean."

"We've had a development here. Any chance we can have another conference call with Dr. Matheson?"

"I'm sure it can be arranged, but we'll need at least twenty-four hours to make it happen."

"I take it you have him in a secure place, don't you?"

"He's not even in the state."

"The politician he referred to is Senator Emily Soon."

"I won't ask how you found it out."

"Probably best, Charlie. She is also the sister of JR's wife, Mia. Which means, they have hidden her identity."

"Why?"

"We think to keep anyone from discovering who her father is. That's why we need to have another discussion with Matheson."

"Give me a day. I'll get it arranged."

CHAPTER 26

Somewhere in the Colorado Rocky Mountains

Tim Gonzales stepped out of the cabin and trudged through the snow to the adjacent building. High in the Rocky Mountains, the FBI maintained a series of small hunting lodges for the sole purpose of hiding high-profile witnesses.

Ethan Matheson answered the door after the agent knocked.

Without being invited in, Gonzales entered and turned. "Close the door. We've had a development."

Leaning against the now-closed entrance, Matheson said, "Good or bad?"

"Definitely not good."

"What?"

"Your house was ransacked."

"Not surprised. When?"

"Except for the first hour after we took you into custody, we've had your home under surveillance 24/7. We think it happened then."

A slow nod came from the computer expert.

"Do you know what they might have been searching for, Ethan?"

"My notes."

"And?"

"I kept them in my home office desk. I'm sure they were found. Which means, they now know what I suspected. And the minute you guys stop protecting me, I'm dead."

"We won't let that happen, Ethan."

"Eventually, you'll stop. These guys don't forget and are very patient."

"There's something else."

"Might as well tell me." Matheson folded his arms.

"We are now in possession of DNA proving Emily Soon is the daughter of the Manchurian and Judy Ling. Which means she is Mia Diminski's younger sister."

Closing his eyes, the former employee of Twin Peaks said, "Shit."

"I take it you didn't know."

"No, I didn't. But a lot of things I've overheard now make sense."

"Give me a for-instance."

"There were numerous closed-door meetings between Becker and members of the security team. All of them were imports from China. I heard two of them discussing what they felt was a threat to their plan coming out of Missouri." He paused. "I found that statement a bit odd. What could possibly be a threat in Missouri? Then I saw an email referencing the death of a woman from that state. I didn't put the connection together until just now. JR Diminski lives in Missouri, doesn't he?"

Gonzales contemplated Matheson for several moments. He then said, "You realize we really need to know what the Manchurian has in mind, Ethan."

"Before I do that, I want, in writing, an immunity from prosecution agreement. Once I have it, I'll tell you everything I know."

Without saying a word, Gonzales left the small cabin and returned to his own. After closing his door, he pulled out his cell phone, checked the strength signal, and made a call.

***

Randall Becker finished reading the pages taken from a file on his desk.

The man with the pockmarked face sat across from him and pointed at the page. "That was found in Matheson's home office."

"Where is he?"

"The FBI's got him hidden."

The lawyer glanced at the page again. "Here in San Francisco?"

"No. We have a source inside the local bureau, and he's not there."

Taking a deep breath, Becker let it out slowly. "The Manchurian will not take this news well." He held up the file. "Matheson knows everything we've accomplished. However, he didn't know the why."

His guest stood. "He knows enough."

"He must not be allowed to discuss our plans with the FBI."

"He won't be. We'll know where he is soon." The tall man turned and exited Becker's office.

***

"Tim, the Attorney General will grant Matheson immunity if the information will let us build a case against Twin Peaks." Charlie Brewer held his desk phone receiver to his ear and tapped a pencil on his desk while he waited for the reply from Gonzales.

"That's a catch-22, Charlie. He won't talk until he's granted the immunity. I think he knows more than we think he does."

"Very well, I'll tell the AG we need a witness immunity agreement with Matheson."

"He'll want it in writing before he'll talk."

"Check your email. I'll have it to you within the hour."

When the call ended, Brewer stood and walked out of his office. He found his administrative specialist at her desk and said, "I'll need a standard witness immunity agreement drawn up."

Angela Bowman looked up. "Sure, Charlie. Who's it for?"

"Leave the name blank for now."

"Very good. Any other details I need to know?"

"No, only that the witness is at our Colorado protection site."

She smiled at her boss.

***

Two Days Later

Somewhere in the Colorado Rocky Mountains

Having deployed to Afghanistan during Operation Enduring Freedom while serving with the US Army, Tim Gonzales recognized the sound of a Switchblade suicide drone. Standing on the front porch of his cabin, the sound of the small aircraft grew louder. Knowing what would be next, he made a mad dash toward Matheson's cabin. He did not arrive in time to evacuate the computer expert.

In the darkness of midnight, the blast momentarily blinded him as the cabin where Matheson slept erupted into a ball of flame. Hitting the ground, he covered his head as pieces of the wooden structure fell to the ground around him.

A second FBI agent appeared beside him. "You okay, Tim?"

Standing, Gonzales brushed himself off and said, "Yeah."

"What the hell happened?" Agent Richard Marshal stared at the burning building.

"Someone discovered where Matheson was staying, and that someone has access to Switchblade drones." Taking his cell phone out of his pocket, Gonzales made a call he really did not want to make.

By dawn, a team of FBI forensic technicians from the Denver field office swarmed over the burned-out cabin. Gonzales watched as a body bag holding the remains of Ethan Matheson was loaded into the back of a black Suburban.

Marshal walked up next to him and said, "They found the launch site."

Turning, Gonzales asked, "Where?"

Pointing to the north, Marshal said, "A clearing on that next peak. It's a little over five miles from here. For some reason, they left the launch tube there."

"They wanted to make sure we knew their capabilities." Folding his arms, the ex-Army Ranger took a deep breath. "Richard, you realize this raises two serious questions."

"I do. First, how did they know where to find him and second, how did they get access to a Switchblade."

"Exactly." Gonzales pulled his cell phone out of his back pocket and placed a call.

"Brewer."

"Charlie, like I suspected, it was a Switchblade rocket drone. We found the launch site and the tube used to deploy it."

The San Francisco Special Agent in Charge remained quiet for several moments. Finally, he said, "Then we have a leak here in the field office."

"Who would have known where Matheson was?"

"Me, you, and Marshal. Unless—" He did not finish his sentence. "I'll have to get back to you, Tim. Keep me posted on any details you discover."

***

Brewer pulled the personnel list for the field office up on his laptop. He glanced over it, stood, and exited his office. He shut the door to the administrative assistant's office and asked, "Bob, how many temps do we have working here right now?"

Turning his attention away from the computer screen, Robert Trent frowned. "We don't have any temps. Why do you ask?"

"We've got a leak."

"There's a painting crew that comes in after hours."

"Do you know who the contractor is?"

"Yeah. Let me get the paperwork."

Five minutes later, Brewer had the owner of the painting company on the phone. "I need the list of the painters you've had working at the field office last week."

"What are you talking about, Charlie? We're not scheduled to start that project until the thirteenth."

"Then who the hell's been painting our offices?"

"Not my company."

"Shit."

After ending the call to the painting company, Brewer drummed his fingers on his desk. Picking up his cell phone, he dialed a number he had memorized a week ago.

"Gonzales."

"Tim, it's Brewer. How are things going now?"

"Not much for Richard and me to do here. Denver field office has jurisdiction."

"Then you and Marshal get back to San Francisco as fast as possible."

"What's happened?"

"I don't want to go over it on a cell phone. Let me know when you two are back."

CHAPTER 27

Southwest Missouri

JR listened without comment as Kruger and Brewer discussed the drone attack on Ethan Matheson's cabin.

Kruger concentrated on the Polycom conference phone while he listened, his hands clasped together. JR knew the news was not going over well with his friend.

The San Francisco SAC's voice bellowed out of the box. "We believe a fake painting crew here at the field office found the information on the whereabouts of Matheson, which led to the Switchblade drone attack. Gonzales and his partner are on their way back to San Francisco and should be here within the hour."

"What about security camera images?"

"Four-man crew. Two actually painted, and two rifled through desks and gained access to our computer files."

"Who were they?"

"Same four guys who broke into Matheson's home, Sean."

"How do you know?"

"Matheson had multiple security cameras installed inside his house."

"So, they have Ethan's files and the files from your office."

"That's about the size of it."

"Charlie, did any of the files from your office mention JR and Mia?"

"No."

"What about the evidence we have about Senator Soon?"

"We think the files from this office were copied before we had the DNA information."

"What about our conference call with Matheson?"

"Same."

"I know it is none of my business, but what's the FBI gonna do now that you know terrorists have access to Switchblade technology?"

"It's been kicked upstairs, Sean."

"And that means?"

"The director is now involved. Which means, a whole bunch of FBI agents will descend on San Francisco."

"Good. Any word about where the Manchurian is?"

"Nothing on our radar."

"Does the director know about Senator Soon?"

"He will as soon as he gets here."

"Charlie, how are you gonna explain the DNA evidence? I don't want my source burned."

"I understand, but the director has a soft spot for that particular source."

"He knows?"

"Of course, he knows, Sean. He knows you and your source have solved more difficult cases than he cares to admit. He's told me numerous times, if this age thing didn't exist, you'd still be with the bureau."

Kruger smiled. "Yeah, I know."

Brewer continued. "He looks the other way and

appreciates the fact you only do so on rare occasions."

The retired FBI agent did not respond. Brewer continued. "How fast could you and JR get to San Francisco?"

Looking at JR, Kruger raised his eyebrows.

JR wrote on a legal pad and showed it to him. *I'm good to go.*

Making an OK sign with his fingers, Kruger said, "As soon as we can get the plane serviced and a flight plan filed. Why?"

"The director is bringing a federal no-knock search warrant for Twin Peaks. The plan is to serve it at 8:15 a.m. tomorrow."

"Why do you need us?"

"According to the director, both of you are considered FBI consultants."

"Yeah."

"He feels you know more about Twin Peaks than anyone and that JR has a skill set way above any FBI computer expert. We can use both of you."

"We'll be there tonight."

"Great. Let me know when you arrive."

The call ended, and Kruger looked at JR. "Things could get interesting tomorrow."

"It needs to be over, Sean. It's ridiculous for Mia and Joey to have to hide at Joseph's house."

"I've told you several times, we have plenty of associates who've volunteered to keep your family out of harm's way."

"I know, but it's still ridiculous she has to hide from her father."

"I don't disagree."

"So, let's do something about it tomorrow."

***

San Francisco

Kruger sat in his rented Mustang with JR next to him in the passenger seat. The retired FBI agent's right index finger tapped the steering wheel as he checked the dashboard clock.

Glancing at his friend, JR asked, "You miss being in the center of the action, don't you?"

"Watching and waiting like a spectator is not my idea of being involved."

"You and I have no business being involved at this stage."

Sitting in the back of the parking lot, waiting for the FBI team to arrive and serve their no-knock search warrant, grated on the ex-agent's nerves. "Sitting on the sidelines is frustrating. I understand the why, but I don't have to like it."

JR pointed to the arrival of five black Chevy Suburbans and two Lenco BearCat Armored Tactical Vehicles. "Apparently, it's showtime."

Glancing at his watch, Kruger nodded. "Charlie always likes being on time."

The Suburbans screeched to a halt near the entrance to the main building containing Twin Peaks' administrative offices. Four agents, dressed in either dark jeans or utility pants, exited each of the black vehicles. Some clutched long guns; others held Glocks.

Charlie Brewer led the agents inside.

Kruger, dressed in jeans and a navy windbreaker, stepped out of his rental and proceeded to follow the agents inside. JR hot on his heels.

The lobby of Twin Peaks contained disgruntled associates and a heated discussion between Randall Becker and FBI Special Agent in Charge Charlie Brewer. Getting within earshot, Kruger heard, "Mr. Becker, this is a federal warrant, not a State of California one. You can call the state AG all you want, but he has no jurisdiction in this matter."

"You can't walk in here and start seizing computers and files."

With a smile, Brewer answered, "On the contrary, we can and we will. Now, back off if you don't want to be escorting the files when we leave."

Becker crossed his arms. "I'm an attorney. I know my rights."

"Well, you might be a corporate attorney, but this is a criminal investigation." Brewer leaned in closer to Becker. "One more word, and I'll have you arrested for obstructing a federal investigation."

Placing his hands on his hips, Becker gave the SAC a smirk. "I dare you."

Turning to Gonzales, who stood on Brewer's right, he said, "Agent Gonzales, read this man his rights and place him under arrest. I have far more important matters to deal with than him."

He turned and walked away as Gonzales cuffed the lawyer and informed him of his rights.

Brewer motioned for Kruger and JR to follow him.

***

The computer room already contained numerous FBI agents sorting and boxing evidence. Brewer turned to JR. "The assistant IT director acknowledged the information mentioned in the search warrant can be found through this terminal. But he refused to access it for us. This type of contingency is the exact reason why you're here, JR."

"What are you trying to find?"

"Data from the houses you guys discovered."

"Okay, let's see what's in this thing." The computer expert sat in front of the terminal. After studying the setup for a few moments, he started typing.

Kruger watched and then turned to Brewer. "He'll be uncommunicative for a while. Why did you need me?"

"We need to know more about the man they call the Manchurian. Since we've arrested Becker, I'd like for you to interrogate him. You were always good at getting people to talk who were reluctant to do so."

"Where did you take him?"

"The little scene you saw in the lobby was preplanned by Gonzales. He's got him stashed in an office on the first floor."

"You'd better watch Gonzales. He'll be taking over your job one day."

With a chuckle, Brewer said, "Already in the works."

"Excuse me?"

"Sean, we aren't that much different in age. This time next year, I'll be calling you for a job."

With a raised eyebrow, Kruger said, "I'll look forward to the conversation."

***

Five minutes later, Kruger sat at a conference table with Brewer on his right. Across from them was Randall Becker and he was not smiling.

Becker's hands were cuffed and in front of him. He eyed the retired FBI agent with his head defiantly back. "Who are you?"

"My name is Sean Kruger."

"Are you with the FBI?"

Brewer interjected. "We'll ask the questions, Mr. Becker."

The managing director of Twin Peaks glared at the San Francisco SAC.

Kruger said, "Where is Ling Mao Chun?"

"Who?"

With a sly smile, Kruger said, "Mr. Becker, we know more than you think we do. Ling Mao Chun is known as the Manchurian. Where is he?"

The momentary surprise on Becker's face told Kruger a lot. He continued. "We also know the bungalows, originally built for commune members, now function as data terminals designed to attack and manipulate computers of state and local governments. They are also being used to compromise utilities, power and water treatment plants."

Becker did not answer, but Kruger observed his knuckles turn white as he clasped his hands tighter.

"We also know that a certain US senator from California is not who she claims to be. She's the daughter of Ling Mao Chun and Judy Ling. You had the mother killed to keep that secret from leaking to the media."

"I have no idea what you are talking about, Mr. Kruger. I want an attorney."

"I'm not an FBI agent. I'm not authorized to get you one."

Nodding toward Brewer, Becker said, "He is. Now, get me an attorney."

"Since I'm not with the FBI, this is not an official interrogation, Randall. I'm trying to determine a few facts."

"That is the definition of an interrogation. I want an attorney present."

"Who ordered the death of Judy Ling?"

The attorney's eyes widened slightly. His composure returned almost as fast. "She died of natural causes."

"If that's the case, why was her house so full of blood? We have pictures and samples. DNA analysis confirms it to be the blood of Judy Ling."

Becker blinked several times.

Kruger continued. "We also have evidence that, after Judy's death, you tried to unlawfully obtain contents of a lock box belonging to her." He smiled. "We also know you sent someone to kill Mia Diminski and her husband. She's alive, Becker. We have proof she's Senator Emily Soon's full sister. We also have pictures of you meeting the good senator at a reception."

The attorney shifted in his chair and glanced at the room's entrance.

"No one is coming to rescue you, Randall." Kruger leaned forward, his palms flat on the table. "With all the evidence the FBI has, you are facing a lengthy stay in a California penal institution. I'm sure once the FBI finishes investigating you, they'll find more laws you've violated. Care to comment?"

Becker stared at the top of the conference table, his. hands cuffed in front of him. Turning his attention to Charlie Brewer, he said, "Get me a deal, and I'll tell you what I know."

Standing, the FBI supervisor left the room.

Turning to Kruger, he said, "You never told me who you are?"

The retired FBI agent stood. He walked to the door of the office and turned. "The person who is going to expose Twin Peaks for what it truly is. A clear and present danger to the United States."

CHAPTER 28

San Francisco

"Damn."

Kruger observed his friend who sat in front of a computer terminal. "What's the matter, JR?"

"I hate quantum computers."

"So, you have said on numerous occasions. Why?"

"Binary computers are simple to understand."

"If you say so."

"No, really, they are. You have a one or a zero. An on state or an off state. Quantum computers have multiple states."

"Uh-huh."

"It's true."

"Whatever."

Turning to glare at his friend, JR remained quiet for a brief moment and then laughed out loud. "Thanks for bringing me back to reality."

"Don't mention it. I wasn't following you in the first place."

Taking a deep breath, JR returned his attention to the computer screen. "I guess I'm getting old. This computer complex doesn't act like a quantum computer should."

"Okay, why?"

JR shot a glance at his friend and then pursed his lips. "Well, let me see, because of the way quantum computers are designed, they are better at solving problems involving unimaginable amounts of data and hundreds of variables. Because of this, they are fast. Incredibly fast."

"And this one is fast."

"Exactly. But not that fast."

"So, what have you found in the Twin Peaks' computer?"

"The vast majority of their system is nothing more than a conventional computer. An extremely large and fast conventional computer, but nothing special. There's an isolated server I haven't been able to gain access to yet. It might be a rudimentary quantum computer, but I doubt it."

"Why do you doubt it?"

"Quantum computers need a specific environment to function. Extreme low temperatures with no vibrations. It would require a special room. A room that does not exist in this building. So, that's why I'm scratching my head about this one server."

Kruger folded his arms. "Do you need help?"

With a chuckle, JR shook his head. "No, I need to get my head out of my ass and figure this thing out."

"Then, I'll leave you alone."

"Not what I meant."

The retired FBI agent did not respond as he walked out of the computer lab.

***

Twenty Miles West of San Francisco
Well Outside US Territorial Waters

Ling Mao Chun, aka the Manchurian, stood on the stern of the ship, a satellite phone pressed to his ear. He listened to the report from the tall, lanky man with pockmarked cheeks. When he finished speaking, Chun asked, "Where is Becker?"

"In custody. Where is unknown at this time. We think he may still be inside the Twin Peaks' building."

"Can you get to him?"

"No."

"Not the correct answer."

"You're not here and don't know the situation."

Ling shut his eyes and kept his breathing steady. "Where are The Four Brothers?"

"Hidden in Chinatown."

"Find Becker and then contact them. They will know what to do."

"Very well."

"I might remind you that if Becker tells the FBI what he knows, they will be knocking on your door."

"I will contact the brothers as you requested. However, I will only tell them where he is, nothing more."

"See that you do."

The call ended, and the Manchurian stopped himself from throwing the phone over the starboard side of the ship. He took a deep breath and then gazed toward the east. San Francisco was a mere twenty miles away, yet, at the moment, he was powerless to stop what he knew to be the first serious threat to his long-term plans.

The chilly breeze from the northwest caressed his face as he concentrated on the problem at hand. The scent of salt and seaweed, a smell he associated with his early childhood, eased the tension throughout his body. Finally, after closing his eyes for a few moments, he knew what he must do.

He punched an international phone number into his cell phone.

***

Randall Becker remained seated at the conference table. His cuffed hands clasped together in front of him as he stared at an imaginary spot on the wall.

FBI Agent Tim Gonzales entered the conference room and took a seat across from the attorney. "My boss, Charlie Brewer, is talking to the DA. Do you have an attorney you wish to contact, Mr. Becker?"

"No. What I wish is to be transferred to a more secure location. Being held here at the Twin Peaks' office is dangerous for me and anyone around me."

"How so?"

Becker gave the agent a grim smile. "They found Matheson, didn't they?"

Gonzales did not respond but kept his attention on the attorney.

"By your failure to comment, I will assume they did. Matheson's dead, isn't he?"

"I'm not at liberty to discuss where Dr. Matheson is, Becker."

"You don't have to. I know these people. The fact the FBI arrested me is reason enough for them to reach out and silence me."

"Then, why did you go to work for them?"

"Money."

"Can't spend it if you're dead."

"The gains outweighed the potential risks."

"Until now."

"Yes, Agent. Until now." He pursed his lips. "If you are

going to hold me, you need to do it elsewhere. These people don't care who they include in their collateral damage. We're both in danger."

Gonzales tilted his head. "Who were the four men who moved in across from Matheson?"

Becker took a deep breath and let it out slowly. "I've never heard their names mentioned. They're referred to as The Four Brothers. Whether they are related, I have no clue. But they are the Manchurian's enforcers." He narrowed his eyes. "And they are ruthless."

Gonzales stood and went to the door of the conference room. He opened it and spoke to someone standing outside. When he returned to the table, he said, "All right. We're moving you."

Becker gave the FBI agent a grim look. "So, Matheson is dead."

"I didn't say that."

"No, but your willingness to move me speaks volumes."

"Stand up, Becker. You're getting your wish. We're taking you to the federal building downtown. Where you'll be afterward is still undecided."

***

"I'll be damned."

"What, JR?"

"Sean, it was right in front me the entire time."

Rolling his eyes, the retired FBI agent sighed. "Go on."

"There was a reason they needed to develop new technology. They needed the computer to be able to hack into every county clerk's office in the country."

"Okay, how?"

"The computer assumes the identity of the county clerk and manipulates the voting data."

"JR, there are over 3,000 counties in the US. How's that possible?"

"The number is more like 3,144 including the District of Columbia. The variables are such that a regular computer would take years if not decades to run through all the calculations and permutations needed. Whereas, a quantum computer would only take a few minutes. The AI aspect of it makes this even more dangerous. This computer site has the ability to manipulate every county election in the United States for all types of elections, local, state, and federal. Elections are now optional, boys and girls."

"How do we stop it, JR?"

"I wish it was as easy as pulling the plug. But it isn't."

"Why?"

"The genie may be out of the bottle, Sean. There's a chance Ling Mao Chun has developed a quantum computer chip that can function at room temperature. If that's the case, he's resolved the main hold-up of quantum computing. Before now, they had to be at almost absolute zero degrees with no vibrations to work. If he has, and I use the word, if, cautiously, he's pushed computer science to the next level."

"If Ling Mao Chun knows how, that means the Chinese government knows how, as well."

JR nodded. "That would be the assumption. But I believe a pretty safe assumption."

Kruger stood and pulled out his cell phone. "This just jumped way above our pay grade."

Returning his attention back to the computer terminal, JR said, "Yeah, and made every computer expert I know, obsolete."

CHAPTER 29

Two Days Later
Washington, DC

The black Suburban parked in front of the West Wing lobby entrance. Blacked-out windows obscured the passengers. One of the two Secret Service agents waiting for the SUV opened the door, and two men exited. Without exchanging words, the passengers followed their escorts into The White House. Kruger and JR were then shown to the Oval Office and allowed to enter. Seated at the Resolute Desk, President of the United States, Roy Griffin rose, walked around the desk, and greeted his old friends.

Shaking the retired FBI agent's hand, Griffin said, "It's been too long, Sean. Good to see you."

"Wish it was under better circumstances, Mr. President."

"Me, too." He offered his hand to JR. "Thanks for coming, JR. I read your assessment of the Ling computer." He paused. "Where are my manners, gentlemen? Please sit." He pointed to the two couches in front of the president's desk.

Kruger and JR sat next to each other, while Griffin took

the sofa across from them.

"Would either of you like coffee?"

Both men shook their head and said in unison, "No, thank you."

"Back to your assessment of the Twin Peaks' computer, JR."

"Yes, sir."

"While I didn't understand the technical jargon, I did appreciate your laying the dangers out in layman's terms."

"It's a dangerous machine, sir. Someone with more knowledge of national security needs to evaluate it."

"I've asked the FBI, the CIA, and the NSA to make understanding this computer a top priority."

Kruger hesitated for a second. "Can they keep it a secret?"

"I've never seen the directors of those three agencies agree on an issue so fast. The Army Corps of Engineers erected a ten-foot chain link fence around the building, and members of a California National Guard MP unit are posted every twenty feet around the perimeter. Their orders are to let no one enter the building except a limited group of individuals. I'm not even allowed inside."

JR tapped his lips with a finger. "Did they shut down the Wi-Fi and the fiber optic landline into the building?"

The president leaned forward on the couch. "Yes. On my last briefing, I was told the corps has already dug up the fiber optic line and removed all the wireless hubs."

"Good."

Kruger asked, "What about the computers at the commune housing?"

"From what Director Clark told me, they've all been removed and taken to a government-owned warehouse near Oakland. It's under guard 24/7."

Smiling for the first time, JR said, "That makes me feel better. Has anyone been designated to analyze the main computer, sir?"

Griffin sat back on the couch and stretched his arm across the top. He stared directly at the computer genius. "Yes, someone has. You."

"Me?"

"Yes, you."

"Sir, I don't have that high a security clearance."

"As of two hours ago, you do." From the inside pocket of his suit coat, the president retrieved an ID and handed it to JR. "You are now a senior technology advisor to the president and entitled to all the privileges the position carries. Your top-secret status has been updated and signed by me." He turned to Kruger. "So has yours, Sean. You'll both be my eyes and ears on this investigation."

With a frown, Kruger said, "Sir, JR will make a great advisor on this matter. However, there are far more qualified individuals than myself to advise you."

"None that I trust as much as you two." He stood and walked to the front of his desk and leaned against it. He appraised his two friends. "There are a lot of talented people here in Washington, DC. But beyond their talent and experience, I don't have a comfort level with them. You gentlemen were instrumental in saving the life of myself and my wife a number of years ago.

"Thank you, sir, but—"

"No buts, Sean. This is one of the most serious threats this country has faced since World War II. Someone is planning to destroy the pillar of our democracy, our free election process. Plus, they are targeting our country's infrastructure. I have to trust the people I have trying to stop it."

Both JR and Kruger remained silent.

"You two discovered this threat and, I believe, together, you both have the best chance to stop it."

"Thank you, sir. I can't speak for JR, but I'll do my best."

The president turned his attention to the computer

expert.

"I'd be honored, sir."

"Good. Now that we have that out of the way, what do you need from me?"

Kruger chuckled. "How about getting my FBI badge back?"

Griffin turned and picked up a leather wallet off his desktop. He handed it to his old friend. "Can't do that, but will this work?"

Opening the leather wallet, Kruger saw a badge and an ID with the title: *Special Agent DHS – Cyber Security Division.* Looking up, he asked, "Homeland Security?"

The president nodded. "Under a special clause, I am entitled to overrule the mandatory retirement age until you are sixty. I've been told you are a year and a half shy of that milestone."

"I am."

"Good. You will have access to all DHS resources. Plus, the director is aware of the situation and welcomes you aboard. However, you will report to me."

"Not sure what to say, sir."

"Yes, would be appropriate."

Kruger admired the badge again. "Yes."

The meeting with the president lasted ten more minutes, after which they were escorted back to where they had entered earlier in the day. Once outside, JR said, "Why do we keep getting ourselves into these messes?"

"I have no idea, JR." Retrieving the badge from his pocket, Kruger stared at it for a few moments. "Never thought I would carry one of these again."

"Sometimes having friends in high places has benefits."

"Yeah, sometimes." He took a deep breath and put the badge case back in his pocket. After glancing at his watch, he continued. "I'll call Stuart and get the plane ready. If we leave now, we can stop in Springfield and sleep in our own beds tonight."

"That would be a novel idea. Do you think it's safe for Mia to move back to our house?"

"As long as someone is watching. I can have Sandy make those arrangements."

"She will be pleased. I'll tell her to take the For Sale sign down."

***

Southwest Missouri

Stephanie Kruger sat at the deck bistro table and sipped a glass of Chardonnay while Kruger flipped hamburgers on the grill. "It's nice to have you home for a few hours. When are you leaving in the morning?"

Before he could answer, Kruger yawned. "Not sure. Now that I've had time to think about it, I need a little guidance on what kind of authority I have with this new title."

She chuckled. "It's not like you, Sean, to forget about details."

"I think it was the shock of seeing the badge and ID with my name on it. Plus, that's not the kind of question you ask the president."

"Who can tell you?"

"I'll call Ryan Clark after dinner and see what he has to say."

She took another sip of wine. In a soft voice, she asked, "How long will you be gone?"

Putting the last hamburger patty on a serving plate, he locked eyes with her. "You're not happy about this, are you?"

"That's not it. I've gotten used to you not traveling as much and…"

"And what, Steph?"

"Not being in the crosshairs of some raving lunatic."

She displayed the smile he loved so much. "I'm being selfish, but I like having you safe and at home on a regular basis."

After wiping his hands on a towel, he stepped over to where she sat. Placing a hand on her shoulders, he bent and kissed her forehead. "I know. Part of me isn't thrilled about the new title. Besides it's only temporary, I have no idea what will be expected of me after we settle this Twin Peaks problem."

"Sean, what about your company and your clients?"

Taking a deep breath, he sighed and shook his head. "That's the other problem, I don't want to leave Jimmy and Sandy holding the bag."

She stood and placed her arms around his waist and buried her head against his chest. "Maybe it's time for Sean Kruger to let someone else save the world."

He chuckled. "That's a little melodramatic."

"I know, but think about it. How many times have you had to put your own interests aside and do what someone else was unwilling to do?"

He did not answer.

"That's my point, Sean. More times than you can count. When we got married, I knew who you were, and I accepted the fact you would be in harm's way most of the time. I've never told you this, but I was glad when you had to retire. Again, I'm being selfish, but the kids are growing and they need their father around."

"I know."

"I love you and don't want to lose you. You're the best thing that's ever happened to me, and I'm gonna fight to keep it that way."

He closed his eyes and held her tighter. "I would like to finish this, Steph. I owe it to JR to help Mia understand the truth about her mother and father."

"Just be careful."

"Always."

CHAPTER 30

San Francisco

Randall Becker sat at an interrogation table. His cuffed hands clasped in front of him. Dressed in an orange jumpsuit, his appearance contrasted drastically from the Brooks Brothers suits he normally wore.

Kruger stood next to Tim Gonzales and watched the prisoner on the closed-circuit monitor. "Has he said anything?"

"Nope. He keeps demanding to have an attorney."

"Did you explain to him he's being held on a domestic terrorist charge?"

"Several times."

"And?"

Gonzales chuckled. "He stares blankly at the wall and repeats his request for an attorney."

"Good. I can use that."

"Want company?"

"No, let's see how he reacts with me in the room." Kruger turned and walked toward the door to the interrogation space. When he entered, Becker glanced at him and then returned his gaze to the wall. Sitting across from the lawyer, Kruger placed a manila folder on the table, opened it, and studied the contents. He did not say a word.

After several minutes, Becker said, "You again?"

Kruger placed his ID and badge on the table. Becker examined them and his eyes grew wide for a split second. He said, "Is that supposed to frighten me?"

Returning his ID to his sport coat pocket, Kruger shook his head. "Nope. Just letting you know who I am and that the charges against you have been bumped up."

"I'm still not going to answer any questions. I want an attorney."

"I'm not here to ask questions. I'm here to explain a few things. You don't have to say a word, just listen."

Becker glanced at Kruger and gave him a smirk.

Kruger continued. "After conferring with the US Attorney General, the charges against you have been upgraded. In accordance with Article III, Section 3 of the United States Constitution, treason is defined as levying war against the US, or adhering to their enemies by giving them aid and comfort."

The prisoner chuckled. "Good luck with that charge."

With a smile, Kruger said, "Under US Code Title 18, the penalty is death."

"The constitution requires two witnesses. Good luck finding two."

"Not a problem. We have more than we need."

Becker frowned. "I seriously doubt that, Agent."

The newly installed homeland security agent gave the prisoner a grin. "Nice try." He flipped a few pages in the folder and skimmed one in particular. "We have a number of computer experts examining the system at Twin Peaks. We know the election of Senator Emily Soon was manipulated to allow her to win. Plus, we've obtained proof she is not who she says she is."

The prisoner's nostrils flared and beads of sweat formed on his forehead.

"I thought that might elicit a response from you. How long has this conspiracy been planned, Randall? Oops, sorry, I'm not supposed to ask questions." Folding his arms on the table, Kruger leaned forward. "We know Soon is the biological daughter of Judy Ling and Ling Mao Chun. Ling is also known as the Manchurian. He's been labeled a terrorist and is now on the FBI's most wanted list."

"You've been busy, Agent. But your facts are wrong."

"Are they? Tell me where I'm wrong."

"I've said too much."

"Not really. The other daughter of Judy and Ling isn't dead, Becker. DNA proves they are full sisters. We also found the original birth certificate for Emily Soon, or should I call her Amy Ling. Someone hacked the California birth records and tried to hide it."

Becker's stare grew cold as Kruger spoke. Finally, he said, "You have no idea who you are dealing with, Agent."

"Oh, I think we do. You see, when you tried to kill Mia Ling, you pissed off her husband. He's one of the top computer hackers in the US, maybe the world. Now his focus is on finding the Manchurian." Kruger stood. "When he finds him, the full fury of the United States Department of Justice will rain down on the man." He moved toward the door. Before he exited, he turned. "Oh, by the way, you have been declared a threat to the security of the US. Therefore, you will not be allowed to speak to a regular attorney. A JAG officer with top secret clearance will handle your case. Sucks for you." He walked out and slammed the door behind him.

When Kruger stood next to Gonzales again, he asked, "What'd our boy do after I left the room?"

With a chuckle, the FBI agent said, "He started to slam his fists on the table but caught himself. He knows he's being watched."

"Good."

As they watched, Becker bowed his head and shook it slowly. Finally, he directed his eyes toward the security camera and said, "I know you're listening. I want a deal."

Gonzales turned to Kruger. "You want to tell him?"

"Let's tell him together. I'll stand and give him my, *you're in deep doo-doo* look, while you explain how this is going to work."

"This is gonna be fun."

The two agents returned to the room. Gonzales sat across from Becker, and Kruger leaned against the wall, the folder held snug against his chest.

The FBI agent said, "Okay, Becker, you want a deal. Here's the problem. Your case has been kicked up to the Justice Department, and the US Attorney General told us no deals. He wants your head on a platter."

After blinking several times, Becker glared at Gonzales for a few moments. "He doesn't know what I know."

Gonzales sat back and folded his arms. He remained quiet.

Becker looked at him and then at Kruger. "Okay, Mr. Homeland Security, I hold the key to understanding the quantum computer. If I don't get a deal, you'll never understand it."

Kruger pushed off the wall, put the folder down, and placed his palms flat on the table. He leaned toward Becker. "Remember the computer hacker I told you about whose wife you tried to kill?"

"You can't prove I was involved, but I remember you mentioning her."

"He's already dissected your so-called quantum computer. He probably knows more about it than you do. Want to try again?"

Taking a deep breath, Becker said, "The Four Brothers."

Kruger returned to leaning against the wall. "Go on."

"I can help you find them."

"Who are they?" This from Gonzales.

"Not until I have a deal."

Standing, the FBI agent turned toward the door. Kruger opened it for him and the two federal agents walked out. Before they could shut the door, Becker said, "They're Triad."

Kruger stopped and turned. "Triad?"

Becker nodded.

Returning to the room, the newly installed Homeland Security agent sat. "Are they brothers?"

The prisoner nodded again.

"From what region?"

"They are members of the Black Society in mainland China. I have heard rumors they are well connected within the government of The Peoples Republic of China."

Kruger shot a glance at Gonzales, who met his eyes. They both returned their attention to Becker.

The prisoner said, "I see you both are familiar with this group. To say the brothers are efficient would be an understatement. They are vicious and have no conscience. Their connections go deep into every law enforcement agency here on the West Coast."

Tilting his head slightly, Kruger asked, "Is the Manchurian a member of the Triad?"

A nod from the man answered the question.

"What do you want, Becker?"

"Agent Kruger, part of my deal is to be transferred somewhere besides here in California. You cannot trust anybody. Particularly in San Francisco."

Gonzales exited, leaving Kruger alone with Becker. He leaned slightly forward, still holding the folder. "You have my attention."

"The Manchurian literally owns The Four Brothers. They are indentured to him."

"In what way?"

Becker shrugged. "Not sure. The Manchurian is not a talkative individual."

"How do we find these guys?"

"As a rule, you don't. They will find you. That's why I must be taken out of California. Otherwise, I will be dead and of no use to you."

Standing, Kruger said, "If we get you out of here, you'd better tell me what I want to know."

"If I change my mind?"

"I'll put your name in bright lights with an arrow pointing to your location." He turned and left the room.

CHAPTER 31

San Francisco

The eldest of The Four Brothers studied the barricades being constructed around the Twin Peaks' office complex. Obscured by a grove of birch trees west of the buildings, his presence remained hidden to those men working at the site. Since his last trip to the facility, an additional layer of security had been added. The ten-foot-tall chain link fence remained. But now a concrete barrier, consisting of twenty-foot-long Jersey barriers, placed end to end, were ten feet in front of the fence. The only gap being where the gate to the complex was located.

He turned to one of his younger brothers. "Each one of those concrete barriers weighs about 3600 kilograms. A car or truck will not move them sufficiently to gain access to the fence."

"I am aware of that, my brother."

"Any ideas?"

"Yes, when I visited Iran, a member of their Revolutionary Guard told me about a similar situation they faced in Iraq. They used a bulldozer to break through the barrier and deliver an explosive to their target."

The older man glanced at his sibling. "Interesting." He returned his attention to the rear portion of the building. "You've been inside. Where is the computer room?"

Pointing toward the structure, the younger brother said, "The rear entrance is at the end of the alcove between those two buildings. The windowless wall to the left of the recess is where they keep the server room. It's on the ground floor to keep vibrations to a minimum."

"So, if we breach the wall, the computer is exposed. Is that what you're saying?"

"Yes."

"Again, interesting." Lowering the binoculars, the eldest brother remained still for several minutes, observing the physical features of the architecture. Bringing the field glasses back up to his eyes, he scanned the concrete barrier again. Finally, he pointed to his left. "There is a wider gap between those two concrete sections. That is where we will breach it. The path also provides a straight line to the computer room."

Handing the binoculars to his younger brother, he said, "Observe for yourself and check my angles."

After a few moments, the other man said, "I agree, the path from those two blocks is straight toward the server room."

"Where can we get a bulldozer?"

***

JR busied himself in the computer room checking code. His studies allowed him to identify the exact section of the large computer which contained the suspected quantum computer modular. The compact design of the unit supported a nagging suspicion about the true makeup of the modular.

The stillness of the room was shattered when a California National Guard lieutenant rushed into the room and shouted his name.

"JR, it's Benson. Are you in here?"

"Yeah. In the back. What's going on?"

"Don't have time to explain. You need to grab your research and get out of here, sir. And I mean now."

JR ran to the server bank with the QC modular. He disconnected it, removed it from the rack and ran toward the front entrance to the room. Benson held the door for him and followed after JR's passing.

"What's going on, Lieutenant?"

"We've got a bulldozer knocking down trees behind the building. It's headed toward the Jersey barrier at full speed. My guys don't see a driver, so we think it's being remotely controlled."

JR followed the national guardsman. "I take it that's not good."

"No, sir."

Behind them, JR could hear a rumble and the wrenching of steel under stress.

"Where are we going, Benson?"

"We're evacuating the building."

"Why?"

"Several of us who were deployed to Operation New Dawn some years ago have seen this before. Use a bulldozer to breach a structure and then set off explosives. This one is headed straight toward the computer building."

The two men exited the main structure and found themselves in the complex's courtyard. A number of guardsmen surrounded a group of workers from inside the building. Benson turned to JR. "We don't know how many attackers there are, but everyone should be safe here."

The ground shook as a deep rumble rolled through the building. Dark smoke and debris suddenly enveloped the occupants of the courtyard as walls of the computer facility imploded.

JR stared at the destruction.

Benson pulled a small walkie-talkie off of his utility belt. "This is Benson, I need all units to check in. Prepare for secondary attack."

Standing next to the guardsman, JR listened to the radio traffic and realized what had happened. He turned to the lieutenant. "There won't be a secondary attack."

"I have to prepare for it, sir."

"I realize that. But they accomplished what they needed to do."

Holding the radio at his side, the guardsman frowned. "What was their goal?"

"They were told to destroy the data center. My guess is they did."

"You think it's over?"

"Yeah, pretty sure of it." He paused and studied the destruction of the building he and Benson had just exited. "The data center was of no importance to them." He pointed to the server modular sitting on the ground next to him. "That is what they were told to destroy."

***

Kruger and JR walked the perimeter of the Twin Peaks' office complex. The retired FBI agent asked his friend, "You think all of this was to destroy the quantum computer?"

JR replied, "Yeah, pretty sure of it."

Firemen and members of an FBI investigative team combed through the wreckage of the southwest corner of the facility. The remains of a large bulldozer could be seen in the middle of the debris.

"What have you learned about The Four Brothers, Sean?"

"They're Chinese Triad and work for the Manchurian."

"Becker?"

"Yeah, he got religion after I threatened to reveal his location to the press." Kruger turned his attention to Tim Gonzales approaching from their left. "Wonder what he's found?"

When Gonzales reached them, he said, "We got a line on the bulldozer."

Folding his arms, Kruger said, "Let me guess. It was stolen."

The young FBI agent pointed toward the skeleton of the dozer. "Stolen from an excavation company."

JR said, "Gutsy."

Gonzales continued. "Yeah, it was. They parked it in a vacant field a half mile from here. A building permit, false, of course, was tacked to a sign on the property. No one thought twice about it being there. Just another upcoming construction site in an area with lots of property development."

Kruger asked, "Did the company know it was missing?"

"Agents found the owner dead in his office late last night. He'd been dead for at least a day. He was a second-generation immigrant from China. We followed up with his father who started the business. It seems the family left China to get away from the Triad over there. Now his son is dead because of that relationship."

Pointing toward the destroyed computer building, JR said, "The Four Brothers will assume the quantum computer was destroyed along with the rest of the server. I say we keep it that way." He looked at Kruger. "I'm flying back this afternoon. I can study the unit better from my office. What are you going to do?"

"Charlie Brewer and I have a conference call scheduled with the FBI director. After that, I have to update the president. His chief of staff has been bugging me for updates."

"Glad it's you and not me. So, when do you think you'll

be back?"

"Don't know yet. It depends on what Ryan Clark has to say."

"I'll let Stuart know you're staying."

"Thanks, JR."

CHAPTER 32

700 Nautical Miles off the Northern California Coast

Ling Mao Chun listened on the secure satellite phone, his free hand clutched tight and shaking. When the individual on the other satellite phone finished his narrative, Ling did not respond for almost a minute.

Finally, he said, "So, Becker is still in the hands of the FBI. Is that what you are telling me, Hao?"

"Yes. They moved him during the night, and our source was not there when it happened. No one is talking, and she is afraid that if she pushes too much, she will come under suspicion."

"Unfortunate."

"Yes."

"I take it you were successful in destroying the quantum computer?"

"Yes. Nothing of the building remains standing. The extra fuel in the bulldozer created so much heat, even the server racks melted."

"Excellent."

"What are your wishes for us?"

"All four of you need to return to Macau. Make sure each of you takes a separate airline. Two will need to go to Los Angeles for departure."

"So, we are done in the United States?"

"For now. Make sure each of you has a satellite phone for secure communications."

"Already taken care of."

"Good." The Manchurian paused. "We will regroup at my office two weeks from today."

"I will pass the word."

The call ended, and Ling stared out over the Pacific Ocean toward the east. He took two deep calming breaths and grabbed the railing on the bow of the cargo ship. Of the twelve passenger cabins on this particular ship, only one held an occupant. His cabin.

The ship owned by the PRC and registered under a flag of convenience in Singapore was used to transport, not only cargo from Chinese factories, but covert agents. According to the ship's log, there were no passengers on this voyage from San Francisco to Macau. This particular run contained high-end wines from both California and Washington state. Wines that would eventually end up in the cellars of elite leaders of the PRC.

Ling paid very little attention to the politics of China. As long as they gave him the resources he needed to pursue his research, he would abide by their wishes. One day, he would not require their protection or money anymore. But that day was not today.

The voyage would take another two weeks; time to plan.

***

FBI Agent Amber Walsh studied the businesses across from the vacant field where the bulldozer trailer remained. The front of the trailer pointed toward the east. From her point of view, the tractor cabin would have been oriented so the driver would have to exit toward the street.

In the middle of the strip mall stood a branch of Bank of America. She crossed the road and searched the exterior of the building. She found what she needed. A security camera pointed directly at the vacant lot. Fifteen minutes later, she stopped reviewing the security video and used her cell phone to call her supervisor.

By 3:16 p.m., eight FBI agents, and a man identifying himself as a Homeland Security special agent, descended on the small branch of the national bank.

At exactly 4:27 p.m., Sean Kruger sent a still from the security video to a facial recognition expert based at the bureau's Quantico, Virigina crime lab. His instructions to the technician: Let him know if they got an ID match as soon as possible.

He had his answer at exactly 6:43 p.m. Pacific Standard Time.

Showing the email to Charlie Brewer, Kruger said, "He's identified as a member of the San Francisco Chinese Consulate-General's general staff. Goes by the name Li Chao. Ever hear of him?"

"No, and I'll bet neither has the Chinese Consulate-General."

"You guys want to handle that part, Charlie?"

"Yeah, I think we probably should. Can you send this to JR? He can probably find a lot more information on this guy than Quantico. Plus, he'll be faster."

"Already did."

"Anything yet?"

Kruger shook his head. "No. I also asked him to check the airlines. If the guy has a reservation or already flew out, JR will find it."

***

Alexia Montreal Gibbs joined JR in the soundproof conference room on the second floor of their company's home office. The quantum computer modular sat in the middle of the long table dominating the room. "So, that's what everyone is claiming to be the end of civilization as we know it?"

"Yup, that's it. Appears innocent enough, doesn't it?"

"How did Ling overcome the instability issues at room temperature?"

"Good question. I haven't opened the case to examine the chips yet. It will be interesting to find out."

The co-owner of JR's company stood and closed the door of the conference room. "JR, I've been doing a little research into Ling Mao Chun's work. It's groundbreaking to say the least. But I think he overlooked something he shouldn't have."

Raising an eyebrow, JR straightened in his chair. "What'd you find?"

"If this device is to be used to hack into county voting records and change them, how does it change the physical backup?"

With a raised eyebrow, JR said, "Go on."

"Between the general election of 2000 and 2004, Direct Recording Electronics grew from 11 percent to 28 percent of all counties. It remained in that range until the 2020 national election. The percent of counties using that method shrank to only 20 percent."

"Because there is no physical backup."

"Exactly. The optical scan system grew to be used in 77 percent of all US counties during that election cycle."

"Because of the physical backup."

Alexia gave him a crisp nod. "Optical recording is fast and almost real-time, plus there can always be an audit done, if the results are challenged. While Ling's combination of AI and quantum computing may be able to hack and change any county election results it wants, it can't change physical data that can be audited."

"What type of system does California use?"

"Currently, they use systems with a hardcover backup, like Optical Scan. But when Emily Soon was elected to Congress, they were using Digital Recording Electronics. Much easier to hack."

"Huh."

"That was my reaction as well."

"So, while Ling was improving his computer power with quantum chips and AI, the industry changed." JR paused and considered the quantum modular sitting on the conference table. "I think it's time we open that thing up and see what makes it tick."

Later that afternoon, JR finished examining a circuit board under a magnifying lamp. "Circuitry is pretty standard."

"The logic system would have to be compatible to integrate with standard computers. The difference would have to be in the actual chip architecture." Alexia stopped consulting her laptop and turned her attention to JR. "Most of the published scientific literature suggests room temperature quantum chips are not possible at this time. At least with today's manufacturing techniques." She paused. "JR, could this be an elaborate hoax?"

"There's always that possibility. But what would be his motive?"

Alexia grinned. "The oldest motivator in the world. Money?"

"Not following you."

"What feeds technical advances?"

"Research."

"Yes, but what feeds research?"

JR stared at her for a long time. Finally, he said, "In the case of China, a group of old men who want to hold on to power and expand their influence across the globe."

"And what do governments possess that companies and individuals do not?"

"The ability to print money."

"Exactly. The ability to print money so they can fund individuals who are willing to help them achieve those goals."

Returning his gaze to the quantum modular, JR said, "Without examining the individual chips, we can't determine how the Manchurian's quantum computer actually works."

"Or…" Alexia's eyes sparkled. "Has he designed a new chip technology that mimics the capabilities of a quantum computer, JR? One of the references I found came from a professor at the University of Texas who claims rare-earth magnets could, at some date, allow quantum computers to work at room temperature." She pointed to the modular. "There are no exotic magnets in that box."

"I've read his paper, and you're right, there aren't any. Which means, we may be dealing with something more conventional. I say we take a circuit board and directly examine one of the chips installed on it."

"I'm ready if you are."

JR reached for the circuit board he previously examined.

CHAPTER 33

San Francisco

Qin Ping, the Chinese Consulate-General, studied the business card. "Agent Brewer, what sort of business might the Special Agent in Charge from the FBI San Francisco field office have with the Chinese embassy?"

"Dr. Ping, we are seeking information on the location of Li Chao."

"I see. May I ask why?"

"Does he work for the consulate?"

The man gave Brewer a shrewd smile. "My answer will depend on why you are searching for him."

Returning the expression, the FBI agent said, "He's a person of interest who may have information concerning an explosion at an office complex yesterday."

Ping crossed his arms. "You believe him to be involved?"

"No. He was seen in the vicinity. He might know something useful to our investigation."

"Agent, even if I knew where Li Chao was, I would not

tell you. He is a citizen of China and not subject to harassment by the American FBI."

"Does he work for the consulate?"

Ping gave Brewer an icy glare. "I do not wish to be difficult, Agent Brewer, but this line of questioning is making me uncomfortable."

"I'm sorry to hear that, Dr. Ping. I was hoping for a little more cooperation."

The man stood still, refusing to engage.

Kruger stood next to Brewer without making a comment during the exchange. When Ping stopped answering Brewer's questions, the retired FBI agent offered his identification. "Dr. Ping, apparently, you are familiar with Li Chao."

"I did not say that."

"But you defended him as a citizen of China. So, you know who he is?"

"I do."

Stepping closer to the Chinese Consulate General, Kruger said in a low tone, "Dr. Ping, your status of diplomatic immunity is in danger of being revoked due to your uncooperative stance. I have the authority to declare your standing as persona non grata and escort you to an airport for your flight home."

"I see."

"Now what position does Li Chao have here at the consulate?"

"He is a consulate employee."

"What are his official duties?"

"He is part of my personal staff and has been with me a long time."

"Then why does the State Department have no record of his being part of the mission?"

"That's nonsense. Li Chao has worked for the consulate for at least two years."

With a shake of his head, Kruger said, "Not according to

Homeland Security. We checked with the State Department, and they've never heard of him. Now, if you wish to remain in the US, I suggest you start cooperating with my FBI colleague."

"I do not have to stand here and listen to—"

"Unfortunately, you do. We have evidence Li Chao committed an act of terrorism here in California. Now, either tell us where he is or..." Kruger shrugged.

Ping alternated his focus on Kruger and then Brewer. He repeated the process several times. "Li Chao does not work in conjunction with this mission. Plus, it would not be healthy for me to expose his whereabouts. He and his brothers are highly connected within the PRC. You will have to trust me when I say I do not currently know where he is. As a favor to me, I would ask you to keep this meeting to yourselves. My life would be in danger if it becomes public knowledge, I cooperated with you or spoke to you."

"How many brothers does he have?"

"There are four of them."

"Are they still in the US?"

"Chao is, but for how much longer, I cannot say."

Kruger smiled. "Then I will do a favor for you. I will file a report explaining how totally uncooperative you've been, Dr. Ping."

"Thank you."

Brewer and Kruger stood to leave the man's office. Before Kruger opened the door, Ping said, "You might want to check apartment B101 at the Mission Bay complex near John McLaren Park."

Neither the SAC or the Homeland Security agent said a word. But as Kruger followed his friend out of the office, he turned and gave Ping a single nod.

***

Tim Gonzales sat in a vehicle parked in the lot of the Mission Bay apartment complex. At least ten other agents in various locations around the area kept watch for the resident of apartment B101.

Kruger slipped into the passenger seat of the bureau SUV. "Apartment manager said he's still there. Apparently, he renewed his lease this morning and paid cash for the next twelve months."

"Maybe he's planning an extended stay somewhere and wanted a place when he gets back."

"You might be right." Kruger pointed toward the north. "Speaking of the devil. Isn't that him?"

A thin man, who resembled the figure in the security video getting out of the tractor hauling the bulldozer, walked with purpose toward the ground-floor door of apartment B101.

Gonzales said into a handheld walkie-talkie, "Suspect is approaching door. Once he has it unlocked, take him down."

As the man began to open the apartment door, four agents appeared and shoved him into the room. Gonzales and Kruger exited their SUV and walked briskly toward the newly apprehended Li Chao.

Entering the apartment, Kruger noted a duffle bag parked next to the front door. The suspect sat on the floor with his hands cuffed behind him. His eyes trained on the carpet while one of the agents read him his rights. Walking past the man now in custody, the newly installed Homeland Security special agent entered the kitchen. Fast-food sacks and carryout boxes spilled over a jam-packed metal trash can. An odor of spoiled chicken and sriracha assaulted his senses.

Gonzales walked up beside him. "You should see the bedroom."

Turning, Kruger said, "Lead the way."

Inside the room, the FBI agent pointed to the ceiling fan and light fixture. "We found a tiny microphone between the bulbs."

"How many others?"

"One in each room and two in the living area."

"So, everything said in this apartment is being recorded?"

"I believe that would be fair to say."

"Huh." Kruger surveyed the room, noting the stripped mattress and the bedding wadded up in the corner. The three-panel bi-fold doors were askew and off their track, revealing empty hangers on the valet rod and a pile of discarded items on the floor.

"Wait till you see the bathroom."

Sticking his head inside the small room, the odor assailed his nostrils. "What the hell is that smell?"

"Under the sink, you can see black mold on the back wall. I'm speculating here, but my guess is our Li Chao wasn't planning on a return. Paying the lease was a dodge to keep the manager out of the apartment for a while. And to throw off any police inquiry."

"How do you figure?"

"If the manager told you the lease was paid for a year, what would you do, Sean?"

"Stake out the place and wait for him to return."

"Exactly."

Kruger backed out and headed toward the living room. "Let's see what our prisoner has to say."

Gonzales approached a tall slender female agent. She wore jeans and an FBI windbreaker, her blonde hair in a ponytail. He said, "Has he said anything?"

Beverly Hammon said, "Claims not to speak English."

Gonzales proceeded to ask the man a question in Mandarin. "You've been in the US for, what, five years, and still don't understand English?"

Li Chao raised his eyes to focus on Gonzales and then shrugged.

With a chuckle, Kruger kneeled down to be at eye level with the man. "Our Mr. Chao may claim he doesn't speak English, but I'll bet he understands it." Standing, he said, "Okay, Agents Gonzales and Hammon, you're with me. We'll transfer the prisoner to the San Francisco field office."

Five minutes later, three agents and one prisoner occupied the SUV Gonzales and Kruger arrived in. The vehicle now headed west.

Li Chao frowned and watched the scenery pass by. When Kruger merged onto the I-80 bridge toward Oakland, the prisoner said something in Mandarin.

Gonzales chuckled. "He said we aren't going the right way to the FBI field office."

Glancing in the rearview mirror, Kruger said, "Oh yeah. I forgot to mention our destination isn't the field office. It's a cabin the IRS confiscated a number of years ago from a family of gamblers."

Chao burst out in unaccented English. "I demand to be taken to the San Francisco field office."

"Thought you didn't speak English, Chao. Sounds like you do."

Chao continued. "I have diplomatic immunity."

Kruger's mouth twitched. "According to the State Department, there is no record of you entering the country. Since you aren't officially here, your ass belongs to the FBI and Homeland Security."

"You are all dead."

"Why's that, Chao?" He waited for a response. When his question did not receive an answer, Kruger continued. "You think your brothers are coming to the rescue?"

The prisoner only scowled.

"Here's the problem as I see it. We are meeting a group of highly skilled FBI Rapid Response Team agents. Before we meet with them, you will be given a sedative. They will then transfer you to one of the most secure prisons in the world. Ever hear of the United States Penitentiary Maximum Facility in Florence, Colorado?"

Chao's scowl only intensified.

"It is commonly called ADX Florence. No one has ever escaped from it. Plus, you will be checked in as a John Doe and kept in complete isolation. The US prison system will not have any record of who you are. The FBI team meeting us will never be told your name. So, since your brothers don't know where you are, and the US prison system has no record of someone by your name being there, it might be hard for them to find you. In other words, Chao, you have officially disappeared from the face of the earth."

"I want a lawyer."

Kruger snarled. "Can't have one."

"Why?"

"I just told you. You don't exist."

"My brothers have ways of finding me."

"If you mean the source they had inside the San Francisco FBI field office, forget it. Angela Bowman is in FBI custody. She figured out telling us what she knew about The Four Brothers was better than being charged with treason."

The scowl returned to Chao's face. "We have other ways."

"I'm sure you do. That's why you're in our custody and where you are going is only known by the three of us in this vehicle."

"I doubt that."

Kruger chuckled. "I'm a special agent with Homeland Security, and I only report to the president of the United States. I have the authority to make those types of decisions. Sucks for you, Chao." After a short pause and another glance in the mirror, Kruger knew he'd gotten through to the man. "Good to see you finally realize the situation you're in."

A glare from the prisoner told Kruger everything he needed to know.

***

Two Days Later

The clock on his Mustang's dashboard told Kruger he pulled into the garage at fourteen minutes past 11 p.m. Stress and exhaustion swept over him as he opened the door leading to the home's interior.

Stephanie sat at the breakfast bar with a stack of papers next to her. When she saw her husband, she rose and quickly walked to him. Their embrace lasted for several minutes.

"Glad you're home. We've missed you."

Kissing her on the forehead, he said, "I've missed you and the kids."

"How long are you home?"

"I hope for a while. We have reason to believe Ling Mao Chun is in China. Where, no one seems to know. But he's definitely not in the United States." The embrace ended, and he asked, "What were you doing?"

"Grading final exam essays."

Furrowing his brow, Kruger asked, "Is it the end of the semester already?"

She chuckled. "Yes, Sean, it is. You've been gone for almost a month."

"I didn't realize it had been so long." He took her into his arms again. "Sorry."

Pressing her head against his chest, she closed her eyes. "I had forgotten how much I miss you when you're gone."

"What've you got going tomorrow?"

"I don't have to be anywhere until noon. Why?"

He broke their embrace, took her hand, and led her to their bedroom.

PART THREE

The Manchurian's Return

CHAPTER 34

Southwest Missouri

A knock at Kruger's office doorframe made him raise his head. He said, "Your door was closed when I got here. Didn't think you were in yet."

Walking into his friend's office, JR collapsed into one of the leather-cushioned captain's chairs in front of Kruger's desk. "I was. The door was closed because I had a disturbing phone call this morning."

Kruger leaned back in his office chair and waited for JR to continue.

"Remember Professor Ravi Gupta? He's been helping me with the Twin Peaks' computer."

"I remember. Hope all is well with him."

"It is. He's been going through the communication protocol on Ling's computer. Very sophisticated and more than a little innovative."

"I'm not going to like this, am I?"

"Probably not. It scares the crap out of me. Ravi feels the same way."

"Go on."

"Ling's been incorporating AI into his interprocess communication protocol."

"I haven't got a clue to what you just said."

"It poses a unique problem."

Kruger stared at his friend. "I won't argue about it."

"Sorry. You know what a cookie is, don't you?"

"Stephanie makes a hell of chocolate chip one."

"Computer cookies, Sean."

"Nope. Want to enlighten my feeble brain?"

With a chuckle, the computer genius said, "I forget about your lack of computer savvy."

"JR, I don't need to be computer savvy. That's your job."

"A computer cookie is a small file used by websites to save browsing information so the next time they communicate with your system, they will remember what you did last time. Normally, they pose zero security threats. Some cookies can, but you can use your browser to delete them."

"I take it Ling's figured out something new."

"Yeah, he has." JR sighed. "Using AI, he's figured out how to embed a rather nasty cookie that creates a custom virus for each machine he needs infected."

"Is he using this technique on every computer he hacks?"

"No." JR rested his elbows on the chair's arms. He made a steeple with his hands and said, "From what we can tell, his targets are specific."

"How specific?"

"Government systems, federal, state, county, major municipalities, utility companies, and water treatment plants."

"Can you detect the cookies?"

"We're working on it."

"Good luck to you and Professor Gupta." Kruger

considered his friend for a moment. "There's been a development on The Four Brothers."

JR's eyebrows rose.

"NSA is reporting a lot of satellite phone traffic between the city of Macau in China and a phone in San Francisco. The location of the phone on the West Coast changes constantly."

"What are the conversations about?"

"Mostly about the weather. NSA thinks it's code. The language is Mandarin, and the same question is asked at the beginning of each call."

"What's the question?"

"Is it sunny or cloudy."

"Let me guess. It's always cloudy."

Kruger nodded. "We think it's because they are seeking information on whether the fourth brother has been found."

"Where is the fourth brother?"

"I forget." He hesitated. "It's not that I don't trust you, JR. But knowing the whereabouts of brother number four places your life in grave danger."

"Sorry I asked."

Looking over his reading glasses, Kruger continued. "There was something else the NSA intercepted."

"The Manchurian is planning a return."

"How'd you know?"

JR shrugged. "I guessed. It's been six months since he disappeared. According to Mia, during the four years her mother lived in Texas, her grandparents told her Judy would disappear for a few days every six months. They never knew why because she would not tell them where she went."

"Is that when she disappeared for good?"

"Yeah. Mia barely remembers her mother. She's more of a fantasy figure to her."

Folding his arms, Kruger frowned. "JR, does Mia have any recollection of how Ling Mao Chun communicated with Judy?"

"You know, that's something I've never asked her."

"Maybe it's time we did."

***

Having dinner with the Diminskis occurred frequently and normally consisted of burgers on the grill or pizza delivery. Tonight, pizza came from a place called Gabby's three buildings west of JR's office.

While the kids played in another part of the Kruger residence, the four adults sat around the dinner table talking.

When the subject of Mia's mother came up, Kruger said, "Mia, did your grandparents ever mention to you if they knew how your father communicated with your mother?"

"No, not really. I think her disappearing every once in a while hurt them more than it made them curious."

"I hope this next question isn't too personal."

"Sean, you and Stephanie are like family to me. Ask away."

Looking at his wife then back at Mia, Kruger said, "How well do you remember your mother?"

She tilted her head slightly and did not respond for several moments. "You know, JR asked me that question a few years after we got married. At the time, I thought I had a good grasp on who she was. But the events of this past year have made me think twice about my perception of who Judy Ling might have been."

JR placed his hand on her arm.

Mia continued. "There is no way I could have known her at all. As you know, she left when I was four, and my grandparents raised me. Judy Ling became this mythical princess I would conjure up and fantasize about. Even the fact she never returned any of my letters didn't destroy the persona I created in my mind. I had pictures of her, but they didn't match the picture of the real woman JR brought back from California. She looked broken and defeated. I felt a deep sense of sadness within her after looking at that picture." She paused for a moment. "You know, my guess is Emily Soon didn't know her, either. Now that I understand what happened to my mother, it raises a lot of questions."

Kruger's mouth twitched. "Do you want to meet her?"

Mia's eyes widened. "Meet who? Emily Soon? No." She crossed her arms. "I doubt very seriously if she would want to meet me, Sean. She's a US senator, after all."

"I'm sure we can find some way to help persuade her."

"Does she know about me?"

"That's a good question. I think Senator Soon has been groomed from a young age for the purpose of being an American politician. She may not even know who her real parents are."

A mischievous grin crossed Mia's face. "Well, then, maybe it's time I told her."

***

The Next Day

JR appeared at Kruger's office door with an ear-to-ear smile. "You might want to come to the conference room. Alexia hit paydirt on Emily Soon."

Rising from his desk chair, the retired FBI agent said, "By all means. Let's see what she found."

When they took their seats at the big table, Alexia Gibbs beamed, her bright teeth exposed by a wide grin. "I think you're going to like this, Sean."

"Let's hear it."

"What if I told you we can trace phone calls from Emily Soon's cell phone to a particular number in California?"

"Not surprising. She's a senator from that state."

JR said, "There's more."

Alexia turned her laptop around and showed Kruger a diagram. "The number she calls is a router. The router will transfer calls from her number directly to a specific cell phone, no matter where in the world the device happens to be."

"Even China?"

"Particularly China."

"Can you identify whose number it is?"

"Yes. The number was issued by China Unicom. We were able to hack into their main server and discovered who the number belongs to."

"Ling Mao Chun."

"Yeah, and better still, the bill is paid by the People's Republic of China."

Kruger chuckled. "So, Emily Soon is calling a phone number on a regular basis that is connected to a cell phone owned by the PRC." He felt the pieces of a puzzle fall into place. "I wonder what the Attorney General and FBI Director Ryan Clark will think of that?"

"I am sure the good senator would be reluctant for them to learn about her activity."

CHAPTER 35

Washington, DC

The Watergate office/apartment complex is a coveted and prestigious address in the Washington, DC area. Situated along the banks of the Potomac River, the building is the home of titans of industry, celebrities, the rich and famous, wannabe rich and famous, and numerous members of Congress.

Once an obscure address, the building became a household name on June 7th, 1972 when five burglars broke into the offices of the Democratic National Committee. Thus began the long and tumultuous decline of Richard Nixon, president of the United States.

Emily Soon, a senator from the state of California called the Watergate home. She occupied a fifteen-hundred-square-foot apartment on the tenth floor of the north building.

After a long day of senate hearings, Emily exited the elevator and sensed someone following her. She chose not to look back to check. When she approached her door, two additional individuals, one on either side of her entrance door, stood.

One, a female in her mid-thirties, stepped forward and asked, "Senator Soon?"

She stopped, glanced behind her, and saw two men in suits five yards away. "What's this about?"

The woman repeated her request. "Are you Emily Soon?"

"Yes. What's this about? Who are you?"

The woman opened a credential wallet, exposing her badge and ID. "FBI, Senator. We need to ask you a few questions."

"Do you realize who I am?"

"Yes, ma'am. Can we step inside your apartment? This is a rather delicate situation."

"No, we may not step into my apartment." She turned and suddenly recognized Ryan Clark, director of the FBI.

Clark said, "Senator, I believe you would prefer we discuss this matter inside and not in the hall."

Staring at the man, she said, "If I must." Turning, she used her key to unlock the door. Two agents entered first, followed by Clark and a man she vaguely recognized. When the door closed, she challenged Clark. "What the hell is this all about, Director? And who is this individual standing off to the side?"

Turning to his companion, Clark asked, "Do you want to enlighten the senator?"

Sean Kruger showed his ID. "Special Agent Sean Kruger, Homeland Security. Should I address you by your true birth name, or do you want me to call you Emily?"

The senator's eyes widened briefly, but a scowl replaced it almost as quickly. "I have no idea what you are talking about, Agent."

"Sure, you do. Your birth name is Amy Ling. Your birth mother's name is Judy Ling. She lived in a commune for years until a few months ago when she was murdered on orders from your father. Your father's name is Ling Mao Chun, aka the Manchurian. He is currently a fugitive wanted by the FBI for terrorism and murder. You might not know this, but you have a sister who is five years older."

She raised a hand, palm toward Kruger. "Stop right there, Agent. I have no idea where you came up with this fantasy, but you are out of line." She turned to Clark. "Director, you have made a grave mistake. This is a perfect example of why Congress distrusts the FBI." Just as she said the words, the incident at the ballroom flooded over her. Without thinking about it, she rubbed the spot on her arm where she found blood.

Kruger saw her reaction but did not comment. Instead, he said, "Shall I continue? We have DNA proof you are the daughter of Judy and Chun. By the way, you and your sister look remarkably alike."

"So, you say. Do you have documentation of this fairy tale you've concocted?"

Kruger turned to Clark. "Want to show her, Director?"

Clark opened a leather portfolio he held. From it, he extracted several sheets of paper. These he handed to the senator.

"The first page is a printout of your original birth certificate. The second page is the birth certificate you used to file your notice of running for the senate with the California Secretary of State. Under California Penal Code 115 PC, knowingly filing a false document with the state is considered a felony. However, we at the FBI consider Title 52 US Code § 20511 more appropriate in your case. Whereas, a convicted felon is prohibited from holding federal office." He met her gaze. "Any questions so far?"

She crossed her arms. "I don't have to put up with this."

"I'm just getting started, Senator."

***

Kruger watched the senator. Years of experience interrogating suspects gave him the sense she was getting nervous. Her eyes flicked from the director to the front door and back. To keep her from bolting, he casually stepped over to the door and leaned on it. She glanced in his direction only once and, just as fast, returned her attention back to Clark.

Five minutes later, the director said, "Ms. Soon, as you can see, the evidence against you is staggering. A copy of this report is being handed to the chairman of the US Senate Select Committee on Ethics and to the majority leader as we speak."

The soon-to-be former senator folded her arms. "So, I am accused of all of this without the right of legal counsel."

"Of course, you are entitled to any legal representation you can afford." He nodded toward the man and woman FBI agents.

Before Emily could react, the female agent grabbed her left wrist and twisted it behind her. Without missing a beat, she recited the senator's Miranda rights and secured her right wrist in the handcuffs.

Clark held out another document. "This is a search warrant for these premises. Right now, other agents are searching your senate office with a similarly signed document." He looked at the woman FBI agent. "Please escort Ms. Soon to your vehicle and then to the holding center at Quantico."

"Yes, sir." The two agents led the woman through the apartment doorway and disappeared down the hall.

Clark turned to Kruger. "Let JR know the apartment's empty. Maybe he can find some answers hidden here."

***

Midnight
Emily Soon's Apartment

Kruger stepped up next to Ryan Clark. "Remind you of the good old days when we both actually worked for a living?"

Putting a file down he had been reviewing, he said, "Sometimes I do miss them. Never even imagined I'd be head of FBI."

"One never knows where destiny might take them."

Clark chuckled. "I sometimes have evil thoughts about you for getting me into this mess. Although I keep them to myself."

"Don't blame me. I fought like hell not to get promoted when I was with the bureau. You, on the other hand, did such a good job at all your assignments, you were impossible to ignore."

"I got curious one day and reviewed your personnel file. You were offered more promotions than I could count. You turned them all down."

"I hate paperwork."

At that moment, JR rushed into the living area of the apartment and said, "I think I found something you both should see."

Kruger fell in behind Clark and followed him to the bedroom. On a desk lay what appeared to be a small handheld walkie-talkie.

JR said, "That was hidden in a carved-out volume on her bookshelf."

"What is it?"

"Well, Mr. Director, that is a Huawei Mate 60 Pro smartphone. Not only does it have the first Chinese-developed 5G chip, but it can make and receive satellite calls."

Kruger bent over to examine the device without touching it. "What does that mean, JR?"

"It means, this Huawei phone can support 5G and satellite calls. Plus, the satellite capabilities only work with the Chinese telecom network."

Clark folded his arms. "Will that stand up in court, JR?"

"Will what stand up?"

"The phone is only capable of calling other Chinese satellite phones?"

With a nod, JR said, "Ryan, it's not a question of if, the phones are designed that way."

Kruger used a pencil to move it around. "I wonder whose fingerprints will be on it."

"Not mine." JR held his hands up. "I've been using static-free cotton gloves."

The FBI director produced a Ziploc bag from his suit coat pocket. "Use this to pack it up. With the files in the living room and this phone, we have what we need for the good senator's indictment."

The newly installed Homeland Security agent said, "I see old habits die hard, Ryan."

"Yes, they do, Sean. I keep a few in my suits all the time."

CHAPTER 36

Washington, DC

Jeffery Wainstein glanced at his attorney. The question seemed innocent enough, but his attorney, one Herbert McLain, shook his head and leaned over. "Don't answer."

Wainstein returned his attention to the director of the FBI. "On advice from counsel, I take the Fifth."

Clark frowned. "Mr. Wainstein, I am merely verifying you are Senator Soon's chief of staff."

McLain placed his hand over the microphone in front of him and leaned over to whisper in his client's ear. "While it is a matter of public record, Jeff, you don't have to confirm it." He sat upright and returned his attention to Clark.

"Sorry. On advice of counsel—"

"Yes, I know. You aren't going to answer." Clark turned to Kruger. "Do you want to explain to these two gentlemen Homeland Security's position?"

Kruger stood. He stepped around the table and sat on the edge next to Wainstein. He folded his arms and directed his attention to the attorney. "Mr. McLain, I don't think you grasp the severity of the charges Emily Soon is facing. Your client Mr. Wainstein is, by official senate records, her chief of staff."

"I'm aware of that. Your point?"

"Ms. Soon is being charged with aiding and abetting a foreign government, one hostile to the United States. She is also being accused of providing false identification to obtain her position as a senator. Your client's refusal to answer our questions could be construed as being complicit with the senator's activities."

"My client is not complicit."

"So, you say. If I make the recommendation, The Department of Homeland Security will file charges against your client, accusing him of being a domestic terrorist."

"Go ahead. You have no proof of Mr. Wainstein's acting as a domestic terrorist."

Kruger tilted his head. "Are you a betting man, Mr. McLain?"

"No."

"Mr. Wainstein's fingerprints were found on a Chinese satellite phone. Only his and Ms. Soon's fingerprints were found on the phone. It has been established the phone's only purpose is to communicate with a man named Ling Mao Chun who is wanted for murder and terroristic activities inside the US. Care to comment?"

McLain glanced at his client and then said, "When was this evidence discovered, Agent Kruger?"

"Since Mr. Wainstein has not been charged with a crime yet, you and your client are not entitled to receive information about our investigation."

"And if he cooperates?"

With a shrug, Kruger said, "It depends on the level of cooperation."

"May I confer with my client in private?"

Clark stood, and both he and Kruger exited the interrogation room.

**

Back in Clark's office, the director said, "What do you think, Sean?"

"I don't know either one of them. Is the AG willing to make a deal?"

Clark nodded. "The main reason I'm involved is because of the high profile of Senator Soon. The AG really doesn't need any information from Wainstein, but if he can get additional evidence, so much the better."

"In my mind, it doesn't make sense for her to bring him into her confidence concerning her true identity."

"Why's that, Sean?"

"Too much of a risk. In this town, you have to keep your secrets close to the vest."

"I would agree. Let's see what the attorney says."

***

"Do you know anything at all, Jeffery?" McLain folded his arms as he sat and watched his client pace.

"That's the trouble. I don't know anything. I had no idea she was talking to some Chinese spy."

"Then you have nothing to worry about."

The soon-to-be ex-chief of staff glared at his attorney. "Right. No one will believe I didn't know something. The only hint I had was her trips to California. She's a senator and goes home to her state frequently. But she never provided me with an itinerary. If I needed to contact her, it was via cell phone."

"Then that's what we tell the FBI."

"I want immunity first."

"If you don't have any knowledge of her activities, they won't charge you with anything."

Wainstein took a deep breath. "Herb, you don't believe that any more than I do. This is Washington, DC. The national sport in this town is making stuff up about your adversary, regardless of the truth."

"What are you saying?"

"If she's a spy, terrorist, or whatever, my ability to get a job in this town will come to a grinding halt. I've built an excellent reputation over the years, and I am not about to destroy it. How do I separate myself from her before this all becomes public?"

The attorney smiled. "You resign as of yesterday and tell everything you know about her."

"Call them back in. I'm ready to talk."

***

The interview with Jeffery Wainstein came to a conclusion four hours later. When he and the attorney were gone, Clark and Kruger called JR into the conference room.

"What'd you two find out from Soon's chief of staff?"

Kruger chuckled. "He didn't know anything, JR. He was more concerned about his reputation than helping us. Anything new on your end?"

"I was able to identify the phone numbers the Huawei called over the last several months. Actually, there were only two. One is the router and the other is in San Francisco. The one in California belongs to the Chinese Consulate-General's office. Guess whose number it is?"

Clark said, "Li Chao."

"Yep. The same guy you people have on ice somewhere."

Standing Kruger paced. "This means Soon knew about The Four Brothers and was in communication with her father."

JR nodded. "The good senator is knee-deep in this whole mess."

Clark said, "This gives us plenty of ammunition for an indictment of espionage and being the agent of a foreign government. We can tack on the terrorist charges later." He headed toward the door. "Good job, guys. I'm going to the Attorney General with what we have. I'll keep you apprised of our next steps."

"Thanks, Ryan."

When the director was gone, JR turned to Kruger. "I'm still not comfortable with something, Sean."

"Should I stop the director."

"No."

"Okay, talk to me."

"Thinking back on Alexia finding Amy Ling's original birth certificate seemed like finding the Rosetta Stone. Why did they change the file name and not delete it?"

"JR, I wouldn't know."

"It's puzzled me ever since she found it."

Kruger's mouth twitched. "Unless…"

"What?"

"Okay. Let's chase rabbits for a moment. What if they wanted the ability to bring Amy Ling back to life at some point. Maybe after the persona of Emily Soon has served their purpose."

"Sean, a senator disappearing and someone looking like her with a different name would defy credibility, don't you think?"

"Not if she changes her appearance. My bet is her hair is not naturally the color it is right now."

"You know, Sean, that makes sense."

"It makes further sense the more I think about it. Were you able to determine when the file's name was changed?"

"Yes, six months after the birth."

"She's what, thirty-nine now?"

"Mia's forty-four. Yeah, that's right."

"This has been in the works for forty years, JR."

"Maybe longer. Who knows? Mia might have been the original experiment, but something changed their plans."

Kruger stood and resumed pacing. "Didn't you tell me at

one point that Mia's father was kidnapped when she was a baby?"

"Yeah. That's why her mother took her to Texas to live with the grandparents."

"Do we know the date?"

JR didn't answer. But his fingers flew over the laptop sitting in front of him. He studied the laptop screen and then typed a little longer. Finally, he sat back and said, "Deng Xiaoping became the head of the PRC in December 1978 after he outmaneuvered Mao's chosen successor, Hua Guofeng. By that time, China was becoming disenchanted with communism under the leadership of Mao."

"I vaguely remember those events. What's that got to do with the disappearance of Mia's father?"

"Think about it for a moment. If Ling Mao Chun was in the States due to being ousted by Mao, Deng may have brought him back for some reason. The timing is not a coincidence."

"Mia was born in November of 1978, right?"

JR nodded. "November 25th to be exact."

"That would have made her about two months old in early 1979."

"What are you thinking, Sean?"

"Mia's dad was in the US for political reasons. Mia's mother claims he was kidnapped. What if it was all a ruse to get him back to China? With the old regime gone and a new leader emerging, Ling Mao Chun was taken back to China to help create their technology revolution."

CHAPTER 37

Florence, CO

KKG's HondaJet touched down at the Pueblo Colorado Memorial Airport a few minutes past 11 a.m. Two passengers, one approximately six foot tall, wearing jeans and a navy sport coat, the other two inches shorter, with a backpack slung over his shoulder, departed the small jet. The taller of the two rented a Ford Explorer from Avis and drove west on US 50 toward Florence, Colorado. Their destination, the high-security federal prison south of town, known as ADX Florence.

Sean Kruger presented his Homeland Security credentials to the proper authorities and asked to see a prisoner officially known by the name John Smith. Kruger's companion presented identification showing him to be a United States cybersecurity expert.

Fifteen minutes after arriving at the Supermax prison, Li Chao, the youngest member of The Four Brothers, sat across from Kruger and JR Diminski.

The prisoner tilted his head and asked, "Who are you?"

Kruger held his credentials out so Chao could see them. "Homeland Security."

"So?"

"Do you know a senator by the name of Emily Soon?"

A fleeting smile appeared on the prisoner's lips for a moment. "Never heard of her."

"She called you fourteen times over the last twelve months at the San Francisco Chinese Consulate."

"Never been there."

"We have a recording of you talking to her."

Chao laughed out loud. "I seriously doubt that. Satellite calls cannot be recorded."

Kruger replied, "Didn't say it was a satellite call."

The prisoner glared at the two men on the other side of the security glass.

JR pressed a button on his cell phone. Chao's voice speaking Mandarin could be heard. The voice of a woman responded. This voice also spoke Mandarin.

The prisoner grinned. "That is not me."

The computer expert shook his head. "Sorry, it is. Voiceprints confirm it's you and Senator Soon."

"I hate to tell you, Chao, but the current predicament you find yourself in just got a lot deeper." Kruger clasped his hands and leaned toward the glass separating the prisoner from his visitors. "Soon is in the custody of the FBI. You are in the custody of the federal government under an assumed name. Chances of you ever getting out of here are currently slim to none. You see, no one who might possibly care knows you're here."

"Why are you telling me this?"

"I want the Manchurian."

"He is untouchable."

"No one is untouchable."

"Says you." The Chinese national scowled at the agent. Kruger maintained a neutral expression. Quiet returned to the small space. Finally, Chao said, "And if I help you find him?"

"You might see daylight again."

The man did not respond for several minutes. His eyes flicked back and forth between Kruger and JR. Finally, he said, "If I help you, they will find me and kill me. If I don't help you, what happens to me?"

"You will disappear into the federal penitentiary system under a false name and be kept there until you're an old man." He paused. "Did I mention you'll be in solitary confinement during this period? No contact with anyone."

"If I help you?"

"I've been authorized to let you know we'll send you wherever you want to go. You'll have a new name and face. But it will be out of this country. Plus, there is one stipulation. If you ever try to return to the US…" Kruger smiled. "Make sure you don't even think about it."

"How long do I have to consider your proposal?"

Glancing at his watch, Kruger said, "One minute. Starting now."

Li Chao blinked once and then nodded. "Very well. What do you want to know?"

***

Florence, CO
Midnight

The overcast sky hid a full moon and the dim light of the stars. At one minute past midnight, a black Ford Explorer with an Avis rental sticker on one of the rear windows passed through the security barrier separating the Supermax prisoners from the outside world.

The vehicle sped north on Colorado State 67 and then east on US 50. Fifty minutes later, the SUV pulled up to a small business jet. Two individuals departed the SUV and climbed the plane's airstairs and disappeared inside. At the same time, the driver wiped down the back seat area, smudging any fingerprints that might have been deposited by one of its passengers.

The driver returned the Explorer to the Avis rental center and deposited the keys in an overnight collection bin. He then walked back to the waiting jet.

At 3:02 a.m., Federal Prisoner 15378-042, known within the federal corrections system as John Smith, settled into an isolated cell at the Federal Medical Center in Springfield, MO.

The two individuals escorting the man exited the medical center grounds an hour later and returned to their respective homes located several miles southwest of the facility.

Only two individuals knew that Li Chao, one of the Four Brothers, had been removed from the ultra-secure prison in Florence, Colorado. The pilot of the HondaJet never saw the prisoner or interacted with him.

Even Tim Gonzales, the FBI agent who arrested Chao, was not informed about his transfer.

For all practical purposes, Li Chao no longer existed within the federal prison system. John Smith, on the other hand, was scheduled for a procedure at a local hospital the following day.

***

One Week Later

Kruger watched through a video link as a doctor removed bandages from the face of John Smith. He turned to JR. "What do you think?"

"Add glasses and cut his hair, he'll be unrecognizable. The doctor did a nice job on his chin line, and the nose is thinner."

"I have to agree."

"So, does this mean Li Chou is no more?"

"Exactly. His new name is John Lee. Born in Chicago. We'll have an Illinois birth certificate arriving today via FedEx."

"What if he reneges on the deal, Sean?"

"He won't."

"You seem sure of yourself."

"As I told him in Colorado, there will be consequences. Like a State Department notification to the Chinese Consulate General that Li Chao was found living under an alias."

With a chuckle, JR said, "Okay, now what?"

"He and I are having a briefing this afternoon. I will inform him now that we have kept our side of the bargain, it's time for him to uphold his."

"Good, need a witness?"

Kruger replied, "Yeah, DOJ has prohibited any recordings of his interviews until we have the Manchurian in custody."

"Want me to record it?"

"Hell, yes."

***

John Lee, the man with prisoner ID 15378-042, sat in a chair across from two men on the other side of the security glass. He said, "The surgeon did a nice job. I hardly recognize myself."

Kruger said, "Glad you approve. Now, time to pay up. How do I find the Manchurian?"

"You said the FBI has Soon in custody?"

"Yes."

"Use her as bait. She is really the only person you have available who can recognize the man they call the Manchurian on sight."

With raised eyebrows, Kruger said, "You've never seen

him?"

"No. My oldest brother has, but he's the only one."

"But you've spoken to him."

Lee shook his head. "I always received my orders from my brother."

"Where's he?"

"Probably somewhere in Manchuria. The brothers will be living separate from each other, as a precaution."

"Why?"

"There are factions within China who disagree with what the Manchurian is doing."

JR tilted his head. "What exactly is the Manchurian doing?"

The man now known as John Lee took a deep breath. "He is developing computer chips for AI that will make all other computer chips obsolete. Then he, and he alone, will garner the profits. There are men in China, part of the ruling class, who oppose him. They think he will take over the party. They fear when the current president grows old, they will be shoved aside."

"He has no plans for the United States with these chips?"

"It was a minor part of his overall plan. His goal here was to make the United States government more friendly to China."

"So, he has no plan to interfere with US elections or the infrastructure?"

"I did not say that. I said he wants the US to be more friendly to China."

Kruger asked the next question. "How was he going to do that?"

"The plan included getting certain individuals around the country elected by manipulating voting machines."

Glancing at JR, Kruger stood and left the area.

Lee frowned. "Did I say something wrong?"

"No, you confirmed what we thought was already

happening." JR paused for a moment. "Quantum computing?"

"What about it?"

"How close is the Manchurian to designing a chip for room temperature computing?"

"He gave up on that pipe dream years ago. But he kept talking about it so his research money would continue."

JR stood. "Thanks, John. Kind of what I suspected."

CHAPTER 38

Northern China

"How does someone disappear in the United States, Hao? There are reporters on every corner, and social media reveals all their government secrets." Ling Mao Chun sipped tea as he spoke to the eldest of the Four Brothers, Li Hao on a video call.

"We have a recording of him being arrested in his apartment. The fool allowed his picture to be taken when he parked the truck hauling the bulldozer."

"What did the recording reveal?"

"The FBI planned to take him to their San Francisco field office. He never arrived."

"Unfortunate."

"We had friends stationed who planned to make sure he did not talk."

"What about our source within the field office?"

"Compromised."

"Does she know anything?"

"No. Not about the overall plan. All she knows is how

much money we deposited in her bank account. Which has now been confiscated by the FBI."

"Good." Ling seemed to contemplate his tea for a moment before taking a sip. "The Americans have a compulsion to keep accurate records. Chao will be somewhere in those files. Find him."

"We have several consulate members working on it. No luck, so far."

"Then try harder. Don't disappoint me like you have in the past." The Manchurian disconnected the Zoom call and turned to the view outside his office window. Below his office, the Songhua River split the city of Harbin in half on its northeasterly flow.

With his tea now cold, Ling grimaced with the next sip. Standing, he moved to where a tea kettle steamed. Warming the contents of the cup, he returned to the laptop on his desk. He picked up a satellite phone and punched in a number. After a series of clicks, the unit connected with a router in San Francisco. The call then went to a satellite phone he did not know was in the possession of the FBI in Washington, DC. Voice mail answered.

The Manchurian chose not to leave a message. He never left messages. The owner of the phone would call back at her first opportunity. However, this was the fourth call to the phone without a response or a returned call.

He checked the time. It would be a few minutes before 7 a.m. in Washington, DC. Instead of calling again, he decided to check one of several US news websites he used to keep track of happenings in the country.

Fifteen minutes into his search, he found answers to his questions.

CNN: Senator Emily Soon remains in custody today following the revelation she held regular communications with a known Chinese national who has been charged with terrorism and murder. CNN reached out to her attorney but has not received a reply.

Ling read the article several times before shutting down his laptop. With the Twin Peaks' computer destroyed and the arrest of Emily Soon, his carefully constructed plan teetered on the verge of collapse. He and the remaining members of The Four Brothers would need to return to the US to manage damage control.

Using his cell phone, he made arrangements for passage on the first available cargo ship heading to San Francisco.

***

Charlie Craft watched as the satellite phone belonging to Senator Emily Soon vibrated with an incoming call. The number calling the phone belonged to the router in California. No message was left at the end by the caller.

He picked up his own cell phone and punched in a number. The individual answered on the second ring.

"What have you got, Charlie?"

"That's the fastest you've ever answered one of my calls, JR."

"Extenuating circumstances. What's up?"

"The senator's phone has been called four times since her arrest. No message is ever left, and all the calls are originating from the router service in San Francisco."

"The Manchurian is trying to get ahold of her."

"That would be my guess."

"Thanks, Charlie, I'll let Sean know."

***

As soon as the call ended, JR walked out of his office and down to Kruger's. When he rapped on the doorframe, his friend motioned for him to come in. "We've got to stop coming in this early, JR."

The computer genius sat in front of Kruger's desk and

said, "Charlie just called. The senator's satellite phone has been called four times since her arrest. All from the router in San Fran."

"Huh."

"Charlie thinks the Manchurian is trying to reach her."

Kruger stood and stretched. "I've got to get some exercise." He picked his mug up and gestured toward the coffee service area. "What do you think?"

"I just made coffee. It's fresh."

"Not that. About the calls."

"If I was to bet on it, I'd agree, it's the Manchurian. By now, he knows one of The Four Brothers is missing. So, he's trying to find out what the good senator knows."

Taking a sip of his freshly poured coffee, Kruger said, "All he has to do is search the news sites. Her arrest is all over the media." He grasped the mug with both hands. "JR, how hard would it be for someone to trace John Lee?"

"Difficult, but not impossible."

"Explain."

"First, Chun would have to know when the fourth brother disappeared."

"We can assume he does. The apartment was wired for eavesdropping."

"Okay, it would be easy to locate someone in the federal prison system."

"We didn't use his real name."

"Yeah, but using John Doe was pretty lame. That name alone could draw an alert researcher's attention."

With a frown, Kruger said, "Okay, not the smartest move we've made."

"I'm just saying, it depends on who is searching for him. Moving him in the dead of night to the medical center here in town might have been your best move."

"He was never identified as John Doe there."

"Good. Make sure his records are expunged when he does leave."

Glancing at his watch, Kruger set his coffee mug down. "It's eight. By the time I get to the medical center, John Lee should be available."

"Want company?"

"I hoped you'd be interested."

***

US Medical Center for Federal Prisoners

John Lee sat down across from Kruger and JR and sighed. "When do I get out of here? I've told you how to find the Manchurian."

Kruger raised his hand, palm toward the prisoner. "Not so fast. He's not in custody yet. Remember our deal is once he's captured, you'll be flown wherever you want to go. As long as it's not in the US."

Glaring at the Homeland Security agent, Lee narrowed his eyes. "You keep changing the deal."

Kruger hissed. "And I'll keep doing so until Ling Mao Chun is dead or in prison."

Raising both hands toward Kruger, Lee said, "Okay, okay. Dead would be better. What do you want today?"

"Will Ling return to the US?"

"He has ways of sneaking in."

"Such as?"

"Search any cargo ship from China that has passenger berths. He won't be listed as a passenger. Plus, he travels alone. He does not allow other passengers on the ship."

"So, any cargo ship that can carry passengers but is empty might be a candidate."

"I just said that."

"Where will the ship's voyage originate?"

"Any of the thirty-four major ports and two thousand minor ones. However, he only travels on ships owned by the PRC."

With a frown, JR asked, "When did the Chinese government start owning ships?"

"As of 1997, three Chinese-owned shipping conglomerates merged. They own a lot of ships now. The Manchurian travels on them exclusively."

Kruger asked, "Will he bring your brothers?"

"He doesn't go anywhere without them. Otherwise, he's a paper tiger. But they travel separately."

"By boat?"

Shaking his head, Lee said, "Usually on separate airlines. Never together."

"What else do I need to know?"

The prisoner pursed his lips. "There is an American who helps him as well. I've never heard him addressed by a name."

"What does he look like?"

"Tall and slender, shaggy hair, and his cheeks are scarred by acne."

The retired FBI agent did not respond.

"He does all of the Manchurian's dirty work when it is not convenient for the Four Brothers to do so."

"Is he from San Francisco?"

"I do not know any more about him. Like I said, he does the messy jobs."

"Anything else?"

"No."

Standing, Kruger said, "Thanks for the info."

Lee stood as well. "Don't forget, once he's dead, I want out of here."

"That's the deal."

As Kruger and JR drove back to the office, JR said, "I'll have Alexia start looking for a Chinese-owned cargo ship containing passenger berths with no one registered."

"Don't limit the search to West Coast ports, JR."

"Why do you say that?"

"Because the US has inland ports. For example, the Port

of Tulsa. Shipping comes up the Mississippi and then the Arkansas River."

"Glad you mentioned it. You don't think he'll come that way, do you?"

"JR, I wouldn't assume anything with this guy. Best be prepared."

CHAPTER 39

Superior Court of California
County of San Francisco

Due to the notoriety of the accused, a sitting US senator, the courtroom overflowed with media reporters, law enforcement types, and the simply curious. Whispers and murmurs created an incomprehensible cacophony of voices as the appointed time for the hearing to commence grew near.

A large, barrel-chested man appeared from a side door. Wearing the uniform of a San Francisco County sheriff deputy, he surveyed the room. He cleared his throat and announced in a gruff booming voice, "All rise."

The commotion of multiple individuals standing filled the courtroom. A slender, middle-aged woman appeared from the same side door and ascended the several steps leading to the judge's bench. She wore the traditional robes of the California Superior Court and took her seat behind the elevated desk.

The bailiff continued. "Superior Court of the county of

San Francisco, with the Honorable Judge Georgia Green presiding, is now in session. Please be seated and come to order."

The judge reviewed the information on the computer screen in front of her. She already knew the particulars of the high-profile case but made sure she remembered the details. Directing her attention to the prosecution and defense tables, she said, "This is a preliminary hearing in the case of the State of California versus Emily Soon, a current US senator. I see that California Attorney General Tim Reid is present. Good morning to you, Mr. Reid. Are you serving as lead attorney for the prosecution?"

"Yes, Your Honor."

With a slight smile, she continued. "It's a little rare to see you in my courtroom. Run out of assistant attorney generals?"

Chuckles swept through the crowd. Reid's cheeks flushed a bit.

The judge continued. "No need to answer the question. We've known each other for a while. It's nice to see you."

She looked at the defense table occupied by the lead attorney, a paralegal, and Senator Soon. "Good morning to you, Mr. Lawson. How are you today?"

"Fine, Your Honor."

"I take it you are representing the senator?"

"Yes, Your Honor."

Green continued. "Gentlemen, as you well know, this is a preliminary hearing and not a trial. We are not here to determine guilt but rather to determine if the State has sufficient evidence or probable cause to take this case to trial. The rules of evidence do not strictly apply. Objections will be considered to the extent deemed determinative of a fact. Is this understood?"

Both Reid and Lawson said, "Yes, Your Honor," in unison.

"Very well. Are both sides ready to proceed this

morning?"

Lawson said, "Your Honor, my client Senator Soon is ready to proceed. While not strictly required at this stage in the state of California, we plead not guilty to this outrageous charge and will be holding the State to meet its burden of proof and at trial if necessary. Currently, as of yet, they have not shown sufficient evidence to support the current charge against her, Your Honor."

"Thank you, Mr. Lawson. I did not ask for opening statements, but that will certainly suffice as one." She turned her attention to Reid. "Does the State desire to make an opening?"

"If it pleases the court?"

"Very well, Mr. Reid, proceed."

"Thank you, Your Honor. The people of California will provide evidence to show the current junior US senator obtained her position by knowingly filing, with the California Secretary of State on November 16, 2011, false documentation as to her true birth identity.

"We will also show that the defendant knew these documents to be fictitious as she continued to be in contact with her birth father. The birth mother is deceased under suspicious circumstances.

"We will also show that a person, or persons unknown, did manipulate the defendant's original and legal birth certificate ten years after the original filing. A forged document was created in its place, and the file name of the original document changed on April 18, 1999. This was a Sunday when the Secretary of State's office was closed and the computer files unattended. The assumption is that the defendant intended to resume her original identity at some point in the future for unknown reasons. Otherwise, the original file could have been deleted."

Lawson stood. "Objection, Your Honor. This is speculation on the prosecution's part."

Judge Green contemplated the defense attorney over her

half readers. "Mr. Lawson, let's not start this so soon. This is his opening statement, and you seem to be speculating on what his witness might say. Save your objection for the witness. By the way, I know speculation when I hear it."

"Your Honor," Lawson continued, "there is no evidence showing Senator Soon had such intentions."

"Wait for the witness, Mr. Lawson. Then we'll see. Objection overruled. Proceed, Mr. Reid."

"Thank you, Your Honor. As we stated earlier, knowingly filing a false and forged document is in violation of California Penal Code, Title 7, Chapter 4, Section 115 and a felony. Not only is the defendant guilty under this statute, but her status as a duly elected senator would be null and void.

"The people will also show that the forged document was discovered by a regularly scheduled audit of the Secretary of State's computer files. We will provide, as a witness, a computer expert who will testify in support of this claim. In addition, we will provide a witness who is the biological sister of the defendant. This negates all public documents that state Emily Soon is an only child."

Lawson stood again. "Your Honor, the evidence of Senator Soon being a biological sister of anyone was illegally obtained in violation of the 4th Amendment and cannot be submitted as evidence. There is a motion to suppress already on file with the court."

"Duly noted, Counselor." Judge Green turned her attention to the Attorney General. "Mr. Reid, I do hope Mr. Lawson's statement is incorrect. Because, if it is, your entire case is subject to dismissal."

Reid smiled. "I assure you, Your Honor, the evidence we will present was all properly collected and will be admitted at trial."

***

The hearing lasted another two hours. At the conclusion, after both sides summarized their arguments, Judge Green removed her half readers and said, "It is the opinion of this court there is probable cause a felony has been committed and this defendant committed it. Defendant is bound over for trial.

"Both sides having consented on my hearing the case after being fully advised of their rights, in accordance with local court rules, I will serve as trial judge."

She referred to something on her desk. "Said trial will commence exactly three months from today's date. That's it for today."

The bailiff barked, "All rise."

Standing, the judge exited the courtroom.

At that moment, numerous reporters, who had not been posting live on the various social media platforms available to them, rushed to get on-air to summarize the information.

On-air media types and pundits described Emily Soon's demeanor in the courtroom as aloof and defiant. One of her few staff members who had not resigned told reporters the senator appeared stoic and confident in her innocence.

Two individuals who sat in the back of the courtroom waited until the chaotic moments subsided to exit. Outside the San Francisco courthouse, Kruger turned to JR and asked, "What do you think?"

"She looked scared to death."

"Yeah, I would have to agree." He hesitated for a moment. "Where's Mia and Joey?"

"They're with Joseph and Mary, waiting to see if she will be called as a witness. I'm guessing she'll be spared the experience until the trial."

Kruger stopped walking and turned toward JR. "Something I failed to consider."

"What's that?"

"Media coverage. Preliminary hearings, while public, are not covered by the media very often. But for someone with a high public profile, like a US senator, the media can't help itself."

JR did not respond right away. His eyes widened briefly. "Well, if the Manchurian didn't know about Soon being arrested, he does now."

"That's only half of it. Reid made the statement that Soon's sister would be a witness at the trial. She'd have to be alive for that to happen."

"Damn. You're right. I didn't consider that, either."

"According to John Lee, there is a high probability Ling is already on a cargo ship headed for the States."

JR pulled his cell phone from his pocket and punched in a number. The call was answered. "Alexia, remember what we discussed about the Manchurian before I left for California?" JR grew silent as he listened. "Testimony in court this morning confirmed that Mia is alive. If he learns this, and we have to assume he will, he'll come after her." More silence. "Thanks. I'll be back in the office tomorrow."

The call ended and JR said, "Alexia has some ideas on how to find the cargo ship."

"Good. I think it's imperative for us to get back to Springfield."

"I couldn't agree more."

***

Somewhere in the Pacific Ocean

Using the ship's satellite reception, the Manchurian watched as BBC World News discussed the developments in the American senator from California's legal woes. The more he listened, the greater his need to lash out grew. Unfortunately, his chosen mode of transportation would require another week at sea.

Instead, he used his satellite phone to call the eldest of The Four Brothers.

"Where are you?"

"Hong Kong."

"Why aren't you in the States?"

"I am not sure our traveling there is a wise idea."

Closing his eyes, the Manchurian took a deep breath and then another. Finally, after several more, he felt calm enough to speak. "I was not aware you felt my orders were optional for you and your brothers."

"With the current location of our youngest sibling unknown, we can surmise he is a guest of the American FBI. If that is the case, they will have a description of us and know how we travel."

"Need I remind you there are very important matters you need to handle in America?"

"Being incarcerated by the FBI is not high on my list of important matters, Mao."

"Surely you have located your younger brother by now."

"He has disappeared into the American prison system. We are unable to locate him."

"That is impossible. The Americans are lazy and subject to greed. Find the right person, pay them, and find out where he is."

"We have resources throughout their government. We have already offered money and yet his location is still unknown. Even our cyber warriors are unable to find him. The last time anyone heard anything about him was over the microphones in his apartment."

"He may be dead."

"If he is, Mao, then we are safe. But do we take a chance he is alive and has betrayed us?"

Ling did not respond.

"I do not believe we can take that chance. He knows your patterns and where you go. If he has been turned, he can betray not only his brothers but you as well."

"You raise a good point. Let me think about it. I will contact you later. In the meantime, plan to return to the States a different way. I have learned Mia Diminski is still alive. She needs to be eliminated immediately."

"Why?"

"Her being alive jeopardizes everything about Emily Soon. We don't need to take the chance."

"Very well. I will wait for your call."

CHAPTER 40

Two Days Later
Southwest Missouri

A few minutes before eight in the morning, Alexia Gibbs motioned for JR to follow her into the conference room. After both were seated, she slipped a piece of paper to her business partner.

After scanning the page, JR looked up. "You found him?"

"Maybe. While there is always the possibility the information is wrong, it seems likely he's on a ship called *Sea of Yunfu* bound for the US."

Studying the page, the computer expert mumbled, "Due at the Port of Long Beach in five days."

"It seems likely."

"Sean should be in any minute, I'll let you tell him." He handed the page back to the female hacker.

The conference door opened and Kruger sat down. "Tell me what?"

Alexia handed the sheet to him. "Ling may be on a ship

due in Long Beach in five days."

"That's good news. Although I've been instructed to let the FBI handle any further apprehensions moving forward."

"Why?"

A shrug was his answer.

"Politics?"

"Probably. But I'll bet it's my temporary status."

JR frowned. "Sean, that's BS and you know it. Someone is mad because a small company in southwest Missouri discovered this mess and has done more to stop it than the ten thousand special agents within the FBI."

Kruger stood. "I'm getting coffee. Anyone want a cup?"

Both Alexia and JR shook their heads.

When Kruger returned to his seat, he placed the coffee in front of him and clasped his hands. "I have a tendency to agree with you, JR. Unfortunately, there's another reason. I got a call from Ryan Clark last night. The California Attorney General feels the more we are involved, the more likely Soon's defense attorney will question the legality of the arrest. We've already been taken off the witness list. I'm afraid any contribution we make from here forward will be consulting only."

"I thought Clark supported us?"

"He does, JR. But his hands are tied. DOJ wants Soon to be impeached as a senator and will then file federal charges against her. With her legal woes just beginning, he's right."

"What about Alexia's theory concerning the *Sea of Yunfu*?"

Taking a sip of his coffee, Kruger said, "Send the info to Charlie Craft. He can run it up the flagpole."

Alexia stood and left the conference room.

JR watched her go then turned to Kruger. "If she's right, there's a chance he's coming back to tie up loose ends."

"I agree. I have a call in for Sandy and Jimmy to swing by the office today. Time to beef up security for Mia, Joey, and yourself."

"She's refusing to hide this time, Sean."

Standing, he gave JR a grim smile. "That's fine. But I want one of our KKG guys driving her at all times."

"Are you planning on telling her?"

"Nope. She's your wife."

***

Charlie Craft, the head of the FBI Cyber Division, sent the information about the *Sea of Yunfu* to his boss, the Executive Assistant Director for Criminal and Cyber. Who, in turn, copied her boss, the deputy director. The deputy director then met with the director who forwarded the info to the Director of Homeland Security. Four hours after Charlie Craft sent his first email, the Coast Guard received orders to intercept the *Sea of Yunfu* and take into custody Ling Mao Chun, aka, the Manchurian.

***

Over the Pacific Ocean

Copilot Lieutenant Jason Osborne used binoculars to search the horizon for the ship he and the pilot, Lieutenant Michael Hernandez were charged with finding. The aircraft, an HC-130J Hercules long-ranged surveillance aircraft was halfway through its mission when Osborne pointed toward the west.

"Mike, one o'clock, five miles. Looks like a container ship. Let's check it out."

"Got her." He turned the plane toward the objective. "Let me know as soon as you can read the name."

Staring through the binoculars, the man in the right seat of the aircraft concentrated on identifying the vessel. Two minutes later, he said, "Bingo. *Sea of Yunfu*. Exactly where it was expected to be."

The pilot keyed his radio. "This is Coast Guard Seven-Two-Five-Niner."

"Go ahead Seven-Two-Five-Niner."

"Confirmation on the location of target vessel."

"Go with GPS location."

Osborne recited the coordinates.

"Roger, Seven-Two-Five-Niner. Help is on the way. Can you loiter?"

Hernandez said, "Tell them we can for a couple of hours. No more."

Repeating the information from his pilot, Osborne then ended the call. "They want us to keep the ship in sight. Just in case."

"Got it. Might as well sit back and relax. Want to do circles or figure eights?"

With a chuckle, Osborne said, "Surprise me."

***

Mia Diminski, a diminutive woman of barely five feet in height, scowled at both her husband and his friend Sean Kruger. "I will not hide from this person any longer. Do you even know where he is at the moment?"

Kruger smiled. "Mia, we don't have specific information on his whereabouts. However, we can speculate and make assumptions."

"So, I'm to put JR's and my son's lives on hold while your former agency tries to figure it out?"

"You are the one in danger. We know for a fact your mother was murdered by his accomplices. We have one in custody, and he confirmed the murder was Ling's idea to keep her from telling us his plans."

She folded her arms at the same time her foot started to tap. "Sean, you have known me for almost twelve years now. Have you ever seen me hide from anything?"

"No, Mia, I haven't. But, until we know exactly where

he is, I would be more comfortable if you stayed at Joseph's."

"No." She focused on her husband. "JR, you've been very quiet. Do you agree with Sean?"

"In a way, yes. But I know when you make up your mind, it's hard to change it."

"Well, I've made up my mind. Joey and I are staying here. We will not hide."

The former FBI agent said, "What about Joey's safety?"

She hesitated, her scowl softening. "There is little for him to do at Joseph's. He got horribly bored last time."

"They tried to kill you once. They'll try again. This time, it might be successful, and Joey could be collateral damage. Can you live with yourself if that happens, Mia?"

She stared at Kruger for a long time. "No. I couldn't. But I'm not hiding."

"What about relatives in Texas?"

"Sean, I haven't lived in Texas since college. With the passing of my grandparents, I don't know anyone there any longer."

"What about a vacation?"

"I do not wish to go on a vacation. Besides, where would I go without JR?"

"Maybe, you, Joey, Stephanie, and the kids can go somewhere."

"Where?"

"I don't know, but we need to think of somewhere."

***

Osborne studied the Coast Guard cutter as it weighed anchor next to the *Sea of Yunfu*. The HC-130J was now at an altitude of only 400 feet and flying over the spot where both ships remained side by side with the cutter off the other ship's starboard side at a safe distance.

The pilots observed a small boarding craft returning to

the cutter. The copilot keyed the radio. "This is Coast Guard Seven-Two-Five-Niner. USCGC *Sherman*, what is your status?"

"Target wasn't on board, Seven-Two-Five-Niner. Captain said they were intercepted two days ago and their guest escorted off the ship. Where to, they couldn't or wouldn't say."

Staring at the ship below their position, Osborne said, "Roger. Report your situation. We're returning to Sacramento."

"Roger, Seven-Two-Five-Niner."

Turning to the pilot, Osborne said, "Someone's gonna be pissed."

"Better call it in, Jason. This just got way above our pay grade."

***

With his door shut, Kruger listened to the caller while he drummed his fingers on top of the desk. Finally, he said, "Do they know if Ling is in the States yet?"

Charlie Brewer sighed. "No one has a clue. This has turned into a giant clusterfuck, Sean. Fingers are being pointed, tempers are flaring and jobs are being threatened. You name it, it's happening. Gonzales thinks brother number four might know what their next steps might be. But he was told not to suggest it. No one knows where the brother is. He's not where he was left."

A slight smile came to Kruger's lips. He hated lying to his friend, but he said, "Charlie, have you lost a prisoner?"

"That's what Tim and I are asking. Do you think his brothers got to him?"

"Hard to say. They have resources we don't know about."

"That's what I've been told."

"I do hope all the ports on the West Coast are being

covered."

"With as many agents as we can spare."

"Okay, thanks for letting me know about Ling. If you hear anything, please call."

"Will do, Sean."

The call ended. Kruger stood to grab his keys and headed toward the parking lot. He needed to discuss the current events with someone named John Lee.

CHAPTER 41

Southern California

The white Lexus LS turned north on California State Route 12 heading toward the small city of Sonoma. The soon-to-be ex-US Senator Emily Soon stared out the rear passenger window. "Are they still behind us, Aaron?"

"Yes, ma'am. About a quarter of a mile."

She sighed. "I guess I brought all this on myself."

"I'm sorry, Senator. I didn't hear you."

"It's okay. I'm just mumbling."

The young driver glanced in the rearview mirror at the reflection of the woman in the back seat. His attention was then drawn to a large SUV passing the FBI vehicle following them. He checked his side mirror and saw the big truck close the distance between them rapidly. He noticed it approached their rear bumper.

"Excuse me, ma'am, but something weird is going on behind us."

Her eyebrows drew together, and she spun around to see the problem. As she did, the SUV, a Chevy Tahoe, accelerated and came alongside the Lexus. Instead of passing, the front right quarter panel slammed into the rear driver's side quarter panel of the Lexus.

The impact caused the luxury auto's rear wheels to skid toward the shoulder. Aaron steered in the direction of the spin and pumped the brakes. The Tahoe then slammed into the front driver's side quarter panel, and the young, inexperienced driver lost control. Surprise worked against Aaron as he fought to keep the car from spinning off the road. He failed, and the Lexus came to a halt facing the opposite direction on the right shoulder.

Emily Soon watched in horror as two men, both of Pacific Rim descent, jumped out of the stopped SUV. The man from the passenger side held a Heckler and Koch SP5 machine pistol. He aimed the weapon directly at the window where she sat.

***

FBI Agent Tim Gonzales watched as the large Chevy SUV passed him on the left and accelerated. He said to his fellow FBI agent in the passenger seat, "Heads-up, Anna. This may be nothing, but get ready." He pressed the accelerator to the floor and the FBI vehicle responded by closing the gap to the big vehicle.

The Tahoe veered to the left and struck the Lexus in the rear. As the car spun out of control, Gonzales slammed on the brakes, skidding to a halt twenty yards from the now-stopped SUV.

He flung the door open and saw a man from the Tahoe aim an automatic pistol at the senator's car.

"Halt. FBI. Drop the weapon."

The man of Asian descent turned the weapon toward Gonzales. Before he could fire, the FBI agent discharged his Glock four times. The assailant caught all four bullets in the chest and went down hard. His head bounced on the asphalt and he lay still. The driver of the big truck dashed back behind the Chevy's steering wheel as Anna Graham opened fire with her service weapon. The Tahoe accelerated away from the scene, one of her bullets shattering the rear window.

Gonzales rushed to the fallen assailant and kicked the H&K away from the prone man's grasp. Blood pooled under the individual, who remained still. Turning to his partner, he said, "Call it in, we're gonna need assistance." Kneeling, he felt the carotid artery on the left side of the man's neck. Feeling nothing, he stood and ran to where the Lexus came to rest.

Within thirty minutes, the scene of the attempted attack on Emily Soon swarmed with local, state, and federal law enforcement.

Gonzales leaned against the Lexus' rear quarter panel. The senator sat in the passenger seat, the door open; her elbows were on her knees and her hands supporting her head. The FBI agent said, "Did you recognize the man with the weapon, Senator?"

She lifted her head. "Yes, Agent, I did."

"Who was he?"

"I believe law enforcement calls them The Four Brothers."

Raising an eyebrow, the FBI agent continued. "Do you know which one?"

"Yes, second oldest. The driver was one of his younger brothers."

"You realize what this means, don't you?"

"Yes, Agent, I realize I've been a fool. I am now a liability to them. They won't stop until I'm no longer a threat."

"Want protection?"

She nodded.

Gonzales pulled out his cell phone and made a call.

***

The Next Day
FBI San Francisco Field Office

Charlie Brewer shook Kruger's hand. "I appreciate you bringing Mia, Sean."

"Glad to do it. She's a bit nervous about meeting her but more than a little curious of what she might learn about her father. Hopefully, you'll be recording the meeting."

"Hadn't thought about it."

"I would suggest doing so. You might learn something about the Manchurian you can use to track him." He folded his arms and considered the Special Agent in Charge. "So, why the sudden change in attitude on Soon's part?"

"Her lawyer advised her to resign from the Senate and take a plea deal the California Attorney General offered her."

With a chuckle, Kruger asked, "What did he offer?"

"Testify against The Four Brothers and Ling."

"And what's in it for her?"

"Couple of years at the women's minimum-security prison at Victorville and then parole."

With raised eyebrows, Kruger said, "She took it?"

"Yeah, I think the incident on the highway yesterday scared the crap out of her. Tim Gonzales said, after it was over, she started talking. We learned a lot from the exchange."

"Huh."

"I'll be interested in what she tells her sister."

Kruger turned and headed for Brewer's office door. Before he exited, he turned. "So will I."

***

Interview Room
San Francisco FBI Field Office

Mia Diminski stood next to her husband. They held hands as she watched the hallway next to the room where she would meet her sister for the first time. At the moment, the hall was empty. "JR, I'm so used to thinking about myself as an only child, this is kind of surreal for me."

"I can understand. Don't overthink this, Mia. She's lived a different life, and you two will probably not have much in common."

"That's what I'm afraid of. Nothing to talk about."

"You'll have plenty to discuss. Ask about your father."

"What if she won't answer?"

"She will. Court order."

Pulling her hand away from JR, she took a step away and looked up at him. "The only reason she's talking to me is a court order?"

"No, Mia, Sean's the reason she's talking to you. He suggested it."

They waited in silence for another ten minutes. Mia asked, "What's taking so long, JR?"

"Don't know." He noticed a familiar figure walking in their direction. "Maybe Sean knows."

When Kruger arrived, he gave Mia a hug. "You ready for this?"

She nodded.

"She just finished a Zoom meeting with the Senate majority leader. Her resignation from the Senate was accepted. She'll return to using her birth name, Amy Ling. When she's done meeting with you, the FBI will be transporting her to a safe location where they can protect her."

Mia pressed her lips together and closed her eyes.

Commotion down the hall drew their attention. A woman who resembled Mia both in size and facial features walked toward them. At first glance, the main difference between the two women appeared to be the length of the former senator's hair. It was short.

When she walked up to Mia, the two women stared at each other for a while and then hugged. Amy Ling said, "They told me you and I resembled each other. It's like looking into a mirror."

Kruger opened the room reserved for their meeting and shut it as soon as they were inside. He said to JR, "You're not going in?"

The computer expert shook his head. "Nope. I think Mia needs to work through this by herself. She knows I'm out here waiting and can help if needed."

***

Mia Diminski studied her newfound sister for several moments. "What's he like?"

"You mean our father?"

"Yes."

"Selfish, conceited, doesn't care who he lies to or how those lies affect others. But he is extremely brilliant."

"What happened to our mother?"

A tear formed in the other woman's eye. She wiped it away and said, "She finally grew tired of his lies. When she threatened to go back to Texas, he got rid of her." She stared at the ceiling. "I didn't know the truth for several months; then he told me what happened. I should have seen the writing on the wall." After taking a deep breath, she blew it out. "I enjoyed being a senator and all the trappings."

Without saying a word, Mia continued to study her sister.

"I was never told about you, Mia. No one ever

mentioned your name. One of those family secrets, I guess."

"Sorry, Amy. We may share the same DNA, but you are not my family. The last time I saw my mother, I was four years old. She never wrote me or called me. It was like I didn't exist. My grand..." There was a catch in her throat and Mia hesitated. She then said, "Our grandparents raised me. They were my family. When I graduated from college, I took a trip to California to try to visit our mother. She refused to see me. My internal fantasy about having a mother who cared vanished during that trip. I'm married now and have a son. I don't mean to be harsh, but they are now my family."

Tears streamed down the face of the former senator. "I'm sorry."

"Not your fault." The room grew quiet for a few minutes. Mia said in a soft voice, "I heard they tried to kill you yesterday."

Ling dabbed at her eyes with a tissue. "Yes."

"They tried to do the same thing to me a few months back. I went into hiding." She raised her chin. "No more. Our father needs to be put in prison. Too many people are dead because of him. Our mother, for one."

"I know."

"Can you help the FBI find him?"

"I don't know."

"Why?"

"Because I never know where he is. I have to call him."

"But you know where he'll be, don't you?"

Amy Ling frowned. "I'm not following you, Mia."

"When you traveled to California all those years as a senator, where did you meet him?"

For the first time since meeting her sister, Mia saw her smile.

"You're right, I do."

CHAPTER 42

Northern California

A lone individual sat in a small, uncrowded café a few blocks off the campus of the University of California at Berkeley. Having graduated from the university in the spring of 1985, he felt a reluctant kinship to the school and the mystique surrounding it.

Except on this particular day, nostalgia for his days in college were far from his thoughts. He waited for a particular acquaintance to join him at his table. Fifteen minutes after the agreed-upon time, the person sat down across from him.

"You're late."

The man shrugged.

"Why is the individual we discussed still alive?"

"You didn't mention she was being followed by the FBI."

The man known as the Manchurian glared at his guest. "What do you mean, followed by the FBI?"

"You're smarter than that, Ling. Think about it. Of

course, they were following her. They believe she can lead them to you. Now, because of your arrogance, one of my brothers is dead and the youngest missing. If he is still alive, he is probably telling them everything he knows."

Ling started to stand. The eldest of The Four Brothers grabbed his arm. "Sit down. Don't draw attention to yourself."

Standing for a few more seconds, the Manchurian sat and glared at his companion.

"Here's the situation, Ling. We have a common problem."

"Perhaps. How do you propose we solve it?"

"We travel to the source."

"And that is?"

"The individual who discovered your plans and his wife, your oldest daughter."

The Manchurian narrowed his eyes. "How does that solve our problem?"

"Do you wish to continue with the project?"

"What if I don't?"

"Someone else will be recruited. The sponsors do not care who achieves the results, just that the results are achieved. Do you understand what I'm saying?"

"Yes."

"Good, because I don't work for you, I work for them. We, unlike you, did research on this man. He is a well-known computer expert and has ties to the US government. Plus, he is smart and willing to wait for you to resume the project. The fact his wife is your daughter makes it imperative they both are dealt with." The eldest brother leaned forward, his palms flat on the table. "I and my remaining brother, will handle the details. If we fail, the task will fall to you."

With a grim smile, the Manchurian said, "Very well."

***

The roar of the HondaJet engines provided a steady white-noise background. Mia and JR sat in the back row as the plane soared over the Rocky Mountains, heading east toward home. During the last forty-five minutes, Mia stared out the window next to her while JR held her hand, his eyes closed.

"JR, are you asleep?"

"Almost." He opened one eye and saw her red puffy eyes. "Have you been crying?"

"What will happen to my sister?"

Sitting up straight, JR said, "A question best directed toward Sean."

"I know. But I was hoping you might have an idea."

"Why do you ask, Mia?"

She resumed staring out the window, but her grip on JR's hand tightened. "I'm torn between wanting her in my life and forgetting she exists."

He placed his other hand on top of hers but did not make a comment.

"JR, you're an only child as well. What if you suddenly found out you had a brother or sister. How would you feel?"

"First, I'd want to understand why I didn't know about them. But you already know why. Second, I'd want to get to know them a little before I made the decision to form any kind of relationship."

"That's the question I'm struggling with. I'm not sure I want to know her."

"You've only known her for a few hours, Mia. She's probably going to be in a women's prison in California for a while. Why don't you write her and see what happens. You can make up your mind later. It's not like she is going to be next door. Almost two thousand miles will separate you from each other."

"I really hadn't thought of it being so far."

"Kind of a barrier, if you ask me."

They lapsed back into a comfortable silence married couples tend to experience. When the plane flew over the plains of Kansas, Mia asked, "JR, should we be concerned about my father?"

"I think we have to be concerned. Sandy and Jimmy are putting a plan together to keep you and Joey as safe as possible without either of you noticing."

"What about you, JR? You're not completely innocent. After all, you're the one who figured out who he is."

He patted her hand. "We could move in with Michael Wolfe. His place is like a fortress."

She punched him lightly on the arm. "I'm being serious, JR."

With a chuckle, he replied, "I hadn't given it much thought. But you're right. I'd better get Sean back here."

Kruger stood in the aisle ahead of them and gave her a comforting smile. "You have some questions about your security, Mia?"

"Should I be worried about my family, Sean?"

"Not from what Sandy told me a few minutes ago. He's got Bobby Garcia and Rick Evans adding a few features to your house. In addition, you'll have 24/7 human surveillance."

She pressed her lips together.

Kruger continued. "About six months ago, KKG bought a log cabin a little east of Stockton Lake. We needed a tax write-off, and our accountant found the place. We will be using it for clients to stay when they visit our facilities. It's also surrounded by open land we will be turning into a training area for our associates and prospective recruits. If things get intense, the three of you can stay there."

Mia wrinkled her nose.

With a chuckle, Kruger said, "It's as nice as Joseph's log home."

Her eyebrows shot up. "Oh."

"So, you see, Mia, I think we can handle anything the Manchurian throws at us. But I don't want to assume anything. We'll be prepared."

***

Ling Mao Chun unlocked the door to the apartment he and Judy Ling shared after their marriage in the fall of 1984. The building, like many in the area, was owned by a shell company with ties to the PRC. The apartments were designated for Chinese national students attending Berkeley. They were well-maintained and the rent kept artificially low. Applications were closely screened. The only exception to the rule, the apartment Ling used.

Walking to the window, he gazed down at the street where, thirty-nine years ago, his kidnapping had been staged. Every six months, he returned to this apartment for a two-to-three day stay. A knock at the door drew his attention from the window.

Opening it, a lanky man with pockmarked cheeks slipped into the apartment. "Welcome back, Ling."

The Manchurian closed the door.

"How long this time?"

"A few days, maybe more."

The man narrowed his eyes as he appraised the Chinese man. "Understand the senator you sponsored resigned."

"She did."

"Does that affect our relationship?"

"No. But make sure any records you possess of her identity change are destroyed."

"Already done."

"Good. I need a new driver's license and American Express card."

"Sure. No passport?"

Ling shook his head. "Not needed. I'm heading to the

middle of the country."

"Got it. What kind of background?"

"Third or fourth generation Chinese. I'll need a forgettable name."

"Of course. What about a birth certificate?"

"Not going to need the ID that long."

Clasping his hands behind him, the thin man wandered over to the window and peered out. "Can't believe that fake kidnapping we staged was thirty-nine years ago."

Ling did not respond.

After a few minutes, the man walked straight to the apartment door, opened it, and left without saying another word.

The Manchurian decided at that moment, this would be the last transaction he would initiate with the longtime forger and fixer.

***

Jimmy Gibbs waved as Kruger stepped down the airstairs of the HondaJet. The aircraft engines cycled down as JR and Mia followed their friend.

When they shook hands, Jimmy asked, "How was the flight?"

Kruger said, "Better than commercial."

"Good to hear. We aim to please. Are you going to need Stewart for a while?"

"No."

"Good. We've got a job for him."

With a chuckle, Kruger said, "Do we need to hire another pilot?"

"Maybe."

"You and Sandy decide."

"You sure?"

"Yes, Jimmy. You two know more about the company's finances than I do."

"Okay."

"How's the other project going?"

Turning to JR and Mia, who stood next to Kruger now, Jimmy said, "Your house has around-the-clock surveillance. You won't know they're there until you need them. Plus, we've added a few, uh, features. I'll show you when we get there."

Mia hugged Jimmy. "Thank you. I appreciate all your efforts."

"We know, Mia. The cabin at the lake is ready for you, Joey, and JR if needed."

JR started toward the parking lot. "I'm ready to go home."

CHAPTER 43

Southwest Missouri

The KKG security enhancements at JR and Mia's house consisted of behind-the-scene measures. The one critical upgrade was infrared motion detection cameras placed strategically around the dwelling. These replaced the original cameras installed earlier.

The second system added included state-of-the-art communication equipment connected to the KKG offices in town and to their airport hangar. The Greene County sheriff would also receive a notification of any intrusion into the home.

Bobby Garcia and Rick Evans handled the improvements. They were also one of the teams assigned to watch over the house.

Due to his status as a principal of KKG, Kruger received a personal tour of the enhancements.

Garcia motioned toward one of the cameras. "We have these both inside and out. The outside ones are active 24/7, while the inside ones are active only if JR or Mia turn them on."

Examining one of the small units, Kruger said, "JR told me he has the images being sent to a stand-alone server at the office running facial recognition software."

"Yeah, if it works the way we think it should, we'll start offering it to clients. It's pretty slick, if you ask me."

The retired FBI agent surveyed the room where they stood. "Bobby, using all of this equipment makes sense until one realizes it takes time for law enforcement to respond. Particularly at night. Our neighborhood is technically outside the city limits. How's that going to work?"

The ex-SEAL said, "Let's go out on the back deck and I'll show you something." When they stepped out onto the wooden platform, he pointed at the house behind JR's. "We've leased that house. It's been for sale for a while, and we talked the owners into leasing it to us for three months. We'll have team members there in three eight-hour shifts."

Returning his attention to JR's house, Kruger took a deep breath. "I hope all of this is for naught."

"So do I, Sean. But I prefer to be prepared."

Kruger shook Bobby's hand and walked back across the street to his house. As he stood on his front porch, he turned and mumbled, "Even with all of these precautions, I'm not sure we can keep JR and his family safe."

***

Kruger walked through JR's open office door and sat down across from his friend. The computer hacker sighed. "Mia is not leaving the house, Sean."

"I know. You've told me several times. What's it gonna take to get you guys to leave for a few weeks?"

JR shrugged. "One thing I learned about Mia before we got married. Once she has a good reason, it becomes almost impossible to change her mind."

"Does she have a good reason for staying?"

"She's from Texas. No one from Texas likes to be being bullied. It's the way she is."

"JR, these people are cold-blooded killers, not bullies. They don't care she's from Texas."

"I know. But you have to admit, having six retired SEALs living behind us is pretty comforting."

Taking a deep breath, Kruger said, "Think about it for a moment. The Four Brothers found access to Switchblade drones and killed Ethan Matheson with one. What if they use one on your house? How are six ex-SEALs going to protect you?"

"I'd forgotten about the Switchblade drones."

"Yeah, well, I haven't. Plus, what else have they gotten access to? The Manchurian has the resources of the Chinese government behind him. We both know the US border with Canada can be a sieve in certain areas. With the right amount of cash, you can smuggle exotic weapons into the wilderness of western Canada and then across the northern providences. You take them south to the border near northern Wisconsin, and you will never see a soul."

For the first time since he met JR Diminski, Kruger saw a scared man. "I take it you're finally seeing the danger."

A nod was the only comment from the computer expert.

"Can you talk to her, or do you want me to do so?"

JR said, "I'll talk to her, but I need to do some research first."

***

Somewhere in the Southern United States

Seven metal buildings were laid out along a horseshoe-shaped access road. Each structure served a unique purpose for the company occupying the compound. Razor wire sat atop a ten-foot-tall chain link fence which surrounded the four-acre complex. At night, a pack of four pit bulls roamed the interior, searching for intruders.

Most nights were quiet.

At exactly one in the morning, two men, both dressed in black, appeared at a northern corner of the fenced-off property. They waited patiently for the dogs to sense their arrival. It took less than a minute.

Out of the dark, two of the facilities trained attack dogs appeared and growled at the two men. The taller of the two used a hand-pumped insecticide sprayer to dose each dog with a compound designed to render them unconscious.

With the canines sound asleep on the grass, the shorter of the two men used a large bolt cutter to create an opening. After the second cut, two additional dogs showed up and were dispatched exactly like their pack mates.

An hour later, the two intruders were gone, and the dogs experienced the first signs of regaining consciousness. The large gap in the chain link fence remained open for first responders to examine.

***

FBI and ATF agents arrived at the compound by late morning and swarmed over the facility. Lead FBI agent, Special Agent in Charge of the Memphis field office, Jim Nivens folded his arms as he watched the general manager of the site fidget in a chair. The two men were in the GM's office with the door shut.

"Let's go over the list of missing munitions again, Bob."

Robert Mansfield rolled his eyes. "Agent, we've gone over the list several times already. It hasn't changed."

"Humor me."

ATF Agent Cheryl Smith entered the office. "Sorry, I'm late."

"No problem, Cheryl. We were going over the missing items." Nivens returned his attention to the GM. "Go ahead, Bob."

Picking up a sheet of paper, Mansfield said, "Two 40mm single shot launchers, two dozen 40mm smoke grenades, and two dozen thermite incendiary grenades."

"Nothing else, correct?"

"Correct. That's all we can find missing."

"Okay, Bob. Thanks for going over it again. I need to use your office for a few minutes."

Mansfield left the ATF agent alone with Nivens. When the door shut, he turned to her. "What do you think?"

"From what our agents found in the warehouse, that's pretty specific munitions. Almost like they had a shopping list."

The FBI SAC pursed his lips as he reviewed the items again. "Yeah, I agree. It's a shopping list for a specific purpose. I think we need to push this up the ladder."

***

Southwest Missouri

The chime of an automatic text message from a snooper program sounded on JR's cell phone. At this late hour, Mia and Joey were already asleep. Before shutting the laptop down, he checked the message and frowned.

As his fingers danced on the keyboard, he checked the message again. He mumbled, "I think I'd better talk to Sean." With that comment, he hit a speed dial number.

"Since I know you don't know what time it is, I'll tell you. It's 12:21 a.m., JR."

"If I told you the FBI and ATF are investigating a break-in at a company specializing in the manufacturer of military munitions in the early hours of yesterday morning, would you be interested?"

"What was stolen?"

"Smoke and thermite grenades, plus two launchers for

the smoke."

"Where's this company?"

"In our backyard. North Central Arkansas."

"Shit." Kruger didn't respond for a few moments. "Any security videos?"

"Only black shadows. They knew where the security cameras were located, and they disabled four guard dogs."

"JR, I am only going to tell you this one more time. Get Mia, Joey, and yourself the hell out of that house until further notice."

"We'll see. Thought you should know about the burglary."

CHAPTER 44

Southwest Missouri

A dark-gray panel van passed JR Diminski's house, heading east, twenty minutes after two in the morning. It did not stop but slowed as it grew even with the structure. Once past, it sped up and disappeared into the gloom of night.

Ten minutes later, the same van drove by again, this time heading west. It did not slow. The vehicle continued on and turned north.

Little traffic frequented the quiet neighborhood at this time of day.

Not two minutes later, the van returned and parked at the curb in front of JR's home. The side cargo door slid open, and two weapons, resembling old-fashioned bazookas, were directed at the house. Both discharged their shells at the same time. One crashed through a large picture window next to the front door and the other through the formal dining room glass pane. Smoke boiled through the broken windows after the grenades denotated.

A trim athletic figure, dressed completely in black, ran toward the large window and threw a soda-can sized object through each of the three front windows. He scurried back to the black van and tires screeched as it accelerated away from the house.

The three thermite incendiary grenades detonated seconds apart. The resulting explosions produced temperatures of 4,000 plus degrees and ignited any combustible component they came in contact with. The flames spread unimpeded through the house in seconds.

Despite the chaos of the moment, the motion-detecting cameras recorded all of the activity outside the house until they melted in the extreme heat.

***

First responders arrived as the inferno created by three thermite incendiary grenades intensified. They encountered two men who moved with the efficiency of trained military operators and another who calmly directed neighbors with measures to protect their own homes.

After the third fire engine arrived, Kruger motioned for Bobby Garcia and Rick Evans to follow him to the street. "Let's allow these gentlemen to do their job."

"Sean, during Rick's and my brief venture inside, we couldn't locate the family."

"Mia's new Honda CRV's not in the garage. Let's hope they left."

Evans stared at the flames and turned to Kruger. "Whoever did this didn't use normal fire bombs, Sean."

"What do you suspect?"

"Something a lot more powerful."

Kruger turned toward the house. "Guys, yesterday, I received a report about smoke and thermite grenades being stolen from a munitions manufacturer in northern Arkansas." He paused and studied the screen on his cell phone. "I got a ping on my cell phone. Our server at the office received videos from the security cameras you guys installed."

"Want me to check them out? Bobby can stay here. In case you need him."

Staring at the burning house, Kruger said, "Yeah. Call Jimmy and Sandy, let them know what happened here. I'll head that way as soon as I know there aren't any bodies in the rubble."

Evans gave him a grim smile. "Let's hope not."

***

Three Hours Later

Dawn lightened the eastern horizon as the battalion fire chief walked up to Kruger. "As you suspected, we didn't find any bodies in the fire, Sean."

"Thanks, Chief. We haven't located them yet, but at least they weren't in the house."

"We found three flash points. All in the front."

"Can you tell what the combustible might have been?"

"We'll have to run tests, but I can guess."

"Thermite?"

The fire chief gave the retired FBI agent a questioning look. "Yeah, how'd you know?"

Kruger shrugged. "Experience."

"Like I said, I can't say for certain until we run tests. All I can say is it was one of the hottest fires we've had to fight around here." He surveyed the completely consumed residence. "I'm going to leave a unit here for a while to make sure we don't have any hot spots flare up."

"Okay. Thanks for the quick response this morning, Chief."

"Glad we could help." He walked away and started directing the process of cleaning up.

Garcia approached. "Rick said the videos gave him a license plate number."

"Stolen?"

"Yeah, yesterday in Branson."

"Another dead end."

"Nope. He said the van is parked two blocks from the office building, and no one's in it."

"Let's go."

Ten minutes later, Kruger peered through the back window of the dark-gray panel van. "I'm not seeing anything in the back."

"The doors are locked, Sean."

"Have you notified the police yet?"

Evans shook his head. "Waiting on what you think is best."

"Call them. I'll phone the FBI. They need to be the lead on this one. But keep your eyes open. There's a reason they parked it two blocks from our building."

Once back on the second floor in his office, Kruger shut the door and punched a series of numbers on his cell phone. The call went straight to the personal cell phone of Ryan Clark.

"Isn't this a bit early for you, Sean?"

"I've been up since 2 a.m. I know where three of the stolen thermite grenades were used."

"Shit. Where?"

"JR's house last night."

The comment was met with silence for a few moments. "I sure hope JR and his family got out?"

"We don't know. I spoke to him about an hour before the incident. He was home then. But firefighters didn't find any human remains. So, I'm thinking they left before the incident."

"Why would you think that?"

"Because I told him about the stolen thermite, that's why."

"Maybe that gave them the incitive to leave."

"These guys aren't going to stop until they silence everyone associated with JR and Mia. Ryan, I think it's time you send in your best agents."

"On what grounds?"

"Interstate transport of stolen, restricted weapons."

"Hmmmm." He paused for a moment. "Let me guess. You have someone particular in mind."

"Tim Gonzales."

Clark did not respond for several moments. "Can I count on you to leave him alone and let us handle this?"

"Sure."

"Sean, I'm serious."

"So am I, Ryan. This has to be handled by FBI personnel. My guys have plenty to do."

"Good. I'll get the wheels rolling on my end."

***

Kruger parked his Mustang in front of the modern log cabin and exited the vehicle. He stared at the individual standing on the front porch. "You had a bunch of people worried."

"How bad is the house?"

"Best to bulldoze the lot and start fresh."

JR Diminski closed his eyes. "Thanks for being so persistent about us getting out."

"What are friends for? How's Mia doing?"

"She's pissed. Real pissed."

The retired FBI agent stepped onto the porch and shook his friend's hand. "This is a nice place. I think you three will be comfortable here until the house can be rebuilt." He tilted his head. "When did you decide to leave?"

"I closed the garage door at 1:48."

"Good."

"Bobby Garcia told me it was an older-model panel

van?"

"That's what the security videos show."

"Gray?"

"Yeah."

"I think we passed it just before we got on the bypass. Not that many cars out that time of night."

"Then you missed it by less than twenty minutes."

"Yeah, I'd say that's about right."

"JR, I've got a few things we need to discuss. May I come in?"

***

Bobby Garcia glanced in the rearview mirror as he drove north on Highway 13. "Rick, we've got company."

"Oh. Who is it?"

"A dirty twenty-year-old F-150. It's been following us since we left the office."

"Really. Where is he now?"

"Four vehicles back. Whoever it is knows what he's doing, but he's made a few mistakes."

Evans checked behind them and spotted the truck immediately. "Well, we can't lead him to Sandy's or Jimmy's place."

"Nope." With a grin on his face, Garcia glanced at his partner. "Wanna lose him?"

Reaching under the Chevy Tahoe's front seat, Evans extracted a Remington pump-action shotgun. "Beers are on me if you can do it in less than five minutes."

"You're on."

Garcia sped up when he saw the exit for County Road BB coming up in half a mile. He checked the side mirror to make sure no cars were approaching in the left lane of the northbound section of the divided highway. He glanced in the mirror again and saw the F150 speed up. He slammed on the brakes and made a left turn onto BB. He crossed the south bound lanes, barely missing a tractor-trailer unit as he accelerated west.

"Did he make the turn, Rick?"

"Yeah. And now he's trying to catch up. He knows we know."

"Good. In about a mile is Farm Road 115. I'll turn right and about half mile later is a hairpin turn. We'll use the Tahoe to block the road and wait for him."

Checking the side rearview mirror to check on their pursuer, Evans grinned. "I like it."

Once Garcia turned right, the road narrowed and turned to gravel. A plume of dust bloomed out behind him as he pressed his foot farther down on the accelerator. After making the turn, he skidded the big vehicle so that it blocked the narrow two-lane country road. They could follow the forward motion of their pursuer as dust boiled up behind it in the distance.

"He's gonna make the turn here in a few moments." Garcia reached under the driver's seat and extracted a similar shotgun to the one Evans brandished.

The F-150 came around the curve and immediately skidded in the loose gravel of the road. When it came to a stop, two men jumped out and aimed AR-15s at the two ex-Navy SEALs. The resultant firefight lasted only a few moments.

CHAPTER 45

Southwest Missouri

Sheriff's deputies closed the road at the junction of BB and County Road 115. Only emergency vehicles and two SUVs, containing FBI agents, were allowed to pass. When the FBI arrived, they took over the investigation while EMTs attended to Bobby Garcia's wound and covered the body of one of the attackers.

Rick Evans answered what he could as the federal agents peppered him with questions.

"You said the truck followed you from your office."

"I did."

"How can you be sure it's the same truck?"

Evans smiled. "I was trained to make those types of observations, Agent."

"Navy SEAL, right?"

"Ten years."

"What about Mr. Garcia?"

"We served together. I need to check on him, Agent."

The young agent hesitated, turned his attention to the

wounded man being attended to by emergency personnel. "Go ahead, but don't go anywhere."

Evans rolled his eyes as he hurried toward his friend. He squatted next to his partner who lay on a gurney being prepared to load into an ambulance. "How bad is it, Bobby?"

"EMT said the bullet missed all the important stuff. But it's gonna hurt like a mutha for a while."

"Well, then, I'll expect you back at work tomorrow." A toothy grin accompanied the remark.

"Right." Garcia chuckled. "What happened to the second guy?"

"Don't know. He tried to start the truck even while steam boiled out from underneath the hood. He took off running toward the north. We must have hit something vital."

"They both looked Chinese, Bobby. So, I checked before the cops got here. The dead one didn't have an ID on him."

"Figures. Have you spoken to Sean?"

"Briefly. I let him know what was going on. He said JR and his family are safe."

"Kind of figured they might be." He grimaced.

Placing a hand on his friend's shoulder, Evans looked at the EMT who stood nearby. "When are they gonna let you get this man to a hospital?"

"As soon as he's ready to go."

Turning his attention to Garcia, he said, "You ready?"

The wounded man grimaced again and said through clenched teeth, "Yeah, I'm ready."

The two EMT drivers loaded their patient into the ambulance and headed south.

***

Kruger arrived at the scene twenty minutes later, having

received reluctant permission from the lead FBI agents already there. He pulled Rick Evans aside. "How's Bobby?"

"I think he'll be okay, but he lost a lot of blood."

With a nod, the retired FBI agent pointed at the covered body in the road. "Have they ID'd him yet?"

"No. Appears Chinese, early fifties, and no ID."

Folding his arms, Kruger stared at the deceased man. "I may have a way to ID him." He walked over to one of the local FBI agents and said, "Hey, Ted, I might be able to help you with an ID. Can I take a picture of him?"

"Sure. Any help would be appreciated, Sean."

He uncovered the face of the dead man, and Kruger froze. "I don't have to take a picture. That's the oldest of The Four Brothers."

Ted Morgan, an FBI agent assigned to the local FBI field office, stared at Kruger. "The one they issued a national BOLO on?"

"One and the same."

"Shit." Morgan turned his back on Kruger, pulled out his cell phone, and walked away.

Folding his arms, Kruger stared at the dead man. "So, only one brother remains, and he's loose in Southwest Missouri."

***

Blood dripped from the left arm of the only member of the Four Brothers not dead or in prison. The geography of this part of Missouri, a transition from the flatness of the Osage Plains to the heavily wooded area typical of the Ozark Mountains, caused him to stumble through the white oak and black walnut trees native to the region. Underneath the canopy of trees, various species of grasses and weeds further hindered his progress.

In the distance, to his south, the wailing of sirens

converged on the area where he and his brother ran into the ambush. The two men they followed led them into the trap. With his eldest brother dead from a shotgun blast in the center of his chest, he was now alone in the middle of a large country in a state he knew nothing about.

The only comfort he felt came from the AR-15 he still carried and the two extra mags of ammunition he had grabbed before abandoning the stolen pickup truck.

When he came to a clearing, he saw a narrow asphalt road ahead with a well-kept farmhouse on the other side of the road. Without hesitation, he made his way toward the building.

***

By midafternoon, Ted Morgan faced a larger problem than a dead Chinese national in the middle of a backwoods country road. A live Chinese terrorist remained loose in the area. Both the Greene County and Polk County Sheriff's Departments were organizing a search of the surrounding area, including a search-dog team.

Standing off to the side, Kruger realized dogs would be the most efficient way to search. Recognizing one of the deputies handling a German shepherd, he walked over to him and shook his hand. "Glad to see you out here, Robert."

Robert Greenly smiled. "Thought you retired, Sean."

"Doing some temp work for Homeland Security."

"Who we searching for? Do you know?"

"Chinese national, member of the Triad on the mainland."

"What the hell's he doing in Greene County?"

Kruger asked, "What have you guys been told so far?"

"Not much. Only that the guy has an AR-15 and isn't afraid of using it."

"Who's your partner today?"

"It's just me and Nova here. Why?"

"Want company?"

"If you're referring to yourself, hell yes."

Knowing and having worked with a large number of the law enforcement members in this part of Missouri gave Kruger an edge. Acceptance among their ranks. Those who had worked with him in the past knew he was a team player and would not take credit for their efforts. Even if he was instrumental in solving a case, he always gave credit to the local guys.

So, when Greenly returned from getting approval for Kruger to work with him, he grinned. "We're good to go. The local FBI guys can't seem to get on the same page as my boss, so he wants us to stop wasting time."

Kruger, who had been studying the land around the F-150, pointed to a red spot on a fallen leaf. "What does that appear to be, Robert?"

Kneeling, the deputy picked up the leaf and examined it. "Blood."

"I agree." The retired FBI agent motioned for him to follow. He pointed to another spot. "I think our fugitive is wounded. Why don't you see if Nova can pick up a trail?"

The German shepherd muzzled the leaf and then the additional spot Kruger found. She looked up at her handler and panted.

"She's got a scent, Sean."

"I've got the radio, let's go."

***

Knowing the area where the confrontation between Garcia, Evans, and the men in the F-150 occurred, caused Kruger to change into jeans, hiking boots, and a black windbreaker before leaving his house. He wore his Homeland Security badge on a lanyard around his neck.

Greenly followed the German shepherd through the

wooded area with Kruger right behind. The dog stopped every once in a while, to sniff the leaf-strewn underbrush. She would then raise her head and follow the scent deeper into the woods.

With a walkie-talkie hooked to his belt and his Glock 19 loaded with hollow point ammunition in his right hand, Kruger felt good to be on the trail of a bad guy in the Ozark woods. An occurrence he had not experienced since his retirement.

Both men communicated with hand signals as the dog silently followed the scent. The only sounds audible to Kruger were the soft padding of the dog's paws on dried leaves and branches, plus the shuffling of their boots through thick underbrush.

Nova trudged ahead through the woods and stopped when a clearing of grass and asphalt road opened before them. Greenly stood next to the dog and stared across the road. "Sean, Nova is signaling the trail leads to the house."

"She seems to sense something wrong."

Checking his partner, Greenly said, "Yeah. That's her something's-not-right stance."

The dog gave a low growl. Greenly said, "Back." The dog retreated into the cover of the trees. His left hand pushed Kruger back as well. The sound of a bullet ricocheting off a tree to their right broke the silence.

Kruger grabbed the walkie-talkie off of his belt and relayed their location.

***

Sirens in the distance converged on the farmhouse located on Farm Road 6. Nova lay inside the tree line, panting, her attention fixed on the building across the asphalt country road.

Kruger watched the dog and asked Greenly, "Who trained her?"

"I did."

"You two make a good team. Ever thought about applying to the FBI?"

"Nah. The wife likes it here. So do I, plus both of our families are here. When Nova retires, she'll stay with me. I'll probably find something else to do at that time."

With a smile, Kruger said, "You know how to get a hold of me, don't you?"

"Yeah, I still have your card on the bulletin board. Why?"

"The company I own needs teams like you and Nova."

"Doing what?"

"The exact same thing you two did today."

"Let me think about it."

"I hope you do."

CHAPTER 46

Northern California

Amy Ling, formerly known as Emily Soon, stared at the ankle bracelet on her right leg, her world now shrunk to a hundred-and-fifty-foot circle around the base unit next to her home office desk phone. As a nonviolent, first-time offender, the court authorized the house arrest.

Thoughts of escape wandered in and out of her mind. But they were only thoughts; no actionable ideas presented themselves.

She sipped tea in her office as she gazed through her window at the rolling hills outside her Sonoma County home. With her back toward the office door, she sensed the presence of someone at the entrance.

"Nice of you to stop by, Father."

The Manchurian stood in the doorframe. "Did you hear me come in?"

Keeping her back to the man, she shook her head. "No, but your appearance has been expected."

"Why did you resign from your senate seat? We could

have weathered this storm."

She turned her office chair around to face him. The change in his appearance since their last face-to-face meeting startled her. His proud chest-out posture slumped. His handsome face was gaunt and ashen. "What's happened to you?"

"Nothing a little loyalty from my colleagues wouldn't cure."

She chuckled. "Father, one thing I learned in the Senate: Loyalty is a scarce commodity. Who's betrayed you now?"

"You, for one."

With a shrug, she ignored the accusation.

"The Four Brothers are no more. Two are dead and two are missing, thanks to the FBI."

"Let me guess. You've been abandoned by your benefactors in China."

"For the moment, they deem me unworthy of their support. But I will regain their confidence by creating a computer chip far superior to any they can manufacture."

"Why tell me?" Pointing to the ankle bracelet, she said, "I am no longer free to help you."

"Oh, but you can."

"And how is that, Father?"

He stepped into the office and moved to the front of her desk. He leaned forward, palms flat to support himself. "By creating a diversion so I can get to the Port of Ensenada in Mexico."

Her eyes narrowed. "You want me to sacrifice myself so you can escape? Is that what you're suggesting?"

"Not sacrifice. You're already in trouble. Helping the FBI to look in another direction is all I'm asking."

She stood and walked around the desk. He straightened to face her. She said, "And when they discover I'm aiding and abetting you, how's that not sacrificing myself?"

His nostrils flared, and he raised his arm to backhand her. She caught it as he brought it toward her face.

She screamed. "How dare you?" With a twist of his arm, she brought him to his knees with severe pressure on the rotator cuff of his shoulder. "You ordered my mother and a sister, I didn't even know about, murdered. For what? To keep a secret you have hidden from everyone."

Struggling, he managed to release his arm from her tight grip and scrambled to his feet. He glared at her and backed away. "I have no idea what you are talking about."

"No, I don't suppose you do. There are those in British intelligence who served in Hong Kong before the Chinese took over in 1997. They knew the truth about you then. The only reason the CIA was never told was because those men were greedy bastards. They didn't even tell their own government."

"What did they tell you?"

"The great Ling Mao Chun, the man who would lead China out of the age of the abacus to being a cyber technology juggernaut, is a fraud." She paused and gave him a sneer. "Your father convinced Deng Xiaoping of your importance. What he failed to tell him was you were an impostor. The computer chips you supposedly designed were actually based on blueprints you stole from Steve Wozniak. You had a stable of engineers who did all the work. All you did was collect the money and promise more and more advanced chips."

Ling glared at his daughter as his breathing rate increased.

"I see from your response, I'm right."

"You benefitted from my work as well."

"Yes. I enjoyed being a senator. So, I kept your secret. Now"—she spread her hands, palms up—, "I have no need to keep it. I'll bargain my way out of trouble with the information."

"You wouldn't dare." He started to approach her.

She stepped around to the back of her desk and reached into the open top drawer. She withdrew a Glock 48. A slim-profile automatic pistol chambered in 9mm ammunition. "Don't come any closer."

Stopping, he smiled. "Emily—"

"My name is Amy."

"Emily, I can still help you." He stepped forward two steps.

She pulled the trigger. The pistol spat, and a red stripe appeared on his left bicep. Blood oozed from the open wound. "I told you to leave. The next one will be in the center of your chest."

The Manchurian spun around and ran out of the room. She heard footfalls outside her office window. She sat in her chair and kept the pistol pointed at the door.

***

Tim Gonzales studied the Glock 48. "How many others do you have, Ms Ling?"

"That's the only one, Agent. I need you to remember, I have not been convicted of a crime at this time."

"I'm aware of that, Ms Ling. If I were you, I'd keep the Glock in a safe place."

"If I had, we wouldn't be having this conversation."

He walked to the opposite side of the room and found the bullet embedded in a thick volume on the floor-to-ceiling bookshelf. "No, I don't suppose we would be." He returned his attention to her. "Did he tell you where he was going?"

"He mentioned the Port of Ensenada in Baja."

Gonzales made a note in a small journal. "How did he get here?"

"I have no idea. He just appeared at the door of my office."

The FBI agent walked to the opening and surveyed the area. "You said you heard someone running outside your office afterward, correct?"

"Yes, that's right."

He walked down the hall to his right and saw the front door. He returned to the office. "Did you hear a car or anything?"

"No."

"How bad was he wounded?"

"I saw blood on his arm, halfway up from the elbow."

"We have agents searching the grounds for blood trails."

"Good." She paused. "Agent, can I relocate to somewhere I might feel safer?"

"As you said earlier, Ms. Ling, you have not been convicted of any crime at this point. However, you are under house arrest."

A female agent walked up next to Gonzales and whispered something into his ear. He smiled and returned his attention to Ling. "They found a blood trail. It stopped at the end of the driveway."

The ex-senator did not respond verbally.

"I might mention, someone made an attempt on your sister and her family early this morning."

She snapped to attention and glared at the FBI agent. "Was she hurt?"

"No, but they have relocated."

"Somewhere safe, I hope. It was probably one of The Four Brothers. They do all of my father's dirty work."

"I'm not at liberty to discuss their location."

Amy Ling did something Gonzales did not expect. She looked at the floor and a tear came to her eye. She let it slip down her cheek.

"What's the matter?"

"Nothing, just thinking."

"Would you like us to put you in protective custody?"

Looking up, she said, "It seems my father is bound and determined to eliminate all traces of his family. Maybe joining my sister in witness protection would be a prudent thing to do."

Reaching into his sport jacket pocket, he retrieved a cell phone and made a call.

CHAPTER 47

Southwest Missouri

Deputy Sheriff cars blocked traffic on Farm Road 6 from the west and from the east. A command post, set up by the FBI, buzzed with activity two hundred yards to the east. Trees hid it from view of the house.

Kruger alternated his focus between the house, where the last of The Four Brothers hid, and Nova. No noise emanated from the farm home, but Nova did not take her eyes off the dwelling.

With the radio now in the hands of Nova's handler, Kruger let him do the communicating with those in the command post, keeping his promise to Ryan Clark. However, he saw a possible way to solve the current problem. "Robert, how hard would it be for you and Nova to get across the road and in behind the home?"

Greenly studied the geography in both directions. "I think we could do it from the east. The west is too open, not as many trees close to the road."

"Mind if I suggest something?"

"Not at all. This has rapidly become a stalemate."

"I agree. What if the suspect is holding the homeowners hostage in there? The last thing any of us wants is more deaths. I think if the suggestion came from you, it might be readily accepted."

Studying the former FBI agent, Greenly tilted his head. "Want to tell me what that means, Sean?"

"Let's just say certain local FBI agents aren't too excited about my presence."

The deputy stifled a smile and said, "I'll take care of it."

Twenty minutes later, with Greenly and Nova in position behind the house, two deputy-sheriff SUVs screeched to a halt on the country road in full view of the home's front picture window. Four men exited the vehicles and positioned themselves so the SUV served as a shield. Three carried AR-15s, which they aimed at the house. The other deputy held a bullhorn. "Li Ning, you are surrounded; there's no escape. Come out with your hands up?"

The answer came with a rifle report and an instantaneous thump on the north side of the SUV. The deputy with the bullhorn then announced, "You have ten minutes to surrender before we force you out."

Only silence came from the dwelling.

Fearing the situation would soon get out of hand, Kruger made a quick phone call and then followed the tree line to the command post. The lead FBI agent saw the retired FBI agent approaching his position. Giving Kruger a scowl, he threw down a pencil he was using to mark a map.

"What the hell are you doing here, Kruger? You were told to stay out of the way."

Showing his Homeland Security badge, the retired FBI agent glared at the younger man. "I think the question should be, what the hell are you doing to end this situation, Ted?"

"Tear gas is the best way to clear the suspect out. We have everything under control."

"Control? Do you know if there are hostages in the house? Do you have a plan to keep them safe or get them out, for that matter? What if they have health issues? Tear gas could do more harm than good. How are you going to utilize the manpower you have? My guess is your answer will be you don't know."

Ted Morgan's face grew crimson as he glared at the older man standing in front of him. "I can have you removed."

"I don't think so, Skippy." He held up his badge. "I outrank you. Now, let the sheriff's people do their job. They know what they're doing and, despite what you believe, are better trained than you think."

"I will not allow—"

Holding his hand up with the palm toward Morgan, Kruger turned to the sheriff. "Paul, I'm taking over. You got a problem with that?"

With a half grin on his face, the sheriff said, "About damn time. What've you got in mind?"

"We need to know who lives in the house."

Using his thumb to gesture toward the young FBI agent who was now being ignored, the sheriff said, "Skippy here didn't bother to ask. We have an elderly couple by the name of Glover and their granddaughter. The couple is in their seventies, and the young lady is nine."

Kruger took a deep breath and let it out slowly. "Okay, we can't use tear gas. Too many risks."

"I agree. You have anything in mind?"

"I do," Kruger told him.

***

Thirty minutes later, six members of the Greene County SWAT team approached the house from a blind spot on the west side. Along with the SWAT members, Robert Greenly and Nova moved toward an outside basement door. After contacting the office of Building Permits and Blueprints, Kruger had called the builder and explained the situation. The man offered several options but felt the basement approach would be the safest for the family.

The sheriff's department entourage gained entry and disappeared inside.

Three-year FBI veteran Ted Morgan stood watching as Kruger and the Greene County sheriff took over the command post and directed the activities of the deputies on scene. He pulled out a cell phone and dialed a number. It was answered on the second ring.

"Glad you called, Morgan. I was about to call you." His tone matter-of-fact, now with an edge, he continued. "What the hell are you doing down there? The report I just received told me you're putting civilians in jeopardy."

"Sir, we had the situation under control until Sean Kruger showed up."

There was silence on the other end of the call. Finally, a strained voice said, "Sean Kruger is there?"

"Yes, sir. He and the sheriff waltzed in here and took over."

"I highly doubt that, Agent Morgan. I've known Sean Kruger for a long time, and he doesn't just waltz in. If he did, he had a reason. The report I received informed me you wanted to use tear gas without knowing if there were any hostages. Is that correct?"

"Uh…" Morgan shut his eyes tight and said, "It was an option."

"Did you know who the homeowners were and whether they were present?"

"Not at that time."

"But you do now?"

"Yes."

"How did you find out?"

"Uh, well, the sheriff knew."

"But didn't tell you. So, did you ask him to find out?"

"No."

A heavy sigh could be heard on the other end. "Morgan, did you offer to help the sheriff, or did you barge in and take over?"

"My advanced training in hostage—"

"Doesn't mean shit. That sheriff has to think of all the residents of the county and their safety. I happen to know the sheriff. He is a well-trained law enforcement officer. You would do well to get to know him better and soak up some of his experience. Why do you think Kruger is so well-respected in Greene County?"

"I have no idea."

"See? There you go. As an agent, Kruger sought out help from the local sheriff and police departments. That's why they listened to him and not you."

Not knowing what to say, Morgan remained quiet.

"We will discuss your performance when the hostages are safe. In the meantime, do whatever Sean Kruger tells you to do. Do I make myself clear?"

"Extremely."

"Good."

The call ended.

***

Robert Greenly stood at the top of the stairs behind a closed door. Nova sat patiently by him. He listened for sounds coming from inside the house. A soft whimpering from a child could be heard from somewhere in the house. The other sound was a one-sided conversation in Mandarin. The voice grew loud as it approached the door and then softened as the individual moved away from the door.

With one hand on the doorknob, he held up the other hand and used his fingers to count down for the SWAT team members on the stairs below. At the appropriate moment, he opened the door, and Nova sprang silently forward and attacked the suspect.

***

The radio in the command center crackled with an incoming message.

"Suspect down. Hostages safe. Over."

Kruger smiled as the sheriff responded and ordered more deputies inside the residence. Agent Morgan stood behind Kruger. "How did you know to use the dog?"

Turning, the retired FBI agent placed his hand on the young agent's shoulder. "Knowing and utilizing your resources are the mark of a good FBI agent, Mr. Morgan. As you grow in your career, you'll find looking down your nose at local law enforcement will get you absolutely nowhere and, in dangerous situations, possibly dead."

He turned and walked toward the house.

***

Entering the home through the front door, Kruger saw an elderly couple sitting on a flower-patterned sofa, with a young girl sitting next to them being embraced by the older woman. The husband summarized their experience to two sheriff's deputies as they took notes.

Walking into the kitchen, he saw Greenly checking a wallet. Nova sat next to the prone prisoner, who lay face down on the kitchen tile, his hands cuffed behind his back.

Kruger asked, "Who is he?"

Greenly looked up. "ID shows he's a PRC diplomat. Name's Wu Dong." The deputy addressed the prisoner. "What's your name?"

"Diplomatic immunity."

Greenly gave the German shepherd a hand signal. The dog produced a deep-throated growl.

The prone man screamed. "Keep that damn dog away

from me."

"Answer our questions, and I will."

"Wu Dong."

Kruger said, "Bullshit. Your name is Li Ning, and you are one of The Four Brothers and a member of a Hong Kong Triad. Oh, by the way, did you know you are the last surviving brother?"

Li struggled to turn his head to look at Kruger. "Diplomatic immunity."

Turning to Greenly, Kruger shook his head. "This clown doesn't have diplomatic immunity. He's now your prisoner. Do what you need to do." He turned and walked toward the home's entrance.

"Where are you going, Sean?"

"I've got a meeting to attend."

CHAPTER 48

Southwest Missouri

Kruger waited patiently in the visitation cubicle at the federal medical center. A guard escorted John Lee into the area. When the prisoner sat across from Kruger, he said, "You are going to tell me the Manchurian is in custody and I will be released, yes?"

"No, I'm going to tell you that your two oldest brothers are dead and the other is now in custody. So, guess what, I'm changing the deal."

"Typical American. No integrity."

"Here's the deal, John. Everything you've told me so far has been BS. We're no closer to capturing the Manchurian than when I started working with you. Now that your brother's under arrest, he seems more than willing to help." Kruger knew this to be a lie but did not care at the moment. "So, give me specific information on where the Manchurian is, or I go to your brother, and he gets the deal. Not you. Your decision."

Lee glared at the retired FBI agent. "Not my fault you

don't follow directions."

Kruger narrowed his eyes. "I'm extremely tired of your games, John. What happens if your whereabouts are suddenly made public. I gave you a new name, I can also take it away. How long will it take for someone to get to you?"

"You would not do that?"

"Want to find out?"

The man now known as John Lee blinked twice and said, "No, I do not wish to find out, Agent Kruger." The federal prisoner took a deep breath and sighed. "He will be reluctant to accept any phone calls. He will only respond to a text message with specific code words."

"Go on."

"I can send the text message and then tell him whatever it is you want me to. Only then will our agreement be complete, and you will release me."

"Nope, only when he is dead or in custody. Not before."

The youngest of The Four Brothers glared at Kruger. Neither man moved or looked away. Finally, he said, "Very well. When do you want me to do this?"

"Now would be a good time."

***

JR set up his laptop in a secure room of the federal medical center. The plan was for the text message and phone call from the youngest brother to appear to originate somewhere in South America. He looked at Kruger. "Where do you want the call to appear to come from specifically?"

"Cordoba, Argentina."

"Any reason why?"

"It's hard to get to, and a lot of Chinese ex-patriates live in the country."

With a slight nod, JR started typing on his laptop. John

Lee sat across from him. Kruger stood with his back against the entrance's door. He watched the prisoner, his arms crossed.

JR turned his head toward Kruger. "I'm ready."

Pushing off from the wall, the retired FBI agent flattened his palms on the table. "Okay, John. If I detect you giving him a message other than the one we discussed, I will break the connection and deposit you in the general prison population. Identified by your real name."

Lee took a deep breath, stared at the man standing next to him, and finally nodded.

"Okay, JR. Let's get this started."

***

The Manchurian sat in his passenger cabin on the container ship and stared at his cell phone. The text message contained the correct code words for The Four Brothers' youngest sibling. He returned the message with a two-word text reply. *Yes, now.*

Two minutes later, his phone vibrated with a caller ID which appeared to originate in Argentina. He answered, "Hello."

"The bird only flies in the light."

It was one of the correct code sentences used to identify the youngest of The Four Brothers. He gave the counter sentence. "But the light can turn to dark." He paused. "Where are you?"

"Argentina."

"Why?"

"I barely escaped the American FBI. I felt this was a safer haven."

"Hmmm."

"Two of my brothers are dead, the other captured."

"Which ones are dead?"

"The two oldest."

The Manchurian paused. "Unfortunate."

"Were you aware both of the sisters are alive and the youngest is talking to the FBI?"

"Yes, I was aware of this. How do you know of it?"

"My brother, the one they captured, told me before it happened."

"Did he know where they were being held?"

"That's why he was in Missouri. To find them, per your wishes."

"So, they are being held in the middle of the country?"

"Yes."

"Do you know where?"

"Somewhere around a big man-made lake in the southern part of the state. The name starts with stock or something like that."

"Find out and let me know."

"No, this is the last time I will communicate with you. I am out of the United States and will not jeopardize being caught again. You are on your own, Ling."

The call ended, and the Manchurian stared at the dead phone. He said, "Then I will take care of it myself."

***

JR cut the connection, closed the laptop, and placed it in his backpack.

Kruger considered John Lee. "I have to admit, you were convincing."

"I want the opportunity to go to Argentina."

"Why?"

"There is a large contingent of Chinese there."

"As soon as the Manchurian is captured, I'll have our company plane fly you there."

Lee stood and bowed. He knocked on the door. A guard appeared and took him away.

The two men did not speak of the phone call until they

were in the parking lot and in Kruger's Mustang.

With the doors shut, JR turned to his friend. "Think it will work?"

"At this point, JR, I wouldn't bet on it. But we need to be ready."

"Why not hand this information over to the FBI?"

Shaking his head, Kruger sighed. "Because after the fiasco near Stockton, I've lost faith in the people they have assigned to this area. Besides, Jimmy and Sandy know the area like the back of their hand. If anybody can capture the Manchurian, they can."

"Sean, I'm not sure I want Mia and Joey to be bait."

"Don't blame you. They don't have to be. Tim Gonzales arrived here with Amy Ling this morning. She has agreed to be the bait."

"Didn't think you wanted the FBI involved."

"I don't want the agents assigned to this area involved. Gonzales is another matter."

"What about me?"

"What about you?"

"I'm the one who started this mess. I should be involved in bringing it to a close."

Kruger glanced at his friend. "When was the last time you got physically involved with a manhunt?"

"Ten years ago. On Joseph's property. If I remember correctly, I saved your bacon that morning."

With a slight chuckle, Kruger said, "That you did. You still up for it?"

"If it means protecting Mia and Joey, hell yes."

***

One Week Later
Near Stockton, Missouri

The black-clad figure moved through the wooded area

surrounding the still waters of the man-made lake. He glided through the area with the efficient moves of a trained athlete. The weapons he carried were simple. A sharp knife and a suppressed .22 Long Rifle Ruger automatic. His final destination, a modern log structure on a large piece of land east of the lake.

The moonless night enhanced his stealthiness. Night vision goggles aided his progress through the woods to the house. When he arrived within sight of his target, he paused and surveyed the area. He checked his watch: 1:43 a.m. He would wait until half past two before continuing into the cabin to kill everyone inside.

***

At 2:32 a.m., the back entrance to the log cabin opened. Not with a flourish but with a slow deliberate motion. The sturdy wood floor did not betray the passage of the assailant with even the tiniest of creaks. Synthetic soles on his athletic shoes kept the sound of footfalls nonexistent. Having memorized the floorplan of the cabin by studying public records at the courthouse, the intruder made his way to the first bedroom on the ground floor.

The door was closed but unlocked. He turned the knob with a slow, careful twist. When the door offered no resistance, he opened it to peer inside. A figure could be seen in the bed. Pointing the Ruger at the head, he pulled the trigger twice. The puff of the subsonic, hollow-point ammunition barely broke the silence of the room.

A violent push from behind caused him to stumble to the floor. A light switch was thrown, bathing the room in a brilliant white light. Two sets of hands grasped his arms preventing him from tearing the NVGs off his face. He screamed as the magnified searing light assaulted his eyes.

***

Sandy Knoll placed the intruder in a wood straight-back chair in the kitchen and used zip ties to secure his hands behind him and his calves to the legs of the chair. Knoll said to his companion, "Nice work, JR. This worked out better than I thought it would."

JR studied the occupant of the chair. Something was wrong. The body type did not match the description given to them by John Lee. He ripped the NVGs and the balaclava off the man's head and stared at the trespasser. The man slowly opened his eyes and returned the stare. The pockmarked cheeks and European face were not those of the man they hunted.

With his breathing heavy, JR clenched his fists. "Who the fuck are you?"

In the slight British accent of someone from Hong Kong, the intruder said, "You must be the husband. I was told to kill you if I had the opportunity."

Knoll bent down and glared at the man. In his most menacing growl, he said, "Answer the damn question. Who are you?"

The man laughed. "Who were you expecting? The Manchurian?"

Neither JR or Knoll responded.

"He sends his greetings. You see, he never does his own dirty work. He always sends someone who doesn't mind getting their hands dirty. That would be me."

"Where is he?"

Returning his attention to JR, the man said, "By now, probably the middle of the Pacific. He's on his way back to China."

"Shit." JR turned and stormed out of the kitchen.

EPILOGUE

Two Months Later

JR walked into Kruger's office and sat down without saying a word.

Turning his attention from his desk to the man now sitting in front of him, the retired FBI agent removed his glasses. He said, "Good morning, JR. Come in, sit down, and take a load off your feet. Can I get you a cup of coffee?"

"Sorry."

He chuckled. "What's up?"

"The Manchurian."

Kruger took a deep breath and sighed. "What now?"

"One of my scanner programs found an email in the San Francisco Chinese Consul General's inbox."

"You spying without permission, JR?"

"I've been in their system since we left San Francisco, Sean."

"A matter of semantics. Okay. Tell me about the email."

"It informed the consultant that Ling Mao Chun's status

as a member of the PRC had been canceled and he'd been assigned to a rehabilitation camp."

Kruger shook his head. "That's BS."

"I don't know. We discovered the name of the ship he sailed on from of the Port of Ensenada. It was boarded by the Chinese Navy ten miles from Hong Kong and a man removed from the ship."

"Really?"

"According to the information I found, yes."

With a half smile, Kruger asked, "Where'd you find the information?"

JR leaned back, clasped his hands together behind his head, stared at the ceiling for a moment, and blew out a breath. "Okay. I hacked into the main PRC server."

Raising both eyebrows, Kruger stared at his friend. "You did what?"

"It's not like they haven't hacked into our government's computers."

"Yeah, but that's…"

"Tit for tat?"

"I hope you didn't leave any traces of your incursion."

"Of course I didn't."

"What'd you find?"

"What I found makes me think the Manchurian may be persona non grata inside his own country."

"Why?"

"Apparently, they discovered his chip designs were basically stolen, borrowed, copied, etc., from concepts developed late in the 20th century. They also shut down all their similar operations around the globe."

Kruger tapped his lip and then grinned. "I'm curious, who made this revelation known to the PRC?"

"I think you know him, Harold Mudd."

A hearty chuckle filled the small office. "Good for Harry." He paused for a moment. "Are we done with the Manchurian?"

"I don't know, Sean. It could all have been a charade. A damn good one, but who knows?"

The two men fell into a comfortable silence. Finally, JR asked, "What's going to happen to Amy Ling?"

"I think after she testifies in front of a closed session of the Senate Security Committee, she might find herself a free woman with restrictions."

"I spoke to Mia the other day. The two women actually came to an epiphany during their two-week isolation during the search for the Manchurian."

"And that was?"

"They have more in common than they thought. Mia said she wants to keep in touch with her sister."

"Good. JR, could the missing pages of Judy's journal have been about her getting back together with her husband and conceiving another child?"

"It would explain a few things. Amy was never mentioned in the diary, and she talks about her husband not being around. Guess we'll never know, since the journal was in the house when it burned." JR sat silently for a moment. "Thanks, Sean."

Tilting his head slightly, Kruger said, "For what?"

"Helping Mia find closure about her family."

"Glad I could help."

Standing, JR moved toward the door.

"Can I ask a question?"

The computer expert turned back to look at his friend. "Sure."

"When will the house be done?"

"A few more months."

"Good. The neighborhood's not the same without you guys across the street."

ABOUT THE AUTHOR

J.C. Fields is a multi-award-winning and Amazon best-selling author. Many of his 12 published novels have been awarded numerous gold, silver and bronze medals in the Reader's Favorite International Book Awards contest.

Over the past three years, many of his numerous short stories have been featured on the YouTube Podcast Fear From the Heartland, a part of the Chilling Tales for Dark Night network.

Currently, one of his novels is under review by Wind Dancer Films for a possible TV or Movie project.

He lives with his wife, Connie, in Southwest Missouri.

Made in United States
Orlando, FL
26 September 2024

52001427R00192